Waking Up
in the Sixties

Waking Up
in the Sixties

A Novel by
William Jordan

West Marin Press
2015

First Printing: December, 2015

ISBN-13: 978-1518765889
ISBN-10: 1518765882

West Marin Press
P.O. Box 902
Woodacre CA 94973

Inquiries: westmarinpress@gmail.com

Cover photo credits:

Paratrooper in Vietnam, 1965. NBC News photo.

Dancer at Love-In, 1967. L.A. Times news photo.

Zen monk. From 2011 article by Tom Hoffarth in L.A. Daily News.

Free Speech Movement demonstration, Berkeley, 1964. Photo by Lon Wilson, UC Berkeley Bancroft Library.

Photo of William Jordan by Forrest Jordan.

Acknowledgements

My gratitude to Charles MacDermed for planting the seed that grew into the inspiration for this story. Thanks to Charles Brown and Barry Franklin for conscientiously reading my early draft and sustaining my effort. Special appreciation to Ace Remas for unconditional help, inspiration, advice, and encouragement. Heartfelt thanks to my wife Dara, whose candid suggestions helped me to complete the story in the way I wanted to write it. Finally, I wish to acknowledge the teachers and companions who have guided and supported me along the years.

Contents

For Dara

Karl

Karl and Adrian lie awake in their beds without speaking. Only the yellow and blue flames of the tiny gas stove in the corner illuminate the room. It is Adrian's first night in Karl's place, a tiny garret built on top of a detached one-car garage behind a classic brown shingle Berkeley house built in the early years of the twentieth century. In contrast to the sterile apartment Adrian has been living in during his first month at Cal, this seasoned dwelling reflects the bohemian life he envisioned when he dreamed of moving to Berkeley from his parents' home in Los Angeles.

Reclining on the thin mattress Karl bought for him at the Goodwill store, in the darkness Adrian gazes at the stars twinkling though the open skylight in the pitched ceiling above him. Occasionally, the cool October breeze makes the flames of the gas stove flicker, casting moving shadows on the white paneled walls of the small abode in which Adrian has agreed to live with his cousin, who is really more like his brother.

Karl breaks the silence with an astounding proclamation.

"Adrian, I want to tell you something. I'll say this only once. You and me and everyone we know —we're all machines."

Karl is silent again. Adrian remains still, thinking about the meaning of his cousin's words. Karl has spoken with such force and conviction that Adrian is sure this is no idle thought. But

1

they both stay quiet. Adrian will have to wait until much later to understand.

Soon, they are asleep.

Karl was the quintessential bohemian. Coming of age in the heyday of the Beat generation in the late fifties, he had shared rooms and lofts with writers, painters, sculptors and musicians in New York, Paris, and San Francisco before settling in Berkeley. Karl was a philosopher, a poet, a screenwriter, an artist, and most of all, a musician. The flash of his red shoulder-length hair and beard was familiar to those who hung out on Berkeley's Telegraph Avenue, along which he appeared several times a day as he walked between his garret and the UC campus. Although he had grown up in a wealthy family, Karl now lived on very little money. Adamant about the necessity of separating creativity and commercial success, he refused opportunities that threatened to spoil his sensitivity or corrupt his work.

Karl and Adrian had always been kindred spirits. When Karl was attending Stanford, he had periodically driven from Northern California to Adrian's parents' home in Los Angeles to spend the weekend. During these visits, Karl shared his current interests with Adrian and introduced him to music, literature, art, and philosophical ideas that Adrian responded to with great interest, absorbing these influences so much that they began to reform his identity. At first, Adrian's parents had welcomed Karl's visits, but they eventually became concerned about Karl's left wing political leanings and began to take steps to keep Adrian away from Karl's influence. They believed their fears were justified when they saw Karl's picture in a *Time* magazine article about the controversial hearings of the House Un-American Activities Committee. A photo showed Karl being swept down the front steps of San Francisco City Hall by powerful streams of water from fire hoses directed at students during a protest demonstration.

At that point, convinced that their nephew had become a communist, Adrian's parents were determined to keep their son away from the liberal environment of Berkeley where Karl had settled. Accordingly, as Adrian's graduation from high school approached, his parents did everything they could to direct him to colleges elsewhere, especially in the South. But Adrian didn't want to leave California, and so as a compromise, he and his parents agreed that he could enroll at the University of Southern California in Los Angeles on the condition that he pledged a fraternity there. However, neither the academic environment at USC nor the fraternity culture appealed to him. Another life was calling to him. It was inevitable that he would find his way to the University of California at Berkeley in September 1963.

Glad that Adrian would be in Berkeley, and knowing that he was enrolled for the fall semester, Karl had gone to the central directory in the campus registrar's office to find out where Adrian was living. By a stroke of serendipity,

Karl arrived there to find Adrian flipping through a bank of directory cards, looking for his cousin's address. When Karl surprised Adrian, they greeted one another with great camaraderie and Adrian suggested they go to the apartment he had just moved into. As they drove there in Adrian's MGA roadster, Karl expressed surprise at how far the apartment was from campus. Adrian explained that, being from car-crazy Los Angeles, where everyone drives everywhere, it hadn't occurred to him that one might find a place to live within walking distance to school. And of course he had no way of knowing that in just a few days his car would be totaled in a head-on accident in San Francisco's North Beach.

Adrian had been glad to host a visitor to his apartment. Sitting in the only two chairs there, which Adrian had just bought at a second-hand store on Ashby, the cousins talked about what had been going on in their lives while consuming Gallo salami and Safeway beer, which was all that Adrian had in his fridge. Adrian told Karl of the pain he felt about what surely was the impending break-up with his girlfriend, who had followed him from Los Angeles to attend San Francisco State College but was now attracted to a life apart from Adrian with people she was meeting in San Francisco.

As he listened, Karl examined his cousin more carefully. He felt a renewed appreciation of Adrian's boyish good looks, with his full head of wavy dark brown hair, bushy eyebrows, brown eyes, elegant nose and broad shoulders. Feeling sympathetic toward Adrian's suffering

4

over his romantic breakup, Karl encouraged him to forget his ex-girlfriend and embrace the new life that was opening to him in Berkeley. Adrian appreciated his cousin's advice, which he felt was just the support he needed to begin to put the affair behind him. Then Karl went on to tell Adrian in enthusiastic detail about his own current work with music and writing. When it was time to drive back to Karl's place, Karl had urged Adrian to move in with him. Adrian would be within walking distance to campus, they could share the rent, but most of all, they would be together. Without thinking long about it, Adrian had agreed, saying he would give notice to his landlord the next day.

Now that they were living together, Adrian shared all aspects of Karl's life. On Adrian's first weekend there, he helped prepare the food for one of the Sunday spaghetti dinners Karl regularly prepared for those who happened to show up. The two of them worked closely together in the tiny kitchen, which was just big enough to turn around in. A prodigious quantity of pasta swam in a large stainless steel pot centered on one of the two gas burners of a miniature stove as Karl stirred basil, garlic, pepper and wine into the deep red tomato sauce. Standing next to him, Adrian breathed in the rich aroma as he washed and assembled the ingredients for a generous salad.

When the meal was ready, Karl served his guests in the yard down below the garret, as there wasn't enough room to eat inside. There were a couple of old wooden benches there, but most of the visitors sat on the grass or just ate standing in the warm Indian summer sun. Karl passed around a gallon jug of red wine he had recently picked up at a small Italian family winery in Fairfield. Although Adrian was shy, Karl introduced him to each of his friends, putting him at ease with gentle affection. Soon, Adrian was talking freely with a young man in charge of cultural events at the student union, who described the New Wave film festival he was planning. Then Adrian met a vagabond writer in Berkeley for only a few days on the way from Portland to Los Angeles, where he was scheduled for a jazz and poetry gig in a club on Sunset Strip. In that setting with those people, Adrian saw his world view expanding before him.

Professors and Poets

Once classes were underway, Adrian discovered how intense the demand at Cal was going to be. He would have to suffer through a couple of required science courses that didn't inspire him, but found his English classes to be exhilarating in spite of the long list of books he would have to read. His favorite course was The Age of Milton, taught by a brilliant young professor from New England who introduced his students to entirely new ways of approaching literature. In one session, the teacher managed to demonstrate in experiential terms how both Bacon and Milton used paradox to transmit ideas to the subconscious mind that the ordinary mind cannot grasp. With the professor's help, some students were able to understand — at least momentarily — that a passage from Paradise Lost can evoke both 'yes' and 'no' at the same time, leaving the everyday intellect in confusion while Milton conveyed his precise meaning to another intelligence in the reader. These lectures were so alive and provocative that many people not officially enrolled in the class dropped in to hear them, even though it meant standing for the full hour and a half at the back of the small lecture hall.

At the end of each day of classes, Adrian joined Karl for dinner in the campus cafeteria. Several other students also attracted to Karl began to join them. Sitting around one of the large round cafeteria tables, they talked about film, art, music, poetry, philosophy and psychology, and sometimes even politics. As their mentor, Karl introduced them to new ideas, new music, new artists. Karl's followers listened with keen interest to everything he spoke about, wishing to embark themselves on the new pathways he was showing them. Determined to find meaning in their lives, they were hungry for new experience.

One evening, Desmond, a sociology major who had become a regular member of this cafeteria troupe, brought a new girl with him to dinner. She was barefoot, dressed plainly in jeans and a cotton serape, and had long dark brown hair that fell straight down all the way to her waist, completely covering her back and shoulders. Framed by this lush growth, her pale thin face was small by contrast. Her eyes were close-set on either side of a long hawk-like nose and she had an unusually wide mouth. Desmond introduced Sandy to everyone around the table, explaining that though she was only sixteen, she had just started her freshman year as a psychology major at Cal. Her energetic vitality and shining intelligence were particularly appealing to Karl, who began to give her all of his attention. To Desmond's chagrin, Karl suggested that, after dinner, Sandy accompany him to one of the campus piano practice rooms so that he could play for her. Karl invited the others to come along as well.

There was only a piano bench to sit on in the one available music practice room, so everyone but Karl had to make themselves as comfortable as they could on the cold linoleum floor. This was definitely not a problem for Sandy, who preferred sitting cross-legged as close as she could get to the piano. Karl opened the piano lid, turned out the lights, sat down on the bench, and began to improvise. A slow impressionist invocation led into several sections of varying tempo and color—first slow and lyrical, then fast, loud and intense, then soft and quietly romantic. Sandy was enraptured. With her eyes closed, she swung her head left and right and in a circle, trailing her long hair through the air in accord with the music. Karl's improvisation finally came to an end with a crashing climax of chords. Everyone listened without moving as the final vibrations of the piano strings gradually died out. When it was quiet, each of them remained sitting still in the dark room, even though they were uncomfortable. Several minutes passed. Then, when Karl got up from the piano bench, the rest finally felt free to move from their cramped positions on the floor. As they left the practice room, Karl quietly asked Adrian if he would delay his return to the garret for a couple of hours. Adrian agreed, knowing that Karl wanted to be alone with Sandy, saying that he had his books with him and could study in the lounge area of the student union.

When Adrian got home much later, Sandy was asleep in bed with Karl. She was there every day after that and soon moved in. Although in general Adrian and Sandy got along well, a kind of sibling rivalry developed between them. But over the next few weeks the trio became inseparable, going to movies together, eating with friends on Telegraph Avenue or at the cafeteria, and sitting around the garret in the evenings discussing every topic under the sun after Sandy and Adrian had finished their homework.

Since Adrian's accident in North Beach the week before he'd moved in with Karl—a crash from which he'd miraculously walked away without injuries—none of them had a car, so they went most places on foot, seldom leaving Berkeley. But when Karl was invited to a party in San Francisco one Saturday night, he borrowed a friend's Edsel and invited Sandy and Adrian to go along with him.

The affair would be at the home of Karl's friend Damien, who was preparing his first volume of poetry for publication by City Lights Books, the North Beach bookstore which had already made several important early works of Beat writers available to the world. Karl explained to Sandy and Adrian that the party was in recognition of Damien's forthcoming book and that many local writers and artists would be there. Adrian was reluctant to go. As much as he was attracted to the culture and literature of the Beats, he was uncomfortable at parties. He particularly resisted putting himself in this situation, as he worried that he would come off as conspicuously dull and inhibited in the midst of the free-spirited flamboyance of the bohemians there. But when Karl dismissed his anxiety and insisted that he come with them, Adrian gave in.

As they approached Damien's cottage, which was situated behind a nondescript house on Scott Street, they heard the sounds of an Indian raga pouring out into the cool night air. The music got much louder when a young woman in a long dress opened the door for them to a room lit only by candles and filled with the mixed aromas of frankincense and marijuana. As their eyes adjusted to the dim light, they made out people in the room, some standing and talking, others sitting on the bare wooden floor. A woman in the middle of the room was moving in time with the raga.

While Karl went to find Damien, Sandy and Adrian stood watching the woman dance. She had dark eyes, bright red lips, and her hair was woven into thick dark braids wrapped around her head. A candle on the other side of the room occasionally penetrated her diaphanous blue dress when she passed in front of it, the flickering light momentarily revealing silhouettes of her swaying breasts as she moved with the music. Little bells hanging from anklets on her bare feet rang out as she surrendered to the unrelenting acceleration of the sarod and tabla intertwining in a rising climax. When the raga ended, the spent dancer retreated from the light.

Then Damien moved to the place vacated by the dancer. Conversations hushed around the room and all eyes turned to him. Looking upward to the ceiling as if addressing the gods, he began to recite one of his new poems, his resonate voice filling the room.

> *In a pirate's patched quilt*
> *From a cavern of golden wide*
> *I watched the apple-toothed sun*
> *Bite the far end of night.*

O renegade visions
Of scar-streaked angels
Lighting the pathway
To a miracle dressed in white.

Spattering the blood feast
Straddling the stones
Rending the nightmare
Retching the bones.

Starlighting my foundster
And ringing my knell
The blackluster call
Broke the last pool of hell.

Innocence wound its cameled way
To a foundling's past
In a midday cave there
In the bushy hide of my age.

Damien bowed his head. First silence, then applause all around. With an appreciative smile, he called out, "Enjoy yourselves!" and went to speak to Karl. Everyone began talking about the poem, with enthusiastic exclamations of "wow," "far out," and "beautiful" heard all around the room.

"What did you think?" Sandy asked Adrian.

"Actually, I thought it sounded a lot like Dylan Thomas' poetry, in a sort of Beat style," Adrian replied.

Karl motioned them to join him. He wanted to introduce them to Damien. The poet was a small, attractive man with fine features. With his olive skin, dark eyes, black hair and beard, he might be mistaken for an Arab or North African. Despite the power of his recitation, his conversational speech was soft. He smiled, laughed a lot and exhibited no arrogance. Adrian liked him immediately.

Another man joined them. As Damien introduced him, Adrian realized that he was a famous poet who had published several collections already. Though clearly an American Jew, he was wearing Middle Eastern clothing. Putting his hand into his tunic, he withdrew a small cigarette-like object, which he put to his mouth and lit with a match. After taking a deep drag, he passed it to Damien. Smiling, Damien put it to his lips. Then to Adrian's surprise, the poet passed it to him. Adrian hesitated, not knowing what the thing was. He hadn't smoked pot yet, but he was sure that this was something different.

"It's opium," explained Karl, seeing Adrian's reticence. "It's okay, just try a little to see if you like it."

Now feeling obliged to smoke it, Adrian put the tube to his lips and inhaled. Knowing that you're supposed to hold marijuana smoke in your lungs for few seconds, he figured that must be true of opium as well. But when he did, he started coughing violently. The laughter that followed embarrassed Adrian, who told himself that the others saw him for what he was, a naive kid from Los Angeles. That's why he hadn't wanted to come to the party in the first place. Now he wished he'd stayed home.

As the conversation turned towards Damien's poetry, sweat broke out on Adrian's forehead and his gut began to rumble. Thinking it must be the opium, Adrian told Sandy that he needed to go to the bathroom. Damien overheard him and stopped what he was saying long enough to point

Adrian to a hallway nearby. Feeling that he had to throw up, Adrian headed in that direction, weaving between groups of people gathered in the dimly lit room. As he considered which of the closed doors in the hallway led to the bathroom, a woman emerged from the one at the end. Adrian waited for her to pass. When she came closer, he recognized her as the dancer he and Sandy had been watching. She must have seen the spark of recognition in his eyes, because she stopped and smiled at him. Moving closer, she lifted his hand and pressed it to her breast. For a moment, her warm softness made Adrian forget his stomachache.

However, in the next instant that tactile invitation to pleasure was overridden by an intense urge to vomit. Without thinking, he freed his hand from her and hurried down the hall to the bathroom, where he slammed the door closed behind him, sank to his knees in front of the toilet, and threw up. Then he threw up again and again. When it was finally over, he got up off the floor, turned the water on in the sink and put his mouth under the faucet. He swished, gargled and spit several times to clear the foul taste, then washed his face and hands. He couldn't bring himself to use the dirty damp towel bunched up on the rack, so he wiped his hands on his pants and left the bathroom with his face still wet. He was more than ready to go home.

When Adrian re-entered the living room, another raga was playing and the woman was dancing again. Recalling the sensation of her breast in his hand and wanting to feel it again, he wondered if there was any chance of resuming contact with her. But then, he didn't even know who she was. She might even be the girlfriend or wife of one of the poets. He persuaded himself that he didn't have the energy to get involved with her now and decided that it was better to avoid her altogether. Besides, he just wanted to go home. Looking around for Karl and Sandy, Adrian saw them talking with another couple across the room. He moved toward them, trying to stay out of his dancing lady's sight. As he drew near to the two couples, he heard them talking about *Red Desert*, a new Italian film he wanted to see.

"It's typical of Antonioni that in his first attempt to film in color, he would use different hues to convey meaning about his characters and settings. I read that he even had plants, trees, and fruit painted over to convey psychological states."

"But the landscapes were so grim after those beautiful Italian views in his other films, even if those were in black and white."

"That's because he's trying to show the malaise of industrial society."

Karl looked up as Adrian joined them. "Where have you been? Why is your face wet?"

"Um, I had to go to the bathroom and there wasn't a clean towel. Hey, I'm not feeling so well. Do you think we could go pretty soon?"

"Sorry, man. Sure, we can split. Okay with you Sandy?"

"Could we just wait a little? I think there's about to be another poem."

Karl looked at Adrian to see if he was willing to wait a little longer for Sandy. Wiping his face with his hand and taking a deep breath, Adrian reluctantly nodded acceptance, though he could hardly stand to stay much longer. He was uncomfortable, disappointed, and disillusioned. So much for the romantic bohemian life of ecstatic states, transcendental poetry and free sex he had imagined.

The man in Middle Eastern attire who had brought the opium now stepped into the middle of the room, calling for everyone's attention. Loudly, he recited one of his poems, injecting what sounded like an Anglo Saxon inflection to his pronunciation.

> *Being chased,*
> *I somersault along the incline*
> *That slides until stop.*
> *The city glows below.*
>
> *An amulet bag*
> *Of grasshopper skin*
> *Hums in a gray mist*
> *Around my neck.*
>
> *Ghosts-in-waiting*
> *Leap home*
> *Through the spider's*
> *Trap-shorn navel.*
>
> *Enemies woven*
> *From silver thread*
> *Laugh and glisten with*
> *The strangled seamstress.*

As before, a respectful silence ensued as all present remained under the spell of the poem for a few seconds longer. Then, applause. Now more than ready to flee the scene, Adrian looked hopefully at Karl. Acceding to his wishes, Karl rose to go and Sandy followed. The three of them said goodbye to Damien, left the little house, and made their way in the cool thickening fog down Scott Street to Karl's borrowed Edsel.

Premonition

Having stayed up late writing a paper on Sinclair Lewis one Thursday night a week before Thanksgiving, Adrian overslept. Karl and Sandy had already left without waking him, apparently judging that he needed to sleep. But it was okay. Friday morning meant Astronomy, which was the one class he didn't mind missing. This wasn't due to a lack of interest in the heavens. The problem was the professor, from whom Adrian received no feeling at all about the celestial science. His dry lectures were composed of nothing but numbers and names.

His second class was not until after lunch, so he had time to make coffee in Karl's Chemex and eat a bowl of Cheerios before setting off at a leisurely pace to campus. When he finally arrived at Sproul Plaza, he was confronted with a completely unexpected scene. Normally, people would either be crossing the plaza to and from Telegraph or be gathered in the cafeteria or one of the restaurants in the student union building. But now everyone was just sitting. Some were on benches around the plaza, some on the stairs of the student union. All looked to be in shock. Girls were crying on the shoulders of their boyfriends. Young men had tears in their eyes too. Some stared straight ahead, seemingly stupefied. TV monitors that Adrian had never seen before hung lowered from their wall mounts all around the student union building. The same news program was playing on all of them. Adrian was still too far from them to see or hear what was being broadcast, so he walked toward one of the monitors. As he got closer, he recognized the face of Walter Cronkite.

"President Kennedy died at 1 pm Central Standard Time."

The impact of Kennedy's assassination pervaded life on campus and within the community. With the capture of Lee Harvey Oswald and his subsequent murder, the news and all the discussions that emerged from it filled the days until Thanksgiving. For Adrian and the others gathered around Karl, the tragic death of that respected young president further provoked their questioning of the status quo.

Adrian returned to his parent's home in Los Angeles for Thanksgiving, but the usual disagreements about moral values and politics didn't come up; such discussions were displaced by the gravity of events. With his mother and sister, Adrian sat in sober silence at the Thanksgiving dinner table as his father said grace.

Back in Berkeley, life slowly returned to a relatively normal tempo. December brought a series of storms, leaving students soaked day after day as they walked to campus. Overall, the cold rain and dark days emphasized the gloom that had settled over the community. But when they were warm and dry at home together, listening to the rain on the roof of their garret, Adrian, Karl and Sandy drew hope and comfort from the basic impressions of life.

At Christmas break, Adrian returned to Los Angeles to be with his parents. As he approached them in the visitor area outside the gate in the airport, something startling occurred. Having identified with the culture of the Berkeley hippy community, Adrian had let his hair grow long. His parents had already seen that at Thanksgiving and had finally accepted it. But since then, he had continued to let it grow even longer and had also started a mustache. As soon as his mother saw him, she shrieked with anger and embarrassment. Refusing his embrace, she turned and walked quickly ahead of him as they made their way out of the airport. Adrian's father didn't join in her reaction. Instead, he treated Adrian with kindness, staying close at his side. In the car, they rode home in silence to the Santa Monica apartment to which they had moved since Adrian left home. After arriving there, very little was said between them and Adrian's parents soon retired to their bedroom while he went to the guest room.

Lying in bed, Adrian felt a certain compassion for his mother's outburst. But he was still hurt and angered by her reaction and the unquestioned priority she always gave to outward appearance and conventional behavior. He had an impulse to get dressed and leave the apartment. He didn't know where he could go. But not wanting to stay there, he got up and gathered his clothes. When he couldn't find his shoes, he quietly opened the bedroom door to see if he had left them in the living room. As he looked for them there, he was startled by his mother's voice.

"I hid them because I was afraid you would leave. I'm sorry for my outburst." Coming into the room in her robe, tears streaming down her cheeks, she finally welcomed Adrian home with her embrace.

Both glad for their reconciliation, Adrian and his mother went back to their beds. As Adrian lay on his back looking up at the ceiling, his thoughts about his relation to his mother led him to recall the extraordinary incident that had occurred when he was in high school, an experience that had convinced him of the existence of a hidden intelligence in people that sometimes surfaces at times of need.

Adrian has returned home on a Saturday night after working late at his job as a box boy at the Brentwood Country Mart. He is surprised to find no one in the house. He knows that his father is out of town on a business trip and he reasons that his sister is probably staying overnight with a friend, but he expected his mother to be there. Tired, he puts on his pajamas and gets into bed. But he can't get to sleep because of a strange feeling that something bad is happening to his mother. Not knowing what else to do, he gets out of bed, dresses, picks up his car keys, and goes back into the garage. He doesn't know where to drive, but feels compelled to search for his mother.

He backs his car out of the garage and drives away from the neighborhood as if he is going to the local grocery store. When he comes to a busy intersection and has to choose which way to go, he decides to continue straight ahead. At the next intersection, he obeys an impulse—whether thought, intuition or instinct, he doesn't know—that directs him to turn right onto a major thoroughfare. Now he is in the westbound lane of a divided boulevard, heading toward the Pacific Ocean. Soon, as he is driving by the golf course of the Brentwood Country Club, his attention is drawn by the flashing lights of a police car parked on the other side of the boulevard. At the first opportunity, he makes a U-turn and pulls up behind the police car.

As he steps out onto the curb, he sees that a car has plowed through the chain link fence that surrounds the golf course. He walks toward the car and recognizes it as his mothers'. Then he sees her standing there. She is talking to a policeman who is writing on a pad. Adrian picks up his step. Coming closer, he sees that his mother looks confused and disoriented. He moves quickly to her now, embracing and comforting her. They exchange only a few words. He looks his mother over carefully to see if she is injured. The bridge of her nose is slightly swollen where it must have hit the steering wheel, but after questioning her about her condition, Adrian feels confident that she doesn't need to be seen by a doctor. Then, he turns to the policeman, who asks for his identification and address. Adrian gives him the rest of the information he wants and consents to have the car towed to a body shop. When he and the policeman have agreed that Adrian's mother doesn't require medical assistance, Adrian is allowed to take her home.

Having relived that mysterious event, Adrian realized that an organic connection between he and his mother existed quite separately from their personalities, political viewpoints, and values. That incident had shown him that in spite of the usual dominance of habitual automatic reactions—which he guessed was what Karl had meant when he said that people were machines—an inner intelligence can take precedence when needed.

Conversation at the Beach

On an unseasonably warm day at the beginning of February, Karl borrowed a car so that he and Adrian could drive to the coast. He suggested they go to Limantour Beach, part of the Point Reyes National Seashore. They drove across the Richmond-San Rafael Bridge, through San Rafael, San Anselmo, Fairfax and other cities of West Marin until they came to the Point Reyes area. Karl turned off Sir Francis Drake Boulevard onto a winding road that ascended through wooded hills and then dropped down toward the coast. They rolled down their windows to breathe in the healing air. As the road made the final steep descent, the mighty ocean appeared spread out in front of them. Karl slowed the car so they could take it in.

They left the car in a dirt parking lot and walked toward the beach, following the path past side trails that led into bird-rich marshlands until they came to a low hill of sand dunes. They took off their shoes, carrying them now as they slogged to the top of the dunes, where they stopped to look down at the wide expanse of sand and sea. Then, feeling like kids, they ran down the dunes to the flat sandy beach, where couples, people with dogs, children building sand castles, and giggling adolescent girls had also decided to spend a part of their day. Seeing a large tree limb in the sand ahead that had been washed by waves and bleached by the sun, they moved toward it.

Karl and Adrian sat close together on the limb, watching the waves coming in and going out again, listening to the hiss of the retreating current as it passed over little shells and stones, and basking in the welcome warmth of the sun. Point Reyes beaches were often foggy and cold, but not on this day. A patient brown pelican flew low above the breaker line looking for prey. Sandpipers skittered silently across the packed sand, seeking insects and shellfish left by the just receding surf. Karl and Adrian sat for a long time without speaking, taking in the rich perceptions of nature. As he listened to the ebb and flow of the surf, Adrian decided to ask Karl to explain what he'd meant on that first night in the garret by saying that they and everyone they knew were machines. When Adrian put the question, Karl closed his eyes and became still. After a fairly long silence, he began to speak.

"Adrian, I know that you consider yourself to be a unique person with some control over your life. Like you, all people imagine that they know themselves and can decide much of what happens in their lives. But in fact, neither of these beliefs is true. The truth is that we live completely in reaction to events according to the habits that have been formed in us. Our so-called thoughts and feelings are just automatic reactions based on previous experiences. Even the physical movements we call our own are variations of a few postures developed during our childhood."

This way of regarding human beings seemed abhorrent to Adrian and made him uncomfortable. "How can you look at our lives in such a bleak way?"

Karl looked back at Adrian steadily, communicating something without words. For a moment, Adrian's discomfort passed as he became aware of the position of his body sitting on that smooth limb and the breeze caressing his face, alert to the repetitive crash of the surf and the shouts of nearby children, sensitive to the intensity of Karl's blue eyes and the feeling of being more fully alive. This overall impression brought with it a strangely familiar sense of himself.

Seeing that Adrian was now listening attentively, Karl continued. "We do have the possibility of becoming complete human beings, but first we have to see the truth of ourselves as we are now. As long as we believe that we're fully conscious and in control of our lives, we won't have a chance. Only if we really see that we don't know ourselves and live always in reaction will we feel the need to develop ourselves."

"If all that you're saying is true, why don't more people know it?"

"It's because we live in a kind of waking dream. We know nothing of the full range of consciousness possible for us. If we did, we'd experience what is actually taking place in ourselves. Throughout our lives, as we grow up, form relationships, have children, create art, conduct businesses, and so on, we only experience a small part of our potential as human beings."

"It sounds like you're talking about developing consciousness."

"People don't really understand what consciousness is because they don't have it. Or rather they live in the lowest states of consciousness, never knowing the higher states that are possible for them."

"Why are we like this? Did something happen to our brains during our evolution?"

"Well, I guess you might put it that way," answered Karl. "Records we have from the ancient past give hints that some people may have lived with full consciousness at one time. But over the centuries, a small mechanical part of the brain has become dominant in most of us, so that our feelings and instincts have been driven more and more deeply into our subconscious and don't often function in our day to day lives. Education, society, materialistic values, and our devolved language have all contributed to that, so that today the associative part of the brain is considered to be primary. But our original state would be one in which the head, feelings and body work together in a balanced way that facilitates a connection with parts of the mind that are the seats of higher consciousness."

"Then how can we escape from this predicament?"

"There are people who, by design or chance, discover the truth of their situation and are fortunate enough to find and be helped by someone who is already on a pathway of spiritual development. Such growth was originally the purpose of the great world religions, but for the most part, these religious teachings have been corrupted and diluted to the point where, if they don't incite Holy War, they merely support the imagination in which people live. At best, they serve only to bring some modicum of comfort to believers."

"But are there still ways in which some people can develop their consciousness?"

"Yes. If a person really begins to feel that something essential is missing in them, they may be attracted to ways that offer the possibility of a deeper understanding of life. Some turn to communities in which one of the traditional spiritual disciplines is still more or less intact. Others, like me, find self-discovery in the creative process, assisted by kindred companions."

Adrian was about to ask more about these ways when Karl got up from their log and walked toward the breakers. After standing near the line of incoming surf and gazing out to sea for a few minutes, Karl came back, telling Adrian that he had to return to Berkeley for a meeting with the head of the music department in a couple of hours. Disappointed in having this long awaited conversation cut short so soon, Adrian accompanied Karl to the parking lot without saying more. But when they were back in the car, Karl turned to Adrian again.

"There's more I want to say to you Adrian, but I have to be very careful not to influence you too much. The ideas I've been speaking about have a way of getting inside some people and changing their lives, whether they like it or not. Let's leave that conversation for now."

Then, as they drove back to the East Bay, Karl talked about the work he had been doing to record his dreams. Adrian became drowsy and nodded off for much of the way. When they were back in Berkeley, Karl parked the car near Bancroft Way and Telegraph Avenue and proceeded toward the student union for his meeting.

Adrian went his own way, walking down Telegraph Avenue, replaying the conversation on the beach in his head as he joined the stream of people of diverse classes and ethnicities flowing away from campus. As he passed Larry Blake's Rathskeller, Adrian mused that he had never been in there and probably never would. That beer joint, with sawdust on the floor and steaks in the broiler, was the gathering place of fraternity and sorority people, where conversations revolved largely around parties and sports. He felt more at home in the Cafe Mediterranean, with its espresso drinks, sandwiches and small round tables where students held forth for hours talking about art and philosophy.

As he approached Moe's Books, Adrian decided to go in and see if he could find something interesting. He ended up in the basement, where he discovered a section devoted to Eastern religions and mysticism. At first, he found nothing, but then for some unknown reason he was attracted by a gray hardcover tucked in at the end of one of the bottom shelves. Pulling it out, he read the title on the spine, *Fragments of an Unknown Teaching*. Not having heard of the book or its author, Adrian opened it at random and read a paragraph. In a discussion with another man, the author was expressing the opinion that people were turning into machines. A chill ran up Adrian's spine at this echo of Karl's words. Without reading further, Adrian took the book upstairs to the counter, paid for it, and left the store.

Continuing down Telegraph with his purchase in a paper bag, Adrian noticed the sign for Payless Hi-Fi, a small record store that he had passed before. Although his parents had been sending him as much money as they could, he was beginning to realize that he would have to get a part-time job to make ends meet. Having worked at an upscale record store in Beverly Hills during high school, Adrian made the quick decision to try his luck getting a job at Payless Hi-Fi. As he walked in, he recognized the style of Bill Evans' piano improvisation playing in the shop. It was Bill's solo on *Blue on Green* from Miles' *Kind of Blue* album. Approaching a tall slender man at the counter, Adrian commented on Bill Evans' lyricism and the unique sound of his rootless chords. Intrigued by Adrian's knowledge of jazz, the man, who turned out to be the manager of the store, interviewed him on the spot. Adrian's timing was good, because an employee has just resigned, leaving a gap to be filled. After only a few more minutes of conversation, the manager asked Adrian to start the next day as a sales clerk.

With his recent book discovery and his new job, Adrian continued toward home feeling lucky. He especially appreciated the warmth of the sun on his face and the beauty of the gardens he passed on Blake Street on the way to their garret. As soon as he arrived, he removed the book from the bag and opened it at a different place than before. What he read seemed to set something inside resonating, as though he was being reminded of something he had known but forgotten. Like a hungry man seated before a table of food, Adrian read on and on. But eventually he had to put the book aside. He had a lot of homework to do.

Chris

When Adrian reported for work at the record store, the manager told him that he had managed to secure an advance copy of *The Beatles Second Album*. He asked Adrian to play it from time to time to attract customer interest. Later that evening, after the manager had gone home, Adrian put the Beatles record on the turntable and turned up the volume. A petite girl with an enchanting smile, who Adrian had already noticed browsing through the bins in the jazz section, now drifted toward the counter. She asked Adrian about the record that was playing. Her deep blue eyes reached out to him and then looked away shyly as she asked the question. Fascinated by her unusual combination of good looks and reserve, he answered briefly, telling her that it was an advance copy of the new Beatles album. When he asked her if she was a fan, a winsome wrinkle appeared on her forehead that Adrian found adorable.

As another customer seemed to be waiting to pay for an album, Adrian could not continue talking with the girl. But he didn't want to lose the chance of meeting her again, so he offered to take her name and phone number, saying that he would call her when more copies of the Beatles album came in. When she took the paper and pen he handed to her, he watched as she wrote her name. Chris

Carter. He liked the name and the stylish flair with which she wrote it. Chris handed the paper to him and smiled, her eyes again bewitching him. Also aware of the customer waiting behind her, she moved toward the door of the shop. Just before she let herself out, she turned and looked back at him. They smiled at each other, each secretly hoping to see the other again.

Adrian waited until he had a day off to call Chris. Something about her chirpy "Hello" told him that she had been waiting for him to call. When he asked if she went to Cal, Chris told him that she was a student at the California College of Arts and Crafts in Oakland but lived only a short bus ride away from Berkeley. She proposed that they meet at the University Avenue entrance to the Berkeley marina, where they could walk along the shoreline. She said she would take the bus from Claremont and suggested that he catch one on University.

Adrian and Chris walked from one end of the marina to the other, talking all the way. Exchanging stories about their backgrounds and families, they shared that special experience of sharing one's own life story and opening to the life of a new person in whom you are interested. As Chris talked, Adrian continued to appreciate the way in which her striking beauty was balanced by quiet modesty. She seemed impressed by things he told her about himself, yet downplayed her own activities and talents. There was something sad in the depths of those elegant blue eyes, though he didn't yet know what it was.

When it started to rain in the late afternoon, Chris suggested that they go to her place to get dry and make dinner. They hopped on a bus traveling up University Avenue, then transferred at Shattuck to another on the Claremont line. Walking a couple of blocks from the bus stop, they came to her building, one of the vintage Queen Anne Victorians found throughout Oakland and Berkeley. All of its rooms had been converted to apartments. They passed through the main entrance and climbed well worn stairs to her studio on the second floor, in the corner turret of the building. She found her keys and opened the door, leading him into a marvelous round room. A stove and refrigerator sat against the wall near the door. On the other side of the door, improvised shelves of white boards and gray bricks were filled with books and records. Across the room, a large window looked out on the neighborhood. Chris' bed, a single mattress neatly covered by an Indian spread and several pillows, lay on the floor under the window.

They took off their wet coats and Chris opened the valve on an old radiator, her only source of heat. She pulled a Modern Jazz Quartet album from the bookcase and placed the record on the turntable of her stereo. She adjusted the volume and then went to the stove to put on a kettle for tea. During their walk, when they had talked about music, Adrian had been happy to find out she shared his love of jazz. Listening to John Lewis improvising on *Django*, Adrian lingered by her bookcase, looking at the titles there. Spotting a book called *The Life Divine*, he pulled

34

it off the shelf and opened it to a page where a bookmark had been inserted. He began to read.

> *For we can say that the inner Presence alone is a Truth and the discordant externality is a falsehood or illusion created by a mysterious principle of Ignorance; our problem is to find some way of escape out of the falsehood of the manifested world into the truth of the hidden Reality.*

The passage struck a chord in Adrian that resonated with the residue of his beach conversation with Karl. Turning to the title page, he saw that the author was Sri Aurobindo. A photograph of the author on the facing page showed an elderly bearded Indian man wrapped in a simple white tunic. Finding something strangely attractive about the man in the photo, Adrian let his gaze remain there for what seemed a long time until he began to feel a faint reverberation in his chest. Noticing Adrian's concentration on the book, Chris approached and touched his elbow. His focus of attention on the photo now broken, Adrian turned to Chris and asked what she knew of Sri Aurobindo.

"I went with a friend to a lecture in San Francisco last month. He told me that Sri Aurobindo died in 1950, but some of his followers have continued his teaching. I don't remember the name of the man who spoke that night, but he was really interesting. When he looked at you, the force that came through his eyes was incredible! My friend loaned me this book, but I haven't read it yet. Are you interested in this kind of thing?"

He considered telling her about his conversations with Karl and the book he'd just started reading, but didn't feel ready to share that part of himself yet.

"Yeah, I've recently gotten interested in Eastern religions, but I haven't heard of this guy before."

Adrian put the book back on the shelf and walked over to look out the window. Being there at that moment with Chris in her place and listening to the happy blending of Milt Jackson's vibes with the sound of rain outside, Adrian felt the same joy he had felt before on rainy days. He always wondered why he felt elated when he heard the rain. Was it because he had been born on a rainy afternoon? He didn't know, but he felt more contented than he had in a long time. Looking out the window, he watched cars passing on the street below, splashing through a pool of rainwater at the corner when they turned.

Chris came up from behind and put her arms around him, laying the side of her head against his back. He waited a moment without moving and then turned around to face her. She was so much shorter than he that her head came up only to his chin. When she looked up at him, he saw the sadness in her eyes again, now more pronounced. He had the feeling that she desperately wanted to be loved but was afraid of being rejected. He took her in his arms and held her close. They stood by the window like that for several minutes, not moving, listening to the music and the rain outside.

Taking his hand, she led him to her bed, where they lay down together with their arms around one another. They remained like that, lost in the delicious sensation glowing from every point at which their bodies touched. When it was time, Adrian began to unbutton Chris' blouse while she watched him in complete surrender, her eyes conveying both vulnerability and trust.

Both Adrian and Chris had only limited experience with sex, but they proceeded with confidence and mutual respect. As they made love, her quiet gentleness in every move she made established a level of refinement that invited the same in response from him.

Adrian and Chris began to see each other every day. Adrian took her home to meet Karl and Sandy, who welcomed Chris, but the new lovers went to Chris' tower room when they wanted to be alone. Reclining on Chris' bed after making love, they listened to jazz or read poetry to one another and then made dinner together in her humble kitchen. For Adrian's birthday, Chris gave him a complete set of A. A. Milne's children's books: *Winnie the Pooh, The House at Pooh Corner, When We Were Very Young,* and *Now We Are Six.* Her fondness for these stories perfectly represented her innocent and childlike nature.

A Dream

Adrian found himself alone for spring break. Chris had gone to New York to visit her father and Karl and Sandy were at a Zen retreat. This gave him time to think. Fragments of his last conversation with Karl, ideas he was discovering in the gray book by Ouspensky and the lines he'd read from the book by Sri Aurobindo kept coming back to him. Then an incident occurred that added to his growing recognition of an unknown intelligence within and the need to understand it.

After having dinner at the apartment of his friend Gary one night, Adrian's stomach began to hurt. When Gary suggested he look for a remedy in the medicine cabinet, Adrian found only Milk of Magnesia. He took some, but his stomachache only got worse and he gladly accepted Gary's offer to take him home. The garret was cold, as he had turned off the little gas stove before leaving. He turned up the burners as high as they would go and climbed under the heavy covers on Karl's bed. The pain in his abdomen kept him awake at first but eventually he fell asleep.

He awoke from a disturbing dream the next morning at the sound of loud knocking on the door. As he rose out of bed, the sudden movement brought a sharp pain in his abdomen. Groggy from sleeping in the stuffy room with the stove burning all night, Adrian walked laboriously to the door and opened it. It was Gary, who, worried by Adrian's complaints of stomach distress the night before, had come to see if he needed help. When Adrian had failed to answer the first taps on the door, Gary became concerned and knocked louder until he finally heard some movement inside.

"Adrian, how are you feeling, man? Your stomachache seemed to be really bad last night. I've been worried about you knowing you're alone here."

"Um, actually, it's a lot worse, Gary. I've got a really sharp pain down here." As Adrian pointed to his lower abdomen, he suddenly remembered his dream. In it, he had been having an appendicitis attack. A thought flashed in his mind. Was his dream informing him that he was actually having an appendicitis attack? He hesitated sharing this with Gary, but the pain in his abdomen was not getting better and he had to do something about it.

"You know, it's funny, but while I was asleep, I was having a really weird dream. The thing is, I dreamt I was having an appendicitis attack. Isn't that strange? I mean, I never thought about that before, so why did it come up in a dream? I know it sounds silly, but I wonder if some part is trying to tell the rest of me that I'm having this attack."

Gary, who had studied Jungian psychology as an undergraduate, didn't hesitate to give credence to Adrian's dream.

"Get dressed! I'm taking you to the hospital, now!"

Adrian put on some clothes as quickly as he could and rode with Gary in his old Mercedes to Cowell Hospital. When Gary told the attending nurse at the emergency room desk that it might be Adrian's appendix, she arranged to have a doctor see Adrian right away. His diagnosis confirmed the dream. Adrian needed to have his appendix removed before it could rupture.

While recovering from the appendectomy, Adrian reflected on the revelation in his dream. Could there be an intelligence that is so well connected to one's body that it can recognize the source of any affliction? While he was coming down with the stomachache that night at Gary's, there had been no mention of the possibility of an appendicitis attack. He had not even thought of it. And yet, something in him knew exactly where the problem lay and had communicated that to his subconsciousness in a dream. What's more, thanks to a connection between his subconsciousness and waking consciousness, he had remembered the dream and been able to relate it to his immediate situation. These thoughts reminded him of the time he had been led by an unseen intelligence to his mother and her crashed car. He wondered about the connection between these two events. The more he thought about this, the more he needed to understand it.

Summer

When finals were over and school was out until the fall, Adrian breathed a sigh of relief. He had been looking forward to the summer vacation. His parents wanted him to come home, but he'd decided to stay in Berkeley. Although many people were leaving for the summer, there was still an active population of students and non-students keeping the coffee houses, restaurants, and theaters full. Chris, Karl and Sandy were planning to be around most of the time, as were Desmond, Jeff and a few of his other friends. Adrian wanted to enjoy the warm summer in Berkeley with them, hiking in Tilden, taking in the latest flicks, attending one of the outdoor Shakespeare plays, going to the Monterey Jazz Festival, and otherwise living the good life. He still had to work part-time at the record store, but he didn't mind now that he was free from the incessant academic demand.

Although he was able to give Chris the attention and affection she continually required, he also liked spending time with his friends Desmond and Jeff, who had initiated him into the practice of smoking pot. Desmond usually had a good supply of grass, which he shared generously. Chris always declined to join Adrian when they were going to get high because she tended to become paranoid. This was fine with Adrian, as he welcomed the male camaraderie. The three friends usually met at Desmond's place, where they would sit in a circle on a small fake oriental carpet in his living room and pass around a long-stemmed pipe filled with Desmond's grass.

During these sessions, they talked about different kinds of mysticism. For awhile, they were into Tarot cards and each of them had his own deck. They spread out the cards on the floor according to a technique Jeff had discovered in a book and waited for the Major Arcana to speak to them. Later, when their interest moved to the I Ching, they threw special Chinese coins on the carpet, looked up the corresponding hexagrams in the Wilhelm translation, and read the judgments to one another. They also shared passages from *Zen Flesh, Zen Bones* aloud, hoping to receive a shock of enlightenment from one of its stories and koans. When they were high, they believed wholeheartedly in their sudden insights, so that a new revelation of some truth would inevitably lead to a long discussion of its implications.

Attracted by the rising flood of interest in Eastern religions, Adrian and his friends shared what they had heard about the various gurus who had arrived in America and formed communities around their teachings. Karl and Sandy had already begun attending weekly meditations with Shunryu Suzuki at Zen Center in San Francisco. Hearing how wonderful Suzuki Roshi was, Desmond and Jeff were planning to go too, but Adrian resisted, for reasons he did not himself understand. Some followers of

Meyer Baba had invited Desmond to one of their introductory talks, but he declined when he learned of their strong rules against any kind of drug use.

The three of them also listened to Alan Watt's talks on the Berkeley public radio station whenever they could. Knowing that Watts lived in Sausalito, they had toyed with the idea of trying to find his houseboat and paying him a visit, but they never did. They were particularly attracted to Watts because of his interest in the relation between psychedelics and the study of Zen. In fact, the new popularity of spiritual traditions was beginning to coalesce with the emerging influence of psychotropic drugs in university towns all across the country. Among the most influential in this movement were three Harvard professors who had been going from campus to campus speaking about their life-changing experiences with LSD.

When Adrian saw posters on campus announcing that Timothy Leary, Richard Alpert and Ralph Metzner were coming to Cal to speak about their LSD research, he excitedly told his friends about it. They all went to the talk at the student union together, joining a capacity audience brimming with anticipation. The three Harvard professors began by describing their initial laboratory experiments with people they had placed under the influence of LSD, mescaline, or psilocybin. After many of their subjects reported having profound mystical and spiritual experiences, the professors began trying the drugs themselves. Their passionate descriptions of their personal experiences left no doubt that their own deep revelations during these psychotropic sessions had transformed their lives.

After the lecture, while many from the audience crowded up to the podium for a chance to get closer to and talk with one of the professors, a representative was selling copies of their new book, *The Psychedelic Experience*, based on the *Tibetan Book of the Dead*. The professors had highly recommended using this book during an LSD trip, promising that it would serve as a guide to free people from the many illusory traps that can appear and help them approach the highest levels of inner enlightenment. Looking at a copy, Adrian noticed that it was dedicated to Aldous Huxley, who had died the previous year, not long after Adrian had heard him speak in Los Angeles about his experiences with psychedelic drugs. When Adrian found himself handing over his money for a copy of the book, he realized that he was going to try LSD himself.

As if by design, a large supply of high-quality LSD became available in Berkeley in the days immediately following the lecture. Matt, a new member of Karl's cafeteria discussion group, was a chemistry student with connections to the people who were making and distributing the drug. He obtained LSD capsules for each of them. Most dropped acid as soon as they received their capsules. Chris declined hers. Adrian accepted his, but put off taking it.

Journeys

Encouraged by reports of his friends about their experiences, Adrian's interest in the promised gifts of LSD eventually overcame his fear of its unknown effects. But he wanted to take it the way the Harvard professors had suggested — in a quiet place with a guide. He asked a friend who owned an apartment building if he could use a vacant room for an evening. Karl agreed to accompany Adrian, to try to be sensitive to his state, and to read aloud to him what he judged to be appropriate passages from *The Psychedelic Experience*. The Harvard professors had emphasized that guidance is essential at certain junctures, both to help the voyager dispel traps of negative imagination and to steer him toward positive inner perceptions. But in spite of all his preparations, Adrian approached his journey with trepidation, concerned that his predisposition to worry might lead him to a dead end of unpleasant hallucinations. Sure enough, as the LSD took effect, Adrian's habitual anxiety soon led him into a frightening landscape.

Objects in the room take on a fearsome aspect. The patterns of wood grain on the wall panels begin to flow and reshape themselves into demonic faces that glare at him with malice. As he turns to Karl for help, his cousin transforms into a hideous creature with a menacing countenance. Adrian remembers a section in the guide on second bardo nightmares but the fiendish look on Karl's face is so threatening that Adrian is unable to ask him to read it. Karl, seeing Adrian's emotional state, thumbs through the book looking for a passage that can help. He finds Instructions for the Wrathful Visions and begins to read aloud. The book reveals that Adrian's terrifying visions are only the projected manifestations of his own thoughts and emotions. Continuing to read, Karl exhorts Adrian to free himself from the hallucinations by recognizing that they come from within himself.

As Adrian accepts the truth of the magical words Karl has read, the demonic visions melt away. Liberated, Adrian enters a new domain of experience. For a time—he doesn't know for how long because he is no longer in time—Adrian opens to the profound experience of his being as pure light and energy.

When Adrian awoke in the afternoon the next day from a long sleep, he felt certain there was another reality in which life could be experienced in a much more meaningful way than he had known before. Ideas he and his friends had discussed from intellectual curiosity now came alive. He enjoyed a fresh appreciation of the literature that had attracted him throughout his life, such as the fairy tales he had read voraciously as a child, the novels of Hermann Hesse, the poetry of William Blake and Samuel Coleridge, the writings of Thoreau and Emerson, and the final works of Aldous Huxley.

Adrian's friends were also deeply affected by their LSD experiences. Before, they had only read and talked about higher states of awareness. Now, they believed they had really experienced these states for themselves. Sharing insights and questions daily, they began to talk earnestly about finding a way toward the practical realization in their lives of the possibility they had discovered. One evening in the cafeteria, they turned to Karl with their questions.

As they spoke to him of what each of them had experienced during their psychedelic sessions, they described dramatic hallucinations, revelatory observations about people, the majesty of nature, the sense assaulting wonderland of city life, and the perception of a mystical connection with everything. But Karl seemed to put all of that aside as he brought them back to consider their ordinary lives and their need to know themselves. He put down his fork, paused as always, and then began to speak.

"With the help of some chemicals, you may have artificially tasted something of the vastness of the mind and discovered a vibrant relation to the world around you. Having been temporarily awakened, you begin to realize that you are usually asleep to the real meaning of your lives. Now you want to find out how to live in a way that leads toward this state of consciousness again. Some of you may return to LSD or try peyote or magic mushrooms and rediscover that other world, but this will not change anything. It may even make it more difficult or impossible to attain authentic and permanent development. You see, real change requires a sustained and difficult work over many years.

"If you begin such work, it will probably take you all of your life, and even then you may not achieve your goal. You must first discover who you really are, just as you are. For this, you need to learn how to study yourselves. Ordinary introspection or guided psychiatric analysis won't bring what you need. You must find a new way to see yourselves. Making outward changes to your life won't help either. Some people decide to 'drop out', but that only leads them away from the goal. You have to start getting to know yourselves precisely where you are now, in the lives you are leading."

Karl stopped speaking and waited for them to respond.

"How can we begin to do what you're suggesting?" Adrian asked.

"You can find important ideas in books," Karl replied, "but to develop a real practice you need to receive help directly from someone who is already working on themselves. It's the same if you want to be a weaver or a potter. You can't learn those crafts from books. You need to work alongside someone more advanced than you who is able to show you the way. Of course, if there are such individuals, they may prefer to give their time to helping many people rather than just one person. So if you are lucky enough to find a teacher, you might have to join a group of people. Even if you normally resist participation in groups, you may come to feel the need for support from others who are on the same path."

They all sat quite still, even though Karl had stopped speaking. He gazed at each of them in turn. When he came to Adrian, he felt what seemed like an intense stream of energy flowing between them. Adrian felt it too. As he had been listening to Karl, something like the vibration of a Tibetan bell had been resonating in Adrian's chest, calling to him to stay within. As a result, he now found himself strangely relaxed and collected, with the ability to listen more deeply than usual, so that Karl's words came alive with meaning.

Karl looked down for a few moments, as if deciding whether to say more. Then raising his head again, he went on.

"There's a group of people in San Francisco who, from a common need, managed to find one another and eventually began meeting together several years ago to try to work on themselves. But they soon came to the conclusion that they were working in the dark. They knew they needed guidance from someone with real experience of the path they needed to take but hadn't been able to find. Fortunately, one of them, a close friend of mine, learned of a master living in New York who had been searching and practicing for many years. They managed to find his address and together composed a letter that described their common quest and asked for his help. They were surprised and delighted when he responded that he would soon be coming to San Francisco and would see them. At the first meeting with him, they knew they had found their teacher. He gave them a general program of study and assigned individual tasks to each of them. He now makes regular trips to San Francisco."

Karl again scrutinized the faces of each of his friends, clearly weighing their response to what he had said. Then he concluded, "If you really want to develop yourselves, I suggest that you find that group and work with them."

They were all eager to hear more, but as no one spoke further, Karl stood up, picked up his dishes and silverware, and headed for the cafeteria busing station. The others followed, leaving the cafeteria and heading off in different directions.

Adrian walked across Sproul Plaza toward Telegraph Avenue. As he waited for a green light to cross Bancroft Way, he had the strange but definite sensation of being between two worlds: the world he was leaving and the world just ahead. Inside him was the vibrating residue of the exchange in the cafeteria. In front of him, he felt the approaching onslaught of energy emanating from the people, lights, and sounds along Telegraph. At the meeting point of these two worlds, past and future moved into the present.

Crossing Bancroft and walking down Telegraph, Adrian continues to feel unusually collected while becoming keenly aware of the life around him. Cars snake up the crowded one-way street. Students of different nationalities in all colors and styles of clothing pass up and down the avenue. The lighted signs and windows of restaurants, coffee houses, and bookstores beckon. As he progresses unhurried down the avenue, he is sensitive to every aroma, now of tamales, now of fried rice, now of roasting coffee beans, now of a girl passing by, now of decomposing food in the garbage can at the side of a Greek restaurant. He is especially aware of the sounds coming to him from all around, from the talk and laughter of people passing by, from the clatter and conversation in each restaurant, from the engines and horns of cars. Even the Beatles song playing in the record store where he works sounds different, clearer and more nuanced.

Now he realizes that what is most interesting is not the drama of the sights, smells and sounds outside of him, but rather the fresh and vibrant quality of his awareness of them. He understands that, in the midst of all these perceptions, he can remain at home in himself rather than being drawn to the outside, as is usually the case.

The vivid impressions faded when Adrian became absorbed by his thoughts again. He considered what Karl had said about the need for a practical way of studying oneself. That seemed to be the next step he and the others had to face if they really wanted to move toward lives with meaning. But why had Karl left so suddenly without telling them more about the group in San Francisco? How could they find it without knowing what it was or where it was? Why hadn't Karl joined this group? Were any of them really willing to put themselves in a group under the direction of a leader? Adrian became so lost in these thoughts that he arrived home with no memory whatsoever of the people and places he had passed during the last ten minutes of his walk.

During the remaining weeks of the summer, Desmond and Jeff continued to experiment with psychedelic drugs. Adrian declined their invitation to join them when they managed to get some magic mushrooms. But in late August, Matt, the chemistry student who had obtained capsules for everyone after the talk by the Harvard professors, persuaded Adrian to take LSD again.

As planned, Adrian joined Matt early on a Sunday morning at an entrance to Tilden Park, where they made a minor ceremony of swallowing their capsules. Without talking much, they embarked upon a beautiful sunlit trail that wound through the hills all the way to the highest point of Tilden. But as was his wont, Adrian began to worry. When he made a remark that revealed his anxiety, Matt grabbed him and pushed him to the ground. Matt held Adrian down, ordering him to let go of all his fears. Adrian was amazed to find that he was able to respond, completely letting go as he relaxed into the dirt and pine needles on the trail beneath him. He was surprised that Matt had done this, but he realized that it was an important lesson. He got up and they continued on along the trail.

But gradually, Adrian felt more and more ill at ease with Matt. In spite of what Matt had done for him, there was something disharmonious in their relationship that made their communications awkward. After an hour, they became separated, partly because Adrian let himself fall behind without really trying to keep track of Matt. Going on alone on a side trail, Adrian came to a grove of redwoods and stopped, looking up to find the tops of the trees that soared straight to the sky.

Everything around him throbs with life. The crystalline voices of the branches creaking in the wind stirs his feeling and demands his respect. Awakened to the vitality of the living earth, he is drawn closer to it. He sits down on the soft accumulation of flat needles and small cones. Somehow, this feast of organic perceptions gives him an appetite for tobacco. He takes a pack of Camels out of his pocket and withdraws a cigarette. Just striking a match is a wonder in itself, the sound of it, the odor of sulfur, and the bright flame. He lights the cigarette and inhales. The warm smoke is vital and pungent. But the real miracle is in the simple sensation he has of the cigarette in his hand, because it feels as much a part of him as the fingers that hold it.

When he has finished smoking, he gets up and continues along the trail until he comes to a magnificent overlook. Looking down at San Francisco Bay with its bridges connecting the cities clustered around it, he thinks about his life. He is convinced now that, to find his way to something like this level of experience naturally rather than artificially, he has to meet people who understand how to wake up. He doesn't know how to navigate the currents of the fast moving river of consciousness. He needs real knowledge. Standing there on that hilltop with the clear sky above and civilization spread out below, Adrian makes a pledge to himself that he will do whatever is necessary to find a Teacher.

Beginning his descent, Adrian followed the trail back down to Strawberry Canyon and the campus below as he also began the slow return to an ordinary state of awareness. He saw with surprise how quickly he welcomed the approaching comfort of a familiar way of being as the intensity of feeling, thought and vision lessened.

When Adrian arrived at home, Karl wasn't there. He took out his *Collected Poems of William Blake* and began to read the "Songs of Innocence." They were full of meaning. Adrian was absorbed by Blake's watercolors when Karl returned, greeting him with only a quiet "Hello." Karl made himself some tea and sat down near Adrian, who felt sure that Karl was sensitive to his state.

"How can I make contact with the group you told us about?" Adrian asked.

Karl looked at him affectionately. "Are you sure you want to take that step?"

"Yes."

Karl sipped his tea. "There's a bookstore in San Francisco that's connected to this group. Go there and look for an older woman behind the counter. Speak to her. Tell her that you've come to the realization that you need to work on yourself but don't know how to begin. Ask her if she can put you in touch with someone who might help you."

Karl got up and opened the top drawer of his bureau. He rummaged through the contents until he found what he was looking for. He handed Adrian the business card for the bookstore. Then, without another word, he turned and got ready to go to bed.

Looking at the card, Adrian felt the excitement of a new possibility. He decided that he would go to San Francisco at the end of the following week. Carefully, he put the card in his wallet. Then he too undressed for bed. It had been a long day.

The Bookstore

After the first weeks of a very full new schedule of classes in September, Adrian soon found himself burning the candle at both ends. It didn't help that he was also working three nights a week at the record store. One afternoon, as he was walking across a bridge over a small stream bed running through campus after leaving his ancient Chinese history class, he felt all at once how tired he had become. Realizing how badly he needed sleep, Adrian walked straight home and went to bed. Karl and Sandy were away for a couple of days and Chris' sister was visiting her, so he had been sure he wouldn't be disturbed. Though he slept soundly for hours, he woke up around midnight with thoughts churning in his mind. Soon he was wide awake.

As he had before, Adrian began to worry again about the possibility of being drafted into the Army. President Johnson had recently reversed Kennedy's policy of disengagement and begun to expand American involvement in the war, citing the "battle against communism" as the rationale. Adrian held a student deferment, but he had only one more year of undergraduate work left and would lose his classification if he didn't continue on to graduate school. Even then, as more and more troops were demanded, there was no guarantee that the government would continue to honor all deferments. For the time being, he was safe, but he felt a future threat laying in wait for him along the unknown road ahead.

Thoughts about the military gave way to reconsideration of the timing for his planned visit to the bookstore. Perhaps it would be better to wait until after mid-term exams, or even until the Christmas break. Clearly, his schedule was too full to add another element. What if the person at the bookstore did put him in touch with someone? Would he have the time to make trips to San Francisco to meet with them? And what if he was invited to other kinds of activities? How would he manage to attend those? He couldn't afford to reduce his hours at the record store. He was making barely enough money as it was.

Catching himself in this line of justification, Adrian became aware of the strange resistance that was coloring his outlook and overtaking his previous intention. What was behind it? What was he afraid of?

Now that it's clear that he won't be able to go back to sleep, he gets out of bed and puts on sweatpants, a sweatshirt, and some socks. He lights the little gas stove and sits staring into the dancing flames. Serious questions begin to present themselves. These are no longer justifications, but sincere inquiries that he doesn't know the answers to. What is missing from his life? What does he want? As he stays with this last question, it seems to open a door. He feels quiet. Closing his eyes, he sits without moving, trying to stay attentive to an inner sensitivity which is emerging. When a thought comes, it's clear that he has to let it go to remain available to what seems like a call from another world within, an influence which he somehow recognizes, a representative of an intelligence usually covered over by the inner noise of thoughts and reactions to the outer demands of life.

For a moment, he knew what he wanted. But when he found himself dreaming again, he let his effort go and got up to get a glass of water. As he drank, his attention was drawn to the book he'd been studying. He picked it up and sat down again to read. But very soon he found himself nodding off, unable to stay with the words on the page. He put down the book and went back to bed.

Two days later, Adrian was on the bus to San Francisco. Getting off on Van Ness Avenue, he walked down Bush Street to Polk Street, where the bookstore was located. He passed restaurant after restaurant—Korean, Chinese, Vietnamese, Mexican and Thai. He was watching for the address on the card Karl had given him, but before he could locate the street number on one of the buildings around him, the store window right in front of him told him that he was already there. Arranged in the window were a variety of books on Eastern religions, occult systems, and diverse metaphysical subjects, as well as decks of Tarot cards and photographs of spiritual masters. One of these photos caught his attention, as the face of its subject evoked a deep response in him, just as the photo of

Sri Aurobindo had when he had seen it in the book in Chris' apartment.

Only one other customer was in the store, purchasing several books from a woman behind the counter. Adrian felt certain she must be the one Karl had told him about. To pass the time until she was finished with the other customer, Adrian began browsing the shelves. There were many books he had never seen before. Entire sections were devoted to Theosophy, Tarot, Occultism, Freemasonry, Hermeticism, Hinduism, Tantrism, Yoga, Tibetan Buddhism, Zen Buddhism, Taoism, Shamanism, Sufism, Madame Blavatsky, Krishnamurti, Rudolf Steiner, Meyer Baba, and others. As he moved slowly down one aisle, he spotted a copy of the book he'd bought at Moe's. On the shelf next to it was a small but thick book by G. I. Gurdjieff, with the strange title of *Beelzebub's Tales to His Grandson*. Taking it from the shelf and thumbing through it, he was attracted by provocative words and phrases that seemed to jump off the pages, but the book appeared to be dense and difficult. Then, looking up, he saw the other customer leaving the store with a brown bag in his hand. Now was his moment, but Adrian suddenly felt resistance to going through with his intention to speak to the woman. Just as his thoughts were offering justifications for putting off the confrontation until another time, the woman looked directly over at him. When their eyes met, he felt that she knew exactly what was going on in him. Without thinking further, he carried the book he had in his hand to the counter.

At first, he acted as though he'd only come to buy a book. Eyeing his selection, the woman looked him over intently for a few seconds. Then she turned to the routine of ringing up the sale. After she had taken his money and was reaching for a small paper bag, Adrian finally got up the courage to speak.

"Uh, can I talk to you for a minute?"

"Certainly." Something in her voice and expression suggested that she already knew what he was about to ask of her.

"Um, recently I've been feeling that something is missing in my life. I've had several unusual experiences that have shown me that something else is possible, but most of the time I'm not connected with it. I've heard there's a group in San Francisco that is following a certain philosophy and I'm hoping that you might be able to help me meet one of those people."

The woman stood still for a moment, then placed his book in the bag. Handing it to him, she held his gaze in hers as though deciding whether to grant his request. Then, without another word, she opened a drawer behind the counter and took out an address book. With a decisive movement, she opened the book directly to the page she wanted and laid it down on the counter. She took one of the store's business cards out of a small stand and copied a name and phone number on the back of it. Then, she gave it to him.

"Mr. Wells is a very busy businessman. Keep trying to reach him until you succeed."

There was warmth in her reply, but something else too, a sense of knowing that emerged from her deep green eyes.

Adrian left the store elated. Tucking the bag with his new book under one arm to free up both hands, he carefully placed the card with Mr. Wells' phone number in his wallet. He put the wallet back in his pocket, took the bag back into his hand, and headed down Polk toward California Street. Bristling with excitement, he walked up California to Van Ness to catch the bus back to Berkeley.

Chris was waiting for him in the Bear's Lair, a casual eating place in the lower level of the student union building. As he was almost a half-hour late, Adrian expected that she might have grown impatient. But she greeted him with a big smile. Chris was nearly always sweet and easy-going, seldom showing any irritation or negativity. Actually, Adrian was beginning to feel that she was a little too nice. But he was glad to see her and sat down close to her on one side of the booth. They exchanged small talk and intermittently scanned their menus. After the waitress had taken their orders, Chris smiled at him again and snuggled closer. As she did, Adrian realized that he ought to try to reach Mr. Wells right away.

"Sorry, Chris, but there's a phone call I've got to make. I'll be right back."

"It's okay, Adrian."

He got up and found the phone booth at the back of the restaurant. Opening the accordion door of the booth, he sat down on the round metal stool, took out his wallet, removed the business card, and placed it on the small metal shelf. Then he waited a minute, trying to collect himself and rehearse what he would say when Mr. Wells answered. When he was ready, he fished a quarter out of his pocket, dropped it into the coin slot at the top of the phone, and dialed the number written on the back of the card.

After three rings, a woman answered.

"South Bay Technical Services."

"May I speak with Mr. Wells?"

"I'm sorry, but he is out of the office at the moment. Would you like to leave a message?"

"No, that's okay. I'll call back."

"Can you try again in about ten minutes?"

Adrian said that he would, thanked her and hung up the phone. Then he returned to Chris.

"The guy wasn't there, so I'll have to call him back. Anyway, tell me about what you're working on at school now."

"Well, I'm starting some studies with pastels. They're fairly new to me, but I really love the colors. I'm going to do a whole series based on views of San Francisco Bay."

As she was talking, Adrian's thoughts began to stray to Mr. Wells again. He looked at his watch to see if ten minutes had passed yet. No, still seven minutes to go. Noticing his distraction, Chris finally began to show some irritation.

"What's on your mind?" she asked.

Adrian wasn't ready yet to tell her about his trip to the bookstore or the reason he wanted to meet Mr. Wells.

"The thing is, there's a really interesting opportunity I'm anxious to talk to this guy about. Hey, sorry I got distracted. Go on with what you were saying about your pastels."

"So anyway, I'm doing a series of views of San Francisco Bay. To get familiar with the full range of pastels, I'm going to do each one in a different color."

Adrian tried to listen as Chris continued telling him about her pastel work, but his body was restless and his thoughts kept drifting off to what he would say when he was able to talk to Mr. Wells. He checked his watch. Ten minutes had passed. He had to call again immediately, without delay.

"Hey, Chris, I'm sorry to interrupt again, but I really have to try to call this guy one more time. Hopefully, I'll get through now."

Chris no longer hid her impatience as he excused himself.

In the phone booth, he dialed the number. This time, the woman in Mr. Wells' office said that he must have gone to his boat and might not be back for the rest of the day.

"But there's still a chance he'll stop by in the next few minutes on his way to the marina," she added. "Can I tell him who is calling if he does come in?"

"Um, my name is Adrian Masters. But I'll definitely call back."

He hung up the receiver.

Chris seemed more annoyed when Adrian returned this time, particularly because their hamburgers had arrived and were getting cold while she was waiting for him. As they began to eat, his agitated thoughts returned. What if Mr. Wells came back just after he called? He might miss him altogether if he waited too long. He looked at his watch. It had been only about five minutes. Looking back up at Chris, who was describing one of her teachers, Adrian tried to let go of his thoughts and follow what she was saying, but he couldn't restrain himself from checking his watch again. Finally, he excused himself.

"Okay, Chris, I'm going to try the call again. I promise that after I talk to him I'll be able to listen to you."

"Go ahead," she grumbled, looking down with a frown.

Once again, Adrian sat in the phone booth trying to relax and quiet his mind. When he was ready, he dropped another quarter into the slot and slowly lifted the receiver to his ear. The woman answered after only one ring.

"South Bay Technical Services."

"Uh, it's Adrian Masters again."

"You're lucky! Mr. Wells just stopped by for a minute and can speak with you now."

Her words triggered a mixture of exhilaration and apprehension in him. He waited.

After a few moments, a very deep, guttural voice came on the line. "Yes, Mr. Masters?"

"Hello, Mr. Wells. The woman at the bookstore on Polk Street gave me your number. I would like to talk with you if you have time."

After a pause, Mr. Wells answered, seeming to know why he wanted to talk to him.

"I could meet you at the Pam-Pam room of the Bellevue Hotel on Geary at 3 o'clock. Can you make that?"

Adrian made a quick calculation of the time he needed to get to a bus stop, catch the right bus to San Francisco, and walk to the hotel. There was barely enough, but it was possible.

"Yes, fine, I will meet you there. Thank you!"

"How will I know you?" he asked.

"I have a mustache and wire-rim glasses."

"Very well, Mr. Masters," Mr. Wells finished, hanging up.

Adrian hurried back to the booth, worrying that Chris might have walked out by now, but she was still there. Without sitting down, he explained that he had to leave right away for San Francisco and would call her later. She was understandably upset, but there was nothing to be done. He had to get to the Pam-Pam room by 3 o'clock.

Mr. Wells

Adrian was lucky enough to catch a bus going down Bancroft right away. He got off on Shattuck and quickly transferred to an F bus headed for San Francisco. From the Transbay terminal, he walked to Market and caught a streetcar to Powell. Not wanting to wait for the next cable car, he walked up the steep hill to Geary. As he walked down Geary toward Mason for the Pam-Pam room, he began to feel the vibes of the Tenderloin district. Strip joints, peek shows, prostitutes and various street characters vied for his attention. In his thoughts, he fancifully compared himself to a seeker in a fairy tale who must pass by the attractions and dangers of a foreign land in his pursuit of hidden knowledge.

As it turned out, Adrian arrived at the Pam-Pam room ten minutes early. A hostess at the front of the lounge greeted him and took him to a small table. A cocktail waitress soon came to ask him if he wanted a drink, obviously wondering if he was old enough to order one. Adrian declined, saying that he would wait for his friend to arrive. He tried to relax, to prepare himself to meet the man who he hoped would be able to guide him. He still had the book he'd bought earlier that day, so he opened it and began to read the first chapter while waiting. But his attention left the page every time someone came into the room.

When Mr. Wells arrived, Adrian recognized him at once. Apparently in his sixties, he was tall and well-built. With his neatly groomed silver hair, mustache and well-tailored business suit, he appeared to be a man of worldly accomplishments. Penetrating eyes and deep lines etched in his face gave him a fierce countenance. As he approached, Adrian stood to greet him and extended his hand. Mr. Wells' hand was warm and firm, and he kept his eyes on Adrian as he held the handshake a little longer than normal. They sat down. Mr. Wells lowered his eyes and seemed to withdraw within himself for a moment. When he raised his eyes, they fell on Adrian's book. He seemed to recognize it, but said nothing.

Adrian felt the unusual intensity of the man's gaze as Mr. Wells opened the conversation.

"Why do you want to get involved with some people you know nothing about, rather than just drinking beer, chasing girls, and raising hell like other college guys?"

Adrian was struck by his plain frankness. He didn't have to think of a reply. It came immediately, surprising him as he heard himself saying simply, "I don't think I have a choice."

"I didn't say you did," Mr. Wells answered in kind. This initial exchange between them was so direct and unexpected that it had the effect of relaxing Adrian. When the waitress returned to take their orders, Mr. Wells ordered coffee and Adrian followed suit.

Adrian began by telling Mr. Wells what Karl had said to him about everyone being a machine and the need to know the truth about ourselves as we are. He related their conversations about the possibility of becoming a man who can act consciously. Adrian went on to tell Mr. Wells how he had come to feel the necessity of seeking someone with real understanding. He had planned not to mention his psychedelic experiences because he had already decided for himself not to take LSD again. He didn't want Mr. Wells to think that he was interested in drugs. But as it was after his last LSD experience that he'd deeply realized his need for help and had promised himself that he would find a teacher, he felt it would be disingenuous for him to leave that out.

"Mr. Wells, common sense tells me that use of drugs is incompatible with the path I want to approach. But I did take LSD twice. Those were powerful experiences that were partly responsible for the need I feel now. They showed me a completely different reality and helped me to understand a lot of the ideas in literature and religion that have been important to me. After the second experience, which was definitely my last, I knew that there is nothing more important than finding the real life inside me. But I realized that I don't even know how to begin by myself. I promised myself that I'd find a teacher. When I asked Karl to tell me more about the group in San Francisco he'd hinted about, he gave me a business card for the bookstore and told me to go there."

As Adrian told his story, he sensed an uncommon quality of listening from Mr. Wells. It was as though Mr. Wells' attention helped him to listen more deeply to himself, so that he became aware of his own impulses to hide, change, or amplify details and felt a demand to speak as truthfully as he could. Hearing that Karl had pointed the way to the bookstore, Mr. Wells looked puzzled for a moment.

"Why has your cousin himself not tried to make contact with someone? It sounds as if he is already well prepared and recognizes the need to work with others."

"I'm not really sure. Karl is first of all an artist and believes that he can develop himself through his creative work. His artist friends feel this for themselves as well. They often refer to what they understand to be the way of development of consciousness followed by great writers, painters, and musicians. Also, Karl is very independent. I think he would be reluctant to submit to the rules of any group."

"I see," said Mr. Wells, nodding.

The waitress brought two cups of coffee with a small pitcher of cream. Mr. Wells quickly dismissed her, dropped the question about Karl, and returned his focus to Adrian.

"Aside from the LSD, which in my view amounts to no more than monkeying with the machine, have you tried anything? Made any efforts or experiments?"

Adrian described the experience he'd had on Telegraph Avenue of sensing that he was between two worlds and his feeling of being at home in himself in the midst of all the attractions of life around him.

"I was so alive. The really important thing was that I felt really there in the midst of things. I knew that I had to keep making room for that awareness if I wanted to keep it. I had to continue letting my thoughts go by and not give them any weight, or I'd lose that special sense of myself. That didn't really seem like what you'd call an effort, because I didn't *do* anything, but there was a constant sense of responsibility for preserving that experience by not getting wrapped up in my thoughts and my reactions to everything."

Mr. Wells had continued to listen intently. Now he nodded, as if to affirm the value of what Adrian had just said. When he replied, it touched Adrian that Mr. Wells seemed to care so much about what he was trying to convey.

"This was a very important experience. It gave you a taste of what it can mean to be present to yourself. It was good that you valued the sense of being in yourself most and gave secondary importance to the magnified sense impressions of the sights, smells, and sounds around you. Quite often, people seek to be stimulated by heightened colors, music that takes them on a 'trip', amplified sensations in sex, and so on. But what is important—and so often missed—is the fragile sense of myself. When that's not there, I certainly am no more than a robot. There's nobody home. But when I recognize the taste of being at home and wish to be in accordance with that, I take a step toward becoming a real human being.

"You also touched a different kind of effort, what I might call active discrimination between energies in yourself. This can help you to begin your work in a new way. Instead of trying to change something or get a result, try to be a student of yourself, as if you were exploring a beach, finding stones and shells in the sand, and turning them over to see what's underneath. Just observe what you find in yourself without judgment. If you can work in this way, you will make many discoveries. Seeing oneself isn't always pleasant, but if I'm in touch with that active discrimination between energies, I can accept what I see because it is the truth and because it is in relation to what is finest in myself. Little by little, you may eventually meet the whole of yourself."

Adrian had never felt it was so important to listen to someone as he did then. It wasn't just a matter of hearing all of Mr. Wells' words. He sensed that it was much more than that. He needed to include the resonance of Mr. Wells' voice, the changing expressions of his face, the gestures of his age-spotted hands. Most of all, Adrian felt that he shared responsibility for keeping the channel open between them by maintaining attention on both what Mr. Wells was conveying and on himself there listening.

Seeming to accept him as a candidate, Mr. Wells gave Adrian some practical exercises. First, he suggested a meditation to try every morning.

"After you've bathed and dressed, but before you've eaten, sit quietly for about twenty minutes. You can use a cushion or sit on a chair, but you'll need to sit quite straight, without tension. Just try to be still inside and watch."

Mr. Wells paused to be sure Adrian understood. Adrian nodded his head, accepting the suggestion, but said nothing as he felt that he should try the exercise before asking any questions.

Then, noticing which hand Adrian used to pick up his coffee cup, Mr. Wells said, "There's another exercise you could try if you like. For the coming week, try to open doors with your left hand."

This sounded like a very simple task, but Adrian was excited to have something practical to try. Again, he accepted the suggestion without asking questions and Mr. Wells said nothing further about it.

Mr. Wells signaled the waitress to bring the check. Anticipating that the conversation would soon come to a close, Adrian tried to think of something else to ask about. He realized that, in addition to the exercises, he should also have some material to read and asked for a recommendation. Mr. Wells gestured toward Adrian's book.

"Read that. It has many important ideas. But most importantly, read it with the whole of yourself, not just with your head as you have always done before."

Adrian felt glad for this suggestion, but said that he didn't really know how to follow it.

"Well, of course you can't *do* it. But you can give some of your attention to your body as you read. Sit in a good position in which your spine is erect and find a way to hold the book so that you can keep your head straight rather than looking down. Try to relax and be still for a few minutes before you begin. All the time you are reading, continue to bring your attention back to the sensation of your body. Don't go on to another page until you know you have understood what you have read. By that, I don't mean that it has to be the ultimate understanding, just some level of understanding. With understanding comes meaning, and with meaning comes feeling. If a moment comes in which your mind, body, and feeling are all present, even a little, then you will be reading more like a man."

The waitress brought the check and Mr. Wells paid it.

"Now you have a program of work. If you would like to meet again next week, you can tell me what you have found."

"Yes, I'd like very much to meet again," Adrian said without hesitation.

Mr. Wells stood and looked around, seeming to take in everything about the people sitting in the lounge. Walking out of the Pam-Pam room together, they emerged into bright afternoon light and the bustle of Geary Street. Like a puppy, Adrian followed Mr. Wells to the corner at Taylor Street. He felt he had found his master! Standing at that noisy intersection in front of an X-rated bookstore, they finalized their appointment to meet again the following week before parting.

On the bus on the way back to Berkeley, in his mind Adrian ran through all the things he could say to Karl about his trip to the bookstore and the meeting with Mr. Wells. Something kept telling him to keep it to himself. Such restraint would be difficult to carry out, as he considered Karl to be his mentor and was in the habit of confiding in him. He decided that if Karl asked him, he wouldn't hide the fact that he had been to the bookstore and met Mr. Wells. But he wouldn't speak about their conversation or the exercises. Adrian reinforced this resolve as he climbed the stairs to their abode.

Karl and Sandy were in bed reading a poem together as Adrian walked into the room. As soon as Karl caught his eye, Adrian sensed that Karl knew where he had been. But surprisingly, Karl didn't ask him about it. Instead, Karl told Adrian and Sandy how excited he was about a new record he had bought that day and asked if they'd like to hear it. Sandy was always enthusiastic about Karl's music and of course Adrian went along with it.

Without touching the grooves of the record, Karl carefully pulled it out of the protective paper sleeve within its cardboard jacket and placed it on the turntable. He started the turntable, lifted the tone arm and delicately lowered the needle into the grooves on the edge of the record. Karl turned up the volume on the preamp until it was quite loud. Then they all lay down to listen. Adrian was relieved that he hadn't had to struggle with his impulse to tell Karl everything after all. Karl understood his need for restraint and was supporting it. Adrian was grateful for his sensitivity.

Meditation

Adrian awoke early the next morning, eager to try the quiet exercise. It wasn't always possible to be alone in their one-room home, but Sandy had persuaded Karl to walk with her to the campus for her 8 o'clock class. As soon as they were gone, Adrian placed a chair under the skylight and sat down. Folding his hands in his lap and closing his eyes, he tried to be aware of himself. But in a short time, he was completely lost in thoughts. He tried to sense his two feet on the floor as a kind of anchor. That seemed to help for a short time. The sounds of birdsong and wind chimes in the garden brought a momentary feeling of tenderness for the life around him. But soon, as if awakening from a dream, he found himself lost in thoughts again. Then he remembered Mr. Wells' words: "Just watch." Not knowing how to do that, he began to consider what it really meant and completely lost touch with himself again. Although he managed to stay in his chair for the full twenty minutes, when he got up Adrian felt that he had failed to achieve anything.

He put the chair back in its usual place and prepared to go to his 9:30 class. After he had closed the entry door and was descending the stairs, he realized that he had already forgotten about his exercise to open doors with his left hand. He made a firm resolve to remember to try it each time he passed through a door for the rest of the day.

Later, while he ate lunch alone in the cafeteria, Adrian mulled over the previous day's date at the Bear's Lair with Chris. Assuming she must still be mad at him for leaving her to meet Mr. Wells, he thought about ways of making it up to her. But as the recollections of his meeting with Mr. Wells were much stronger than those of his interrupted lunch with Chris, fragments of what Mr. Wells had said took over. With a pleasant feeling, he recollected things he had said that seemed to gain approval from Mr. Wells and these he played over again and again in his mind. When he recalled the part of their exchange in which Mr. Wells had given him the exercises, he realized with a jolt that he had completely forgotten to open doors with his left hand all morning. The last time he'd even thought of it was when he had resolved to do it as he was going down the stairs that morning.

Determined to succeed, he pushed the lever on the exit door of the cafeteria with extra force as he went out. There, he thought, I've done it. All he had to do was to keep his mind on it each time he approached an entry. But when Adrian realized that he'd forgotten again after entering Wheeler Hall for his Shakespeare class, a new realization began to dawn. Mr. Wells had given him this exercise to show him how strong his habits were. The routine of using his right hand to open doors was so automatic that he was accustomed to doing it unconsciously.

Adrian's relationship to the others who met for dinner and conversation in the cafeteria began to change. Wanting to keep his new endeavor to himself, he refrained from speaking during open discussions about self-development. He did occasionally try to introduce an idea he had become interested in, but found that the others immediately launched into explanations and answers instead of just being open to the idea itself. Even his relationship with Karl was different now. When Karl finally asked him what contact he had made with the San Francisco group, Adrian told him about his trip to the bookstore and the subsequent meeting with Mr. Wells. But as he came close to speaking about the exercises, Adrian felt the flash of an inner warning and retreated from going into those details. Karl respected his privacy, but Adrian knew that Karl was hurt that he no longer openly shared everything with him as he had done in the past.

We Shall Overcome

While Adrian was at home studying on the last day of September, Karl arrived with someone Adrian hadn't met before. The newcomer was tall and lanky, with curly brown hair. Karl introduced Mario, describing how impressed he'd been by the way the young man had debated with the professor of a philosophy class Karl was auditing. When the class ended, Karl had introduced himself to Mario and invited him home for dinner.

Although Sandy was seldom found in the kitchen, she had prepared the meal that night. As the four of them dug into their vegetarian lasagna, Mario described his recent experiences during Freedom Summer in Jackson, Mississippi. Adrian and Sandy listened wide-eyed as Mario told how some of his fellow volunteers had been ambushed by Klansmen.

Karl was shocked by Mario's story as well, but he was always more interested in philosophy than politics. Wanting to take advantage of the philosophical adroitness of his guest, Karl soon turned the conversation in that direction. For the rest of the evening, Mario and Karl challenged one another along lines of logic. Sandy excused herself from their conversation to study and Adrian was more than ready for bed when Mario finally took his leave.

After his morning classes the next day, as Adrian was walking across Sproul Plaza on his way to meet Chris at the Forum on Telegraph for lunch, he was stopped in his tracks by the drama he saw unfolding in front of him. A campus police car had driven right onto the plaza and stopped near the row of card tables routinely set up there by different social and political organizations to promote themselves and distribute information. A policeman had gotten out of the car and was approaching the CORE table, where a young man was offering leaflets about the civil rights movement. Arriving at the table, the policeman seemed to challenge the young man in some way. They began to argue. Adrian was surprised to see the policeman grab the man's arm and take him to the squad car, where he pushed him into the back seat.

Suddenly, Adrian was aware of the sound of running footsteps and a strangely familiar voice calling out loudly to those on the plaza to surround the police car. Turning to see whose voice it was, Adrian recognized Karl's guest from the night before. Again, with even more insistence, Mario called to anyone willing to help him prevent the squad car from leaving. He was incensed that the police had violated the young man's freedom of speech and wanted others to join him in not letting them get away with it. Though not at all sure about what he was doing, Adrian responded automatically to the emotional power of the call, as did others around him. More and more passersby gradually joined in until, within thirty minutes, there were hundreds of sympathizers blocking the car. Mighty Sproul

Hall, which housed the university administration, loomed up above the plaza as if watching the confrontation below.

Remembering that he was supposed to meet Chris, Adrian weaved his way out of the crowd and headed to the Forum to get her. With some difficulty, he walked down Telegraph against the stream of people who had heard about the demonstration and were hurrying to see or join it. Entering the Forum, he quickly spotted Chris waiting for him at a table. She had already heard the news and wanted to go back to campus with him. Now they joined the flow moving up Telegraph towards the Plaza. By the time they got there, the crowd around the police car had more than doubled. Mario was now standing on the top of the car, speaking with passionate intensity into a microphone someone had brought. The cop and the man from the CORE table were still sitting in the back seat.

Suddenly, in the midst of the excitement and energy around him, Adrian wondered what he was doing there. He had never been politically active. In fact, he had often thought of himself as apolitical. But now, the immediacy of the situation seemed to demand something from him. He felt sympathetic with Mario's stand and was curious to see what would happen, but he distrusted the emerging crowd mentality. Something about the excited tone of the conversation of a man and woman near him made him realize that, alongside the moral values people espoused, they were also animated by other influences, including sex.

Now beginning to feel apart from the crowd, Adrian considered the relation of this momentous external event to his personal need to approach the mysteries of his inner life. What Mr. Wells had already helped him to understand had opened Adrian to an appreciation of a completely different order of values than those represented by the speeches of Mario and others who had begun to join him. What did he really want? What was his purpose in being a passive participant of this demonstration? If he wasn't committed to this cause, why was he staying there? Wouldn't it be more honest to leave and give his attention to something he could feel wholehearted about? With those questions in mind, Adrian turned to Chris and suggested they go home. As usual, she deferred to what he wanted and together they made their way out of the growing throng.

Back at the garret, Adrian and Chris told Karl and Sandy about the demonstration. Though Karl tended to be apolitical, he got excited about scenes of rebellion and civil disobedience. The fact that his new friend Mario was at the root of this event made him especially interested. Karl said he would accompany them to the campus the next morning to see what had developed.

When they got there, Adrian was surprised to see how much the crowd had grown. There were thousands of people surrounding the police car now, so that the perimeter of the throng extended beyond Sproul Plaza, spilling into adjacent areas and filling the sidewalk up and down Bancroft. They got as close to the car as they could, staying to listen to the speakers who mounted the police car, one after another. In the afternoon, Mario announced that the university president had sent a message offering a deal. He read the president's statement to the crowd, and encouraging them to accept the terms of the agreement, asked everyone to disperse.

In the days following, rallies and demonstrations continued off and on until Thanksgiving, when most students went home for the holiday. Adrian again went to see his parents in Los Angeles. He had intended to avoid discussions about the FSM (Free Speech Movement), but the head of the family his parents had invited to join them for the holiday didn't waste any time bringing it up. As soon as Lew saw Adrian, he asked in his typically sardonic way, "Are you one of Mario's boys?"

Although Adrian didn't actually feel aligned with either Mario or the university administrators, Lew's challenge pushed him to side with the students.

"I saw the event that provoked the demonstrations first-hand. There was no question that the police violated the rights of the guy they arrested. I think that Mario is a passionate idealist who acted upon his beliefs, not some Communist puppet as some of the newspapers have led you to believe. People really responded to his leadership. I watched everything that happened as the crowd grew and the demonstrations progressed. Afterward, I read the newspaper articles about the same events. I can tell you that the newspaper stories did not match up with what I witnessed. From now on, I will never believe what I read in a newspaper again."

His statement was strong enough to end discussion on the subject for both Lew and Adrian's father, who wanted to avoid a political argument at the Thanksgiving table.

When Adrian returned to the campus after the holiday, a new FSM rally was in full blossom on Sproul Plaza. Addressing another huge gathering with another impassioned speech, Mario now questioned the motives and actions of the administration. He was joined by Joan Baez, whose albums Adrian had loved as soon as he discovered them while working at the Beverly Hills record store during his last year of high school. Accompanying herself on her guitar, she sang "All My Trials," "Blowing in the Wind," and "We Shall Overcome," encouraging everyone to sing along. As the emotion in the crowd grew, Adrian saw people around him weeping, which intensified his own feelings.

As they sang, Mario invited the crowd to march behind him into Sproul Hall. Although Adrian had not come there to participate in a sit-in, it seemed as if he had no will of his own. He found himself moving as part of the massive organism now flowing into the halls of the administration building. Inside, the FSM leaders, amplifying their voices with megaphones, instructed everyone to sit down on the floor on both sides of the long hallways of the first and second floors. Then they described how to resist when the police arrived.

Although Adrian could not help but feel the emotional power of what was happening, and though he respected the commitment of the other students, when it came time for him to sit down, he found that he couldn't. His heart wasn't in this historic drama unfolding around him. To sit down would be to commit, and he didn't feel committed in the way that others seemed to be. He knew that he didn't belong there. Only the new world of possibility opened by Adrian's relation with Mr. Wells and the promise of the mysterious San Francisco group had real meaning for him now.

The emerging struggle between the magnetic draw of the demonstration and the call to another life inside reminded him of another struggle, one that had taken place when he was fourteen. Having stayed overnight with a school friend one Saturday night, Adrian had gone with his friend's family to their Presbyterian church on Sunday morning. When the pastor challenged those present to step forward and accept Jesus Christ as their savior, Adrian had felt torn between what he thought was respectful obedience toward the authority of the pastor and a natural impulse to be true to himself rather than do something he didn't understand or believe in. In the end, he did not step forward to join those taking communion.

Remembering this, Adrian decided to leave the building. As he made his way out, he felt somewhat guilty as he passed by students singing "We Shall Overcome" again as they prepared to face and resist the police. When he was outside on the plaza, he turned to look back up at Sproul Hall. A movement in the windows on the second floor caught his eye. Students were placing large posters in the three center windows. With one large capital letter on each poster, together they read, "FSM."

When Adrian got home, Karl and Sandy were talking excitedly with some visitors about the sit-in. Not wanting to explain that he had just walked out of it, Adrian immediately turned around and left again. As he walked down Blake Street toward Dana Street, his thoughts about the sit-in faded away as he became more cognizant of his own presence and of each house he passed under the illumination of the full moon.

Sirens invade the quiet of the night. Called to sense the fullness of the life around him, he feels grateful just to be there, walking under the huge sky. Then something tells him to stop. He stands still for a moment, listening to everything around him. He has a fleeting intimation that he is close to a real experience of the present moment, but he knows he is still separated from it. Although people often give lip service to the ideal of living in the present, he knows it isn't so simple. What would it mean to really be fully present, here, now? As he listens to the sounds outside, he becomes aware of the movement of his thought. Then, for a moment, there are no thoughts. A new feeling emerges, the feeling of himself. There is joy in that, and an enormous appreciation of being alive. But then a passing patrol car takes his attention and the experience is over.

The next morning, Karl, Sandy and Adrian were awakened by one of Sandy's friends who had come to tell them what had transpired on campus overnight. She described how most of the students had refused to leave when the police arrived, linking arms in defiant solidarity. She vehemently cursed the cops for what she judged to be their brutal handling of students as they dragged them along the halls, down the stairs, and into buses waiting to transport them to the Santa Rita jail. Adrian felt for the demonstrators, but he had let go of feeling guilty that he hadn't been one of them.

After finals in January, Adrian searched the classified section of the *Berkeley Barb* for a place to rent. He could no longer put up with the lack of privacy in the garret and missed the quiet conditions he needed for study and meditation. Sandy was around whenever she wasn't in class and Karl's friends often dropped by unexpectedly. Furthermore, Chris was becoming more and more dependent upon him. She stayed overnight regularly now, requiring his attention constantly, never really becoming fully absorbed in interests of her own. But what bothered Adrian most of all was the realization that his feeling for Chris had faded. He wanted to live alone.

Accustomed to the independence of the garret, Adrian looked for a small cottage instead of an apartment. Berkeley had many of these, as in the past homeowners had often built small guest cottages in their back yards. Such cottages were rarely available though, as people tended to keep them or pass them on to friends. Adrian continued to look without luck through February. Then, during the first week of March, he saw an ad for a cottage on Addison Street and called the landlord, who offered to meet him that afternoon. When Adrian arrived at the address, the landlord took him through a gate at the side of his house to a cottage in the back yard. Inside, Adrian saw a small living room, separate bedroom, bathroom, and tiny kitchen. Privacy was somewhat comprised because all of the windows faced onto the landlord's back yard, but Adrian liked the place and was excited about having it for himself. He took it on the spot, writing the landlord a check for the first and last month's rent.

On the way to see the cottage, Adrian had noticed a Clown Alley hamburger joint at the corner of Addison and Milvia, just half a block down from where he was now. He decided to walk there and get some lunch to bring back to his new place. While waiting for his burger and shake, Adrian bought a *San Francisco Chronicle* from the machine in front of the restaurant. The headline was about a violent confrontation on a bridge in Alabama between state troopers and people marching from Selma to Montgomery in support of voting rights for Blacks. Adrian took the paper back to the cottage to read while he ate his lunch.

Studying the details of the headline story, Adrian was reminded of what Mario had told them about the beatings and killings of demonstrators by Klansmen. In this case, state troopers had assaulted the unarmed marchers with billy clubs, seriously injuring many of them. Thinking about Mario's wholehearted commitment to human rights and feeling his own ire raised by the newspaper story, Adrian again had to question his own non-involvement. Why didn't he feel called to help? Was it simply fear of what might happen to him? Perhaps partly, but he knew it wasn't only that. He was drawn more strongly by another influence that he didn't understand but had to respond to.

Another front-page story described the escalation of U.S. military involvement in Vietnam. President Johnson was sending 3500 Marines to protect U.S. Air Force bases in South Vietnam, from which air strikes were already taking place. Reading this, Adrian suddenly felt cold. He reasoned to himself that he had nothing to fear because he had a student deferment, but this didn't make his trepidation go away. It was as if, deep in his subconscious, he knew that the tide of the war could easily pull him in.

Chameleon

In May, along with thousands of others, Karl and Adrian were attracted to an athletic field on campus where activists and faculty members had organized a three-day Vietnam war "teach-in." To the displeasure of the university administrators, regular class attendance was decimated as large numbers of students and professors alike attended this massive extended rally. Standing on a roughly constructed stage, the organizers explained that the aim of the teach-in was to spread awareness of the true motives behind the entry of American forces into Vietnam and to show why the war had to be stopped. Mario was a key participant along with other FSM leaders. Several celebrities gave spirited speeches and urged young men in attendance to burn their draft cards.

Sensing the rising wave of emotion generated by the assembly, Adrian became cautious, lest he be swept up in it. Once again, though he was sympathetic with the principle behind the anti-war sentiment, he distrusted the fervor of the crowd and its chanted slogans. His only real interest was in preparing himself for the meeting with Mr. Wells scheduled for the following day. He wasn't at all sure what a proper preparation would be, but he knew that the way he spent his time and the type of conditions he was in mattered. After staying a couple of hours at the teach-in, Adrian finally told Karl that he would see him later, made his way out of the assembly, and returned to his cottage on Addison.

Walking up Geary Street to the Bellevue Hotel the next day, Adrian noted how much more relaxed he was than he had been before his first meeting with Mr. Wells. He even felt more at home in the Tenderloin, smiling at the prostitutes and panhandlers as he passed them. By chance, Adrian and Mr. Wells arrived in the hotel lobby at the same time. As Adrian approached Mr. Wells, he was again struck by the power of his presence. Greeting Adrian with his strong but yielding handshake, Mr. Wells led him into the Pam-Pam room and to the same table as before.

"Well, what did you discover since we met last week?" Mr. Wells asked.

Adrian began by reporting his excitement at the realization that he couldn't remember to open doors with his left hand.

"Occasionally, I do remember, but that's not really the point. What's important is the revelation that I completely forget this task most of the time. I get lost in all kinds of daydreams and just open doors with my right hand, automatically and without even knowing I'm doing it."

"Well, Mr. Masters, that's very interesting," Mr. Wells said in his gravelly voice. He sat looking intently at Adrian for what seemed a long time. Then he went on.

"I'm glad that you've been able to appreciate the results you've received from this exercise. It shows on the one hand that you really tried it, and on the other that you valued seeing the truth rather than getting stuck in a judgmental reaction of failure. We wish to know ourselves, but when we see our real situation we usually don't accept it. Instead, we want to change something because what we have seen doesn't match up with our imaginary picture of ourselves. We need to be able to stay with what is actually taking place, no matter what it is. This is a good first step for you."

Though heartened by Mr. Wells' words, Adrian could convey only frustration about his results from the meditation exercise.

"I've not been able to become quiet when I sit in the morning. I'm constantly finding myself lost in thoughts and no matter how many times I try again, I get lost very quickly."

Mr. Wells made the unusual movement of his face that Adrian had noticed before whenever he stopped to think or withdraw within himself. It was as if a backward movement of his scalp stretched the skin on his forehead so tightly that the deep lines there receded for a moment.

"You don't fully understand yet, but you're beginning to appreciate the paucity of your attention. We live in our heads most of the time and are accustomed to giving credence to our thoughts. I identify with them, believing that they represent me. But there is much more to me than these streams of memories, worries, considerations of what someone said to me, rehearsals of what I'll say to them, excitement about upcoming events, and so on. I need all of myself to participate in this attempt. That's what it means to collect myself—to gather all of my parts together. When you sit in the morning, try giving attention to the sensation of your body. Be aware of yourself sitting there. Sense your feet on the floor, your weight on the chair and the straightness of your back. Try to be aware of tensions in your neck and shoulders, even in your face. Take the decision to give up your thoughts for twenty minutes so that you can really be quiet inside. If you try in this way, you may come to a more stable quality of attention, which will help you to watch what is taking place."

Listening intently, Adrian valued everything Mr. Wells said. At the same time, he began to be aware of his own presence there with him in a new way. For the moment, Adrian's thoughts had become secondary; they were still there, but the need to attend to Mr. Wells was stronger.

As Mr. Wells spoke, Adrian felt something about the man himself. He was both fierce and sensitive, strong and tender, demanding and forgiving. The deep lines on his face and the intensity of his eyes told something of his own years of struggle and suffering. Adrian was curious, but felt it would be inappropriate to ask Mr. Wells personal questions about his life.

Mr. Wells went on to a new topic.

"I think you're ready for another exercise. When you come to the end of your morning meditation, make several appointments to meet yourself during the day. Then, when the appointed times come, try to observe yourself. Don't change anything, just take whatever you see."

Adrian accepted the task.

Wanting to keep the conversation going, Adrian spoke about what he'd been reading. "I'm really interested in the possibility of a higher state of consciousness. One idea that stood out for me was that when you enter a higher state, the lower states don't go away. They're still there, and you have to discriminate between them."

"You have to see these states in yourself. You need to digest this idea, but trying to analyze it or figure it out won't help. You can only understand it through your own direct experience."

Mr. Wells paused for a moment, then smiled as he added, "Would you rather read about fucking or fuck?"

"I see what you mean." Adrian blushed.

Mr. Wells laughed, his eyes twinkling. Then he urged Adrian to try the exercises and go on with his reading.

"If you like, we could meet once more before the summer break."

This surprised Adrian. He hadn't realized that there would be a summer break and was suddenly faced with the unexpected outlook of going on alone without meeting with Mr. Wells.

"Of course I want to meet again."

Mr. Wells took his appointment book out of his inside jacket pocket. They made a date for the following week.

Chris was in the kitchen preparing dinner when Adrian entered the cottage.

"Hi, Adrian! Did you have a nice day? I made lasagna for you!"

Adrian knew that Chris was trying to be nice, but he couldn't help being turned off by her syrupy tone. He made a quick detour into the bedroom, where he removed his jacket and slipped out of his shoes. In the past few weeks he had become increasingly irritated by Chris' fawning adoration. As he carelessly tossed one of his shoes into the closet, he could feel how the energy gathered in the meeting with Mr. Wells was being drawn into a negative reaction. His state of containment was disappearing quickly.

"What's wrong, Adrian? Why aren't you talking to me?" Chris called from the kitchen.

Going into the living room, Adrian stood watching her as she prepared a salad at the kitchen counter. When she turned to face him, he saw that she was afraid of what was about to happen. Wrinkles of concern in her forehead combined with those melancholy eyes to reveal her vulnerability even more than usual. Remembering how much he used to adore her, Adrian felt sad as it dawned on him that he didn't want to be with her any longer.

"What's the matter?" she whimpered, coming close to him.

Adrian took her in his arms, not wanting to hurt her but knowing it was over. She began crying, her head buried in his chest. Adrian held her for a minute longer and then pulled back to look her in the eyes.

"I think I need a little space," he said, trying to hide his feelings.

"Okay, I'll leave you alone. I'll be at my place."

Her tears told him she feared their relationship was coming to an end. After gathering her things, she headed toward the door. As she opened it and gazed back at him with a look that fully expressed her deep sadness, a pang in his gut told him that it would be the last time they would be together. Then she was gone.

At first Adrian was relieved. But soon, he felt remorse for causing her pain. She was such a kind person and they had felt such joy together. But somewhere along the way their relationship had changed. Adrian didn't understand what had happened, but he blamed himself. He thought it must be another example of what he had begun to call his chameleon nature. How would he ever be able to have a real relationship if his feelings were always changing?

Adrian put a portion of Chris' lasagna on a plate, set it between the silverware and napkin that she had laid out, and sat down at the table. This only deepened his remorse as he thought about her effort in preparing dinner for him. He thought of how she had always tried to make him happy. He couldn't eat. Leaving the unfinished plate on the table, he got up and went into the bedroom. He picked up his book and lay down to read, turning to a section in which the author was criticizing contemporary literature, judging all of it to be worthless. Adrian's thoughts continued to circle, taking his attention away from the book so that he had constantly to start over at the top of the page. He gradually became annoyed by what he perceived to be the author's arrogance. Finally, in frustration, he threw the book across the room as hard as he could so that it hit the wall with a bang and fell to the floor. In despair, he turned out the light and tried to sleep. It took a long time before he could.

Adrian visited Karl the next day and told him about the breakup. Karl felt sorry because he liked Chris. But he wasn't surprised it had happened as he'd observed the gradual deterioration in their relationship over the past month or so. He invited Adrian to go to a movie with he and Sandy that night. It helped Adrian some to be with them, but even during the film his thoughts kept returning to that final scene with Chris.

Adrian's attempts with the new exercise—to set appointments to observe himself—brought more impressions of his forgetfulness than he had expected. Usually, he remembered about an appointed time only after it had come and gone. For the most part, his experience amounted to little more than negative self-judgment. But one day something quite different occurred.

Adrian had taken the bus to San Francisco to apply for a summer job at the Emporium, a big department store on Market Street. At a few minutes before 10 o'clock, he was standing on a step of an ascending escalator leading to the third floor, where the employment office was located.

A sudden wave of remembrance informs him that he has completely forgotten about the 9 o'clock appointment he had so earnestly set to observe himself. But instead of falling into his usual reactive judgments about failure, he experiences an unusually full sensation of being there, standing on that escalator high above the second floor, looking down upon the grand expanse of the store below. For a moment, all at once, he is aware of the way he is standing, the weight and balance of his body on the moving stair, his hand resting on the moving rail, the tensions in his face, the feeling of nervous anticipation about his interview, and the words he has been rehearsing for it. He wonders if this was what Mr. Wells had once referred to as taking a snapshot of himself.

Mr. Wells listened intently as Adrian described his observations on the escalator when they met again just after finals week at the end of the semester.

"That was a very important experience, Mr. Masters. Previously, you remembered appointments with yourself only with your head. But this time, you had a direct experience of the whole of yourself, including your body, your feeling, and perhaps even your atmosphere. Maybe all of the efforts you have made up until now were for this experience."

He paused and gave Adrian a mysterious look.

"Or it might even have been a result of an effort you will make in the future."

Adrian started to ask him how results could come from efforts that have not yet been made, but Mr. Wells went on.

"The experience you had is not something you have control over. Be sure of that. It was given to you. But it would not have come without your efforts to remember, to be quiet, and to observe."

Listening to Mr. Wells, Adrian was filled with hope. With a surge of appreciation of the importance of his relation with this man, Adrian once again sensed a channel of energy passing between them. He was sure there was no imagination in this. They shared responsibility for a process. Somehow he knew that at the same time as Mr. Wells was helping him up to the next level, Mr. Wells himself was receiving help.

Smiling warmly as if to affirm Adrian's intuition, Mr. Wells asked him how the morning meditation was going.

"I'm beginning to find a little quiet. I'm still waylaid by my thoughts most of the time, but sometimes, when I remember that I'm here again, there is a subtle valuation of knowing that I've been lost. I realize that I don't have to change anything. I only have to stay here."

Mr. Wells smiled. "You are beginning to understand what it means to watch."

Encouraged, Adrian decided to ask about his break-up with Chris. "I was shocked to see how my feelings for her could change so much. In the beginning, I was crazy about her and we were really happy together. But in the end, I didn't want to be with her any more. When she was gone, I felt sorry for having hurt her."

As Mr. Wells shifted a little in his chair, the skin of his forehead stretched as it moved backward and he sighed. He looked down for a few moments, considering his response.

"Well, Mr. Masters, this is how relationships go for most people. What is interesting is the way in which you have been shaken by these impressions of your changing emotions. You didn't ask me how you could become a better person. Instead, I think you want to understand why you are as you are."

He looked to see if Adrian was following him. Adrian nodded his head. Then Mr. Wells continued.

"You are beginning to see facts that do not correspond to the image of yourself you have had until now. You have believed in a picture of yourself as someone who has permanent feelings towards others and behaves consistently in his relationships. Nothing could be farther from the truth. In fact, we have nothing permanent in us at all. We are changing all the time, reacting automatically to every event, depending upon the influences acting upon us at the moment.

"Everyone talks about love, but most don't understand what real love is. What people call love is either a physical attraction which sooner or later disappears or an emotional attraction which can change into its opposite, as yours did with Chris. There is the possibility of another kind of love, but few people even know about it, let alone achieve it. With this kind of relationship, a lover wishes and strives for the inner development of the beloved. That does not happen automatically. It takes time, and it requires intention and effort from a couple with a certain level of being. But this is far from most of us, so that is probably all we need to say about it now.

"If you really want to understand your emotions, you will need to see much more. So far, you've managed to catch a few glimpses of the truth. To see more deeply and more often, you must learn how to study yourself. This has nothing to do with introspection or ordinary self-analysis. It requires sincerity born of necessity and the practice of an art of inner seeing you can only learn from others. You realized this when you went to the bookstore. It is why you and I are meeting now."

Mr. Wells gazed at Adrian with compassion, his eyes sparkling. "We have a very long road ahead of us, Mr. Masters. But now, we're going to take a break for the summer. Go on with the exercises you have been trying, if you like."

Then he retrieved a book from his briefcase and handed it to Adrian, saying, "I would suggest that you study this book during the summer."

"Thank you." Adrian felt particularly touched, as there was something personal in this gift from Mr. Wells.

Saying that he would phone Adrian in the event of an opportunity for a meeting during the summer, Mr. Wells asked for his number. Then, without warning, Adrian found himself responding in a strange and unexpected way. It happened so quickly that he was helpless to do anything to change it. A part of him that had always feared and resisted involvement with social organizations and spiritual groups, but which for some time had been hidden among the other creatures within that lurked in the background of his consciousness, came forcefully to the forefront and took control. Watching helplessly as this interloper intentionally gave Mr. Wells the wrong phone number, Adrian's heart sank. After the rich and heartfelt exchange he had just shared with this wonderful man, he had betrayed their trust. His chameleon nature had thrown everything into question again.

Margie

Adrian spent most of the summer working. Continuing to sell records at Payless Hi-Fi on some evenings, he now also began working at the Emporium in San Francisco during the day. There, his job was to play the role of a "blue pencil," a position of special status awarded to college students, supposedly because they were considered future candidates for management. The regular sales clerks were obliged to summon them to approve certain transactions, such as when a customer paid by check rather than with an Emporium card. Adrian's job was to judge whether a transaction would go through smoothly and to approve it by signing his name on the sales slip with a special blue pencil. Only once did he hold back his blue signature, when a customer appeared so nervous that Adrian suspected that the check would bounce. Of course, all of the regular sales staff were older than he and many had been with the store for a long time. They were less than enthusiastic about having to call for approval from a young man with little knowledge of the store or its products. This put Adrian and his blue pencil colleagues in an awkward position, but the sales clerks had no choice but to tolerate them.

As Karl and Sandy were traveling in India for most of the summer, Adrian spent his free time with Desmond and Jeff. Most often, they met at La Fiesta on Telegraph, where they exchanged insights over tostadas and beer. But as Adrian didn't want to talk with them about his meetings with Mr. Wells or the exercises he'd been trying, he felt constrained from speaking about what was truly of most importance to him. Further, he could not join in the enthusiasm around their LSD trips, which they continued to have.

On a warm Saturday night, Jeff took Adrian to a party at the Berkeley Hills home of a popular political science professor. They were drinking beer and joking with Desmond and his date when Adrian noticed a striking young woman standing on the other side of the room. She was engaged in a conversation with a man he didn't know. Although she was very attractive, she had another quality that interested him, something that came through the poise of her posture and gestures. When Desmond and his girlfriend moved on to talk with someone else, Adrian pointed the woman out to Jeff.

"Do you know who she is?"

"Oh, yeah, that's Margie. Pretty girl, huh? Hank, that's the guy she's talking to, told me about her. He's hot for her, but whenever he asks her out, she says she can't go because she has to study. He doesn't think it's always just an excuse because she is, like, very disciplined, and hits the books all the time. She's had a four-point average all through school and has gotten great scholarships. So she's obviously, like, very intelligent, but Hank says she's pretty independent and kind of hard to get close to."

"Could you introduce me to them?"

"Okay, sure man."

Adrian followed Jeff to the corner where Margie and Hank were talking. Hank was holding a large paper cup of beer filled from the keg in the backyard, while Margie had a glass of red wine. As Jeff and Adrian walked up, Hank greeted them first.

"Hey, Jeff, how's it going?"

"Cool, man," Jeff replied, turning to acknowledge Margie as well.

Now that he was closer, Adrian couldn't take his eyes off Margie. Standing near her, he could see that she was almost as tall as he was. Her long light brown hair fell softly to her shoulders, framing an oval face with hazel eyes under full brows, a turned-up nose, a small mouth, and freckles that gave her the wholesome look of a country girl. Though gracefully slender, she had broad shoulders and full breasts. Long slender fingers with perfect nails without polish grasped her wine glass. A plaid blue skirt showed off her slim hips and long legs.

"Hi Jeff. Who's your friend?" asked Margie, looking Adrian over.

To Adrian's amazement, he felt the vibration of Margie's voice resonate in his chest, something he was sure had never happened before.

"Oh, this is Adrian Masters. You know that red-headed artist, Karl, that a bunch of us meet for dinner at the cafeteria? Well, Adrian is his cousin."

"Hi, Adrian, I'm Margie." When she looked at him, he felt a wave of energy move through him, from head to foot.

Adrian took Margie's extended hand. Soft and warm, it sent a gentle current of electricity through his hand, up his arm, into his chest and down his spine.

"Glad to meet you," Adrian managed, finding it hard to speak while he was having so strong a response to her.

"I'm Hank," interjected her companion.

Adrian let go of Margie's hand and turned to Hank, whose pumping handshake was overly firm, as though he wanted to emphasize his masculinity.

"Hello, Hank."

"Are you a student at Cal?" asked Hank.

"Yeah, an English major. What about you?"

"I'm in Philosophy, like Margie."

Taking this opportunity to turn his attention back to Margie, Adrian said that he was very interested in philosophy as well.

Margie was about to respond when Desmond and his date joined the four of them.

"Hey guys, I've got some unbelievable grass. Anybody interested in smoking a couple of joints?"

Jeff's body language showed he was definitely interested. But he was reluctant to leave the others, so he insisted that they all go out onto the deck and get high together.

"You guys go ahead," Hank said. "I'll just stick with my beer."

"Come on, Hank, this is incredible weed, almost like hash," asserted Desmond. "Anyway, it'll make you thirsty and you'll like your beer even more."

Jeff contributed to Desmond's coaxing until Hank gave in.

"What about you guys?" Desmond asked, looking at Margie and Adrian.

"Thanks, but I'm not doing grass any more," Adrian said. "Enjoy yourselves."

"How about you, Margie?"

"No, it gives me a headache. I'll stay here and talk to Adrian."

Hearing this, Hank looked uncomfortable. He didn't want to leave Margie alone with Adrian, but he had already committed himself to Jeff and Desmond and really wanted some of that dope.

Seeing Hank's uneasiness, Margie tried to reassure him.

"Go ahead and enjoy yourself, Hank. When you're done, come and find me."

Hank nodded, though he was still reluctant to leave. Then Jeff pulled on his arm and the three of them went outside to a deck overlooking the expansive panorama of San Francisco Bay from the front of the house.

Adrian and Margie recognized a kindred spirit in one other. They talked about various things, eventually arriving at their mutual passion for foreign films. Agreeing that the noise level in the house was becoming too loud, they made their way to the back patio. As the warm summer evening invited them to linger there, they sat down in a couple of chairs and returned to their discussion of favorite films.

"Did you see *Jules and Jim*?" Adrian asked.

"Yes. I think it's one of Truffaut's best. But I'll never forget the impression that *The 400 Blows* made on me. I think that flick changed my life."

"Me too," Adrian agreed. "That last frame, in which the boy's face is frozen, really haunts me. You have to wonder what will happen to him. What about Bergman? Do you like him as well? Have you seen *The Seventh Seal*? Those scenes where the knight plays chess with Death are incredible."

"Yes, of course. That is a very profound film. Did you see *The Virgin Spring*? Bergman really makes you face some essential moral questions in that one. The rape scene is particularly powerful."

"How about *Black Orpheus*? I love the Brazilian music."

"Yes. And it's so interesting to see the myth of Orpheus and Eurydice shown in the setting of Carnaval."

There was something so easy and comfortable about being with Margie that Adrian risked asking her out without waiting any longer.

"Want to go see Fellini's new flick with me tomorrow night?"

"You mean *8½*? That film is supposed to be really long and I need to study for my classes on Monday."

He remembered what Desmond had told him about Margie always turning down Hank because she had to study.

Then, after thinking for a moment, she asked, "Why don't you just come over to my place for a simple dinner tomorrow night? I'll have to get my studying done first, so it might be a little late. Say, around 8 o'clock?"

"Sounds great." Adrian had a big smile.

As Margie wrote down her address and phone number on a slip of paper, Adrian saw Desmond, Jeff and Hank emerging from the back door of the house.

"See you tomorrow night," he said, taking her hand for a moment after she gave him the paper. Again he felt a kind of electricity in her touch. Then, getting up and waving to the other guys as he headed toward the walkway around the side of the house, Adrian made a quick departure. He had to go home and get some sleep so he could be up early the next morning for a full day at the Emporium.

Adrian finished wielding his blue pencil at 6 pm the next day. It was another warm evening, so he walked down Market to First Street and from there to the Transbay terminal to catch the bus to Berkeley. Riding over the Bay Bridge, he caught himself daydreaming about what had happened at work that day and what he hoped would happen that night with Margie.

Then it occurred to him that, for the past few days, he hadn't even thought about setting appointments for himself. He'd managed to continue sitting each morning, but his experience lately had become dry. Remembering how rich his meditations were while he was meeting with Mr. Wells, Adrian wondered if Mr. Wells had tried to call him yet. There were still a couple of weeks left before the end of the summer. Then he remembered that Mr. Wells wouldn't be able to reach him because he'd given him the wrong number. What would Mr. Wells think of him when he found out? It pained him to think of it.

Adrian turned to the book Mr. Wells had given him, from which he had been reading a little each day. As he couldn't talk with Mr. Wells about the ideas in it, he wished there were someone else he could share them with. Then it occurred to him that Margie might be interested. He decided to steer their conversation to one or two ideas while they were having dinner.

He got off the bus at University and Milvia and walked to his cottage. There was plenty of time to clean up, change into better clothes, and make it to Margie's by 8. In the shower, he relived the way Margie's voice had resonated in his chest and the electric charge of her touch. In his mind's eye, he saw her again as he'd first seen her across the room. He went over their conversation again and again. Then, as if coming out of a dream, he saw that he'd been so completely lost in his thoughts that he couldn't even remember whether he'd washed his face or not. He was reminded that, if he'd learned anything from his talks with Mr. Wells, the most important thing was to try to stay present when he was with Margie. It occurred to him that reading a passage from one of his books might help prepare him for the evening.

Adrian opened the Ouspensky book he'd found at Moe's and flipped through the pages looking for something of interest. He stopped on a page presenting the idea that one must struggle with habits in order to observe them. What interested Adrian was the emphasis on getting to know one's habits as they are rather than trying to change or break them. One suggestion was to modify the length of one's stride or the tempo of one's walk in order to observe one's walking habits.

Adrian decided to try this as he walked to Margie's apartment. With renewed interest in studying his habits, he left the cottage and set out on his way to her place. His first attempt involved taking much bigger steps than usual. But that seemed artificial to him and he thought it must look ridiculous to anyone who happened to notice him, so he toned it down a little, trying to take just slightly bigger steps.

As he walked up Bancroft Way, Adrian saw a crowd gathering across the street. Curious, he crossed at the next light and approached the scene. Apparently, someone making a right turn had been hit by an oncoming car. The two drivers were standing between their damaged cars arguing about whose fault it was. As neither was injured, Adrian turned to continue on his way.

Becoming aware that the crowd gathered around the accident had distracted him from his attempt to study his way of walking, he began the experiment again. This time, he tried to walk a little faster than usual. But he continued for only a short time before concluding how silly it was. He didn't seem to be getting any real information about his habits, so why go on with this? Just walk normally and try to observe, he told himself. Why interfere with his usual way of walking?

As he approached Margie's building, Adrian's thoughts revolved around his anticipation of the evening with her. Considering that he might open a conversation about habits, he realized that he had completely disappeared into daydreams as soon as he had reverted to his usual way of walking. With renewed resolve to pay particular attention to each step, he climbed the stairs to the second floor and found Margie's apartment.

She opened the door as soon as he knocked. Margie stood in the doorway, half squinting, half smiling at him with the sun in her eyes, the day's last rays revealing the luminance of her light brown hair, which was now parted in the middle and gathered in pigtails that lay on her shoulders. She looked tomboyish in her denim overalls.

"Hi, come on in." She welcomed him into the living room of a typical one-bedroom student apartment.

"Are you hungry? I've made coq au vin."

"I'm starved!" He didn't know what coq au vin was, but the aroma coming from the kitchen was fantastic.

Margie gave him a quick tour of her apartment and then led him into the kitchen. Removing the lid from a red casserole dish on the stove, she dipped a large spoon into the broth and lifted it to his mouth. Adrian leaned forward to take a sip.

"Wow, that's incredible!" It was one of the best things he had ever tasted.

She handed him a bottle of wine and a corkscrew. "Would you open this, please?"

Adrian didn't know much about wine. From the label, he saw this was a 1958 Pinot Noir, which he guessed was probably pretty good. While he removed the cork, Margie carried the food to a small table in the corner of the kitchen.

"The wine glasses are in the cupboard to the right of the sink," she directed.

Adrian selected two matching glasses and carried them to the table. Margie set out silverware, napkins and plates while he poured the wine.

Finally, they sat down. Margie used tongs to serve a chicken thigh to his plate and drenched it with several large spoonfuls of mushrooms and onions in a thick sauce. Then she served herself. The steaming aroma made Adrian salivate.

Lifting her glass, Margie made a toast. "Here's to our new friendship."

Impressed with her confidence and gladdened by her welcoming spirit, Adrian touched his glass to hers. "To our new friendship," he echoed.

They began to eat. Adrian was really hungry and the dinner was delicious. But reminded that this visit was about much more than the food, he slowed down and opened the conversation. "Which philosophy classes are you taking now?"

"I have a course in metaphysics and another in the philosophy of language, principally related to the work of Wittgenstein. Right now, I'm reading Kant's *Critique of Pure Reason* for the metaphysics class. Have you read Kant?"

"I learned a little about him in a general philosophy survey last year," he answered, already feeling inadequate to the subject. "I can't say I really know his work. But I've talked a lot with my cousin about the ideas of Wittgenstein and find them interesting."

"I think you said you're an English major?" Margie asked.

"Right. But I'm also very interested in philosophy and psychology. Recently, I've been reading a book about the study of consciousness. You might put it in the category of philosophy of religion, but it's not really religious. The ideas in it relate to both Western and Eastern religions, but they are much different than anything I've found before. This book actually describes a way toward self-development in the midst of everyday life."

"What do you mean by self-development?"

Putting down his fork and taking a sip of wine, he wondered how to answer her.

"To give you the real answer, I'd have to describe what I feel is missing in my life, and for that I'd need to tell you more about me and what has taken place since I've come to Berkeley. I'll share all that later, but I'd rather enjoy our dinner now and hear a little more about you." Margie looked intrigued. She really seemed interested. But she let it go and offered him more coq au vin.

"Okay, whatever you like. I think I can relate a little to what you're saying about self-development. Last week, I went with a friend to a meditation at Zen Center, on Bush Street in San Francisco. Suzuki Roshi spoke at the beginning. There was something really special about him. I think he lived in a Zen monastery in Japan before coming to the States.

"Anyway, I didn't really know what I was doing. I had to find a way to cross my legs and sit up straight on the cushion without getting tense. At first, it was hard to relax. I closed my eyes and just tried to let my thoughts float by, as Suzuki Roshi had suggested. After awhile, my body did relax and I felt like I could settle down and be quiet. I opened my eyes once and saw this guy—I think one of the senior students—walking around with a bamboo stick to hit people who signaled him. You can do that if you get drowsy and can't concentrate on your meditation. If you want him to come and strike you on the shoulder, you put your two palms together and bow your head. I saw him go over to this one woman who was signaling him. First, he tapped her twice on the shoulder. When she tilted her head to the left, he hit her a little harder on the right shoulder. Then they went through the whole routine again on the left shoulder. I realized I was getting pretty distracted by that whole scene, so I closed my eyes and tried to start over again."

Margie's story reminded Adrian of his own attempts to sit in the morning. He was excited that they had this in common.

"I've been meditating too," he said eagerly. "But I've only tried it by myself at home in the morning. I understand what you mean about feeling you don't know what you're doing. It's hard to just watch your thoughts because you keep disappearing into them."

"Are you doing Zen meditation too, or are you following another method?"

Adrian decided not to hide anything from Margie.

"Actually, I've been meeting with a man who works with a group in San Francisco. He's given me several exercises. One of them is to meditate every morning, trying to be quiet inside and watch. I've been doing this for about ten months now. At first, I couldn't seem to concentrate at all. I would just get completely lost in thoughts about what happened yesterday, or what I was worried might happen in the future, or about something I wanted. But gradually I found that I could be free from my thoughts for short periods by concentrating on the sensation of my body. Then, like you said, I could settle down and be quiet."

"That's really great that we're both into meditation. But you didn't say what technique you're following. Is the man you meet with a Zen priest?"

"No, I don't think he's a Buddhist. Actually, I don't really know what religion he has, if any at all. His group has been working with a teaching rooted in ancient ideas from the East but formulated for people living in the

116

modern Western world. When I meet with him I feel something special, like you did with Suzuki Roshi."

Margie poured them each another glass of wine. Adrian was beginning to feel pleasantly relaxed. They clinked glasses again.

She wanted to know more. "What other kinds of exercises do you try? I know that in Zen, they also do walking meditation. Is it like that?"

"Not really." Adrian reflected on how to explain the exercise to open doors with one's left hand. "It's kind of hard to describe. One of the main ideas is that people aren't aware of themselves. Everybody thinks they're conscious and in control, but in reality they aren't. But before you can develop consciousness, you have to realize that you don't have it. If you think you do, then of course you'll be satisfied and won't make any efforts. You have to see for yourself that you're really not aware of yourself most of the time. So the first exercise this man gave me was to try to open doors with my left hand. I thought it would be easy, but most of the time I completely forgot to do it, only remembering about it after I'd already gone through a door. I'd tell myself that for sure I'd remember the next time, but then I'd forget again. I began to realize that it's such an automatic habit for me to open doors with my right hand that I do it without even knowing it. I expected to be able to catch myself in the habit, but it turned out that I was always thinking about something else when the time came."

He wondered what Margie was thinking. What he was saying probably sounded a little crazy to her. But the intensity of interest in her eyes suggested that she understood what was important. They gazed at one another for a few moments without words.

Margie offered dessert. "Vanilla ice cream?"

Though already full, Adrian accepted. Margie got up, picked up their plates, and took them into the kitchen. Returning with a pint of ice cream and two bowls, she scooped a generous serving for him but took only a little for herself. Sitting down, she drained the last of her wine before starting on the ice cream. He followed suit.

"I've never tried anything like that," she began again, "but for some reason I'm really touched by some of the things you've been saying. It's sort of like hearing an echo inside me while you're talking."

Looking at Margie through the glow of the wine and the excitement of their shared experiences, Adrian saw how beautiful she was. She recognized his ardent gaze and smiled. Then, she looked at her watch.

"It's going on 11," she said in a matter of fact tone. "I love our conversation, but I have an early class tomorrow and really need to get some sleep." She got up and began to clear the table. Joining her, Adrian took the empty bottle and glasses into the kitchen. On the way, he asked her what class she had to be at the next morning. She said she had three of them, starting at 8 with her linguistic philosophy lecture.

"I can finish clearing up," she insisted. "I'll see you to the door."

He had actually hoped that they might end up sleeping together that night, but Margie had clear priorities.

"Thanks for the incredible dinner."

"Thanks for coming." She leaned forward and kissed him softly on the mouth. With that, they said goodnight.

Bounding down the stairs, Adrian was on top of the world. He thought he had never felt like this before. Beyond the physical attraction, there was a feeling of sharing something important in common. They were clearly compatible, but this was more than that. The way she looked at him affirmed a connection between something unseen in both of them.

Sushi

Adrian woke up the next morning feeling wonderful. He could only think that the evening with Margie had reanimated him. Being able to share his experiences, feeling aligned with her meditation at Zen Center, putting himself in her shoes as she tried to understand the path he was following—all of these renewed his own interest.

Adrian had the day off from both jobs and was eager to see Margie again. He decided to walk to campus and intercept her during a break between classes. Leaving the cottage and recalling his aborted effort to study his walking habits, he was determined to try again. As he emerged from the front gate onto the sidewalk, he attempted to take the measure of his usual stride and then increase it just a little. He continued this way along quiet Addison Street until he came to Milvia Street, on which he turned left towards University Avenue, where he felt the draw of people and traffic much more. Already, he was becoming irritated with the artificiality of taking longer steps. But rather than giving up, he tried something different, reducing the length of his stride. This felt equally unnatural, but he managed to stay with it.

Arriving at University Avenue and heading towards campus, he asked himself what he was doing. He felt he had to try to be sincere about his motives. Had he already lost the thread of study and simply begun to maneuver so he could say he was making an effort? He decided to try something different again, this time returning to the longer stride and walking faster at the same time. This approach was less awkward, but he encountered constant resistance to keeping it up.

As he approached campus, he was ready to give up and return to his normal walk when it occurred to him that the irritation and resistance was simply a reflection of the force of his habit. He realized that his body wanted to return to what was easy and customary. Curious to see if this new recognition would help him see and understand his ordinary walk, he allowed himself to return to it. Immediately, he felt comfortable again.

Margie had told him the night before that her second class was in Dwinelle Hall and her third in Wheeler Hall. The first got out at 11:30 and the second started at 1:00, so Adrian thought she should have free time in-between. He looked at his watch and saw that it was already 11:20. He picked up his step.

Adrian was heading up one of the pathways that wound through campus when he became aware that he had become lost in thoughts again. He remembered the moment of feeling relieved to return to his usual way of walking, but after that, although he had crossed busy Oxford Street, started on the foot path to campus, made his way through a large grove of eucalyptus trees, and passed people coming in and out of the life sciences building, he had no distinct memory of any aspect of that passage. He had been completely absorbed in a pleasant daydream about the previous evening with Margie and thoughts about what he would say when he saw her.

He found a bench on Dwinelle Plaza that faced the exit to Dwinelle Hall and waited. Just after 11:30, people started coming out of the building. He watched for Margie with tense anticipation. When he finally spotted her, his heart leapt in happiness and he got up from the bench to go meet her. But then he saw her turn to a man who had just come out of the building. Adrian recognized him as Hank, the man she'd been with at the party. As he watched the two of them talking and laughing, Adrian felt a pang of jealousy. He considered leaving the scene altogether, but something told him to follow through with his plan. He reasoned with himself that it was ridiculous to be jealous because he had only just met her. Then, seeing that the two of them were walking away together, Adrian hurried to catch up with them. Margie and Hank both saw him approaching and waited expectantly.

"Hi guys, what's happening?" Adrian greeted them, a little out of breath.

"Hi Adrian," Margie said with a broad smile. "Do you remember Hank Stevens?"

"Of course." He shook Hank's hand. "What are you two up to?"

"We're going to get a bite between classes," Hank answered in a slightly offhand manner.

Then, after a pause, Margie asked, "Do you want to join us?"

No, he didn't. Adrian wanted to ask Margie if he could see her that night, but not in front of Hank. However, if he didn't ask her now, he might lose the opportunity.

With some surprise, Adrian heard the sound of his voice as he spoke. "No thanks, I've already got plans for lunch. But I'm glad I found you, Margie, because I came to campus just to ask you if you'd like to get together tonight."

Hank looked uncomfortable, but Margie was calm and unperturbed. In fact, she seemed to enjoy the situation.

"Yes, I'd like to go on with our conversation from last night," she said brightly.

Hank looked rejected. Turning to him, Margie explained, "Adrian and I have a common philosophical interest that we need to finish talking about."

Hank didn't seem assured by her explanation, but he nodded his head in acceptance.

Adrian didn't try to hide his elation. "Great. Do you want to have dinner at the Japanese place near your apartment? Say, around 7?"

"Sure, I think that will work. I'm in pretty good shape for my classes tomorrow."

"Okay, I'll swing by your apartment about 6:45. You guys have a good lunch." Adrian gave Hank a final quick glance and then returned his eyes to Margie.

"See you," she said, showing her smile again.

The hostess at the Kirala Japanese restaurant seated them at a table where they could either sit cross-legged on a thin cushion on the floor or let their legs dangle down into a recess underneath. They chose to sit cross-legged as that seemed in keeping with the conversation about meditation they ostensibly intended to continue. They sat looking at one another for several minutes, both feeling contented just to be together. Adrian found Margie's eyes to be soft and vibrant and she responded to the intensity of Adrian's searching gaze. He felt filled with happiness from the vision of Margie across from him, with her brown hair loose again, falling onto tan freckled shoulders revealed by her white sun dress.

But practical as always, Margie bypassed any small talk they might have had and returned directly to the subject of their conversation the evening before.

"How did you meet the man you told me about?"

"To explain that, I'd have to tell you about all the things that led up to meeting him. It's a long story. Do you really want to hear it?"

"Of course I do, but first let's decide what we're going to eat."

After the waitress had taken their orders and brought tea, Adrian began at the beginning, telling her about his voracious appetite for fairy tales as a child, his adolescent fascination with the spiritual and psychological ideas in *Siddhartha* and *Steppenwolf*, and the mysterious way he'd found his mother the night she'd crashed through a fence. He shared his memory of the provocative lecture by

Aldous Huxley he'd heard in Los Angeles and his continued interest in the experiences Huxley wrote about in *The Doors of Perception* and *Heaven and Hell*. He described how he'd moved in with Karl and quoted his cousin's emphatic statement on their first night together that people are all machines.

When the waitress brought them soup and salad, Adrian motioned Margie to go ahead and eat, but he continued his story, recounting some of the conversations amongst the troupe in the cafeteria, his intimate talk with Karl at Limantour beach, and the book he'd found the same day at Moe's. He described the lecture of the three Harvard professors, his own subsequent sessions with LSD, and his experience of being between two worlds as he walked down Telegraph Avenue. Then he told her about the prophetic dream that warned him he was having an appendicitis attack.

When the waitress brought the sushi rolls, Adrian noticed that, in the urgency to share his experiences, he had eaten little of his soup and salad. He took a sip of his soup, but put the bowl right back down. His need to finish his story was stronger than his interest in the food. So he went on, telling Margie about Chris, how he'd been stunned and saddened to see the change in his feelings toward her, and how he blamed himself for the failure of the relationship. Finally, Adrian recounted his trip to the bookstore and his meetings with Mr. Wells, describing those conversations while leaving out only a few details.

Adrian was finally able to take a deep breath, as though he had been underwater and could finally come up for air. Margie was waiting patiently for him to begin the sushi, which had been sitting there for quite a while.

"That's an incredible story," she said excitedly. "I would love to meet Mr. Wells myself. When are you going to see him again?"

Feeling guilty and regretful, Adrian told her what he had done at his last meeting with Mr. Wells.

"I gave him the wrong phone number. He said he might call me during the summer for a meeting, but if he tried he would not have been able to reach me." After everything Adrian had just told her, he felt foolish.

Margie looked puzzled. "What? Why did you give him the wrong number?"

"I know it seems absurd. We'd just had a wonderful conversation and then I found myself doing that. There's a part of me that resists making commitments and avoids any kind of group. I suppose that part is also afraid of being exposed."

Margie didn't criticize him or analyze what he did. She just proceeded directly to the next practical step.

"Well, why don't you call him?"

So simple. Just call him. Of course, he had thought of this too, but had put off doing it, thinking that he didn't need to call until the summer was completely over.

"Why don't you do it now?" Margie urged. "Do you have his number?"

"Yes, I've got it in my wallet. You're right, I should call him. But I'll do it tomorrow. I'm sure he won't be in his office at this hour."

"Adrian, after everything you've shared with me, you know yourself that you should try to get him now. You've already left your food sitting there a long time and I don't mind waiting for you. There's a pay phone over there."

Adrian had never met anyone like Margie before. It wasn't that she was being bossy. She was smart and practical. She seemed truly interested in his story and knew how important it was for him to re-establish contact with Mr. Wells.

"Okay, I'll try calling him now, but I probably won't get him."

Adrian got up from the cushion on the floor, feeling stiff from sitting in that position for so long. The phone booth was empty. He went in and closed the door. Searching through his wallet, he found the card the woman in the bookstore had given him. It seemed silly to call Mr. Wells office in the evening, but it wouldn't hurt. Dropping a quarter in the slot, he waited for the dial tone and dialed the number. There were a couple of rings, then a click, then a ring with a different sound. He realized that probably meant the call was being forwarded. So it might be worth calling now after all. After another ring, he heard Mr. Wells' unmistakeable deep voice. "Yes?"

"Hello, Mr. Wells. This is Adrian Masters. I thought I'd check and see if there are any meetings I could go to."

"Ah, Mr. Masters. You missed a very interesting meeting with our teacher from New York because you gave me the wrong number."

Adrian felt the stab of regret in his abdomen. He paused, feeling guilty and not knowing what to say. Then Mr. Wells said it for him, as if he knew what Adrian was feeling.

"Maybe this can be your shock to start again."

Adrian felt ashamed. It was useless to try to excuse himself for having given Mr. Wells the wrong number.

"Yes, I would like to start again."

"There is a new group being formed," Mr. Wells went on. "I suggest you call the leader. His name is Robert Eckart. I'll give you his number. Do you have something to write with?"

"Yes." Adrian fished a pen out of his shirt pocket. "Please go ahead."

Mr. Wells gave him the number. "Thank you, Mr. Wells. Will I be able to see you again?"

"I'll be around. But Mr. Eckart is your man now. Goodbye, Mr. Masters."

"Goodbye, Mr. Wells. And thank you again." Adrian felt clumsy, but it didn't matter. Thanks to Margie, he'd been able to talk to Mr. Wells. He felt connected to him again and Mr. Wells had invited him to join a new group! Adrian returned to Margie walking on air.

"I can tell you got him!" Margie said excitedly. "Are you going to meet him again?"

"Not exactly. He gave me the name of another man who is starting a new group. He implied that I could join that group if I got in touch with this man. When I asked if I could meet with him again, Mr. Wells said that this other person is my man now."

Adrian sat down cross-legged on the tatami mat again. The dragon and rainbow rolls were still untouched.

"Let's eat our sushi." With chopsticks, Adrian placed one of the pieces of dragon roll on Margie's plate and one on his own. They ate without talking for a few minutes.

"I'm really interested in everything you told me about," Margie said, breaking the silence. "I want to know more about what you're trying to do."

"I've been reading a book that Mr. Wells gave me that contains ideas related to what we've been talking about. I'll loan it to you."

They finished the sushi and Adrian paid the check. Ten minutes later they were back at Margie's apartment. As it was late and she had another early class the next day, he assumed they would say goodnight at the door.

"It was really great to be with you again," he said, putting his arm around her.

"You're not going anywhere," she replied with an impish smile. Taking his hand, she led him into her apartment and closed the door behind them.

Mr. Eckart

The next morning, during his break at the Emporium, Adrian tried to reach Mr. Eckart. He looked for a pay phone in a relatively quiet place and, as had become his wont, took a few minutes to collect himself before calling. A woman answered. Speaking in a refined and gracious manner with a distinct British accent, she said that her husband was at work and asked Adrian to call back in the evening. Adrian said that he would and thanked her.

He was at Margie's apartment when he tried the call again after dinner. This time, Mr. Eckart answered. His voice was soft and elegant. He too had a British accent.

"Yes, Mr. Masters, I've been expecting your call. Mr. Wells told me a little about you and suggested that you might be a candidate for a new group we are forming. Would you be interested in that?"

"Yes, very much. When will you be meeting?"

"The first meeting will be at our place in San Francisco in three weeks. Our regular time will be at 7:30 on Tuesday evenings."

Adrian remembered that he had signed up for a Tuesday evening class on the poetry of William Blake. This was to be his most important course as a senior. "I have a conflict, Mr. Eckart. My senior thesis class is on Tuesday evening."

Mr. Eckart did not hesitate or bend. He said simply, "I think it will to your advantage to come to the group." His surety was so compelling that Adrian no longer felt he had a choice.

"Then I'll come," Adrian replied, as though echoing his assurance. "Where do you meet?"

"We have the upstairs rooms of a building at the corner of Sagamore and Plymouth streets, where the San Francisco Ballet School used to be. The building occupies the entire corner and the entrance is on Sagamore. Do you think you can find it?"

"I'll find it," Adrian answered with more confidence than he actually had.

"Can you come fifteen minutes early before the first meeting so we can talk a little?"

"Of course," he agreed quickly.

"Very good, Mr. Masters," he said with a formal intonation. "I'll see you then."

"Goodbye, Mr. Eckart, and thank you."

Adrian hung up the phone with mixed feelings. He was excited about coming one step closer to the group. But he had been glad to find the course on Blake at the time he made his fall program; now he needed to find a different class for his senior thesis. He asked Margie if she had the fall course catalog.

"Why?" she asked. "I thought you had your program in place. Does this have something to do with the phone call to that man?"

"Yes. He said the new group is going to meet on Tuesday nights, and that's the time of a course on Blake I was planning to take. I don't really know what else is available, but I've got to find something."

"Didn't you tell him that you have an important course at that time?"

"Yes, but apparently he didn't consider it to be as important as the group meeting. He didn't offer any alternative."

Margie started to say more, but stopped herself. By her expression, Adrian could tell that she had picked up on the influence Mr. Eckart had on him.

She got the catalog and handed it to him. Adrian found the section listing the available courses. He wasn't drawn to most of the authors featured, but one interested him because he had read and liked his poem, "Thirteen Ways of Looking at a Blackbird."

"Have you read Wallace Stevens?" he asked Margie.

"We studied a couple of his poems in American Lit. He was sort of an interesting guy, different from a lot of other artists. He was actually the president of a big insurance company at the same time that he was writing his poetry."

The notion of a creative man with a rich inner life who also managed to thrive in the world attracted Adrian. He checked the time of the Wallace Stevens course in the catalog. It would work.

As Adrian was on his way home after making the course change at the registrar's office the next day, he thought of stopping by Karl's place. He hadn't seen him for weeks and missed him. He couldn't tell him much about his work with Mr. Wells, but he wanted Karl to know a little of what he had been doing. After all, Karl was the one who had pointed him toward his current direction in the first place.

Adrian found Karl alone at home, writing in a tablet. Karl greeted him warmly and offered him a cushion on the floor, pulling one up next to it for himself.

"Adrian, we've missed you! Sandy will be sorry not to have been here for your visit. She's in class all afternoon. How are you? What news do you have?"

"Well, a lot has happened since I last saw you, Karl. I met with the man I told you about, Mr. Wells, in the city a couple more times. He's an extraordinary person who really understands something. I think he's a developed man. I can't tell you all the details about the things he's given me to try, but I wanted to tell you that he has just invited me to join a new group."

"Well, that's quite a significant development," said Karl with interest. "So you really feel ready to give yourself over to someone's authority?"

"I know that would be difficult for you, but I think it's the right choice for me. I've been helped a lot by meeting with Mr. Wells and feel that the group is definitely the next step I have to take."

"Then I fully support you."

"I also wanted to tell you that I have a new girlfriend. Her name is Margie. You'll be interested to know that she's a gifted philosophy student who shares your interest in Wittgenstein. She's intelligent, beautiful, and practical."

"When do I get to meet her?"

"We'll have you and Sandy over for dinner."

"Sounds wonderful. Say, Adrian, I wonder if you'd like to go with me to an event at Zellerbach Hall tomorrow night. I've got two tickets, but Sandy can't go. Have you heard of the Mevlevi dervishes?"

"No, not really."

"Well, they're whirling dervishes. They've come from Turkey. Their order has been in existence for a long time. It was supposedly founded in the thirteenth century by followers of the great Sufi poet Rumi after he died. Through their practice of turning, they reach a state of ecstasy. The Mevlevi don't come here very often, so this is a special opportunity. Do you want to go?"

Adrian thought a moment. He didn't have to work at the record store the next night, so he was free. What Karl had said about the dervishes interested him.

"Okay, I'll join you. What time?"

"The presentation starts at 8 pm, but let's get something to eat first at the Chinese place on Telegraph between Channing and Dwight."

"Great. I'll meet you at the restaurant around 6:30."

The next night, they left the Chinese restaurant and walked up Telegraph to Zellerbach auditorium. There were already two long lines extending onto Zellerbach plaza, one for people who had tickets and the other for people buying tickets. Karl and Adrian got in the line for people with tickets and waited for the doors to open.

"Even though the whirling dervishes are a big tourist draw in Turkey, the government there has outlawed the practice of Sufism," explained Karl. "It's all based on political manipulations that took place a long time ago. But some scholars say that Sufism represents the esoteric core of the Islamic religion. The rising popularity of Rumi's poetry has led to a lot of interest in Sufi practice here in the U.S."

A man emerged from the theater and moved down the ticket buying line, informing people that the show had been sold out. Those who were left in line muttered disappointment and walked away. The doors opened and those with tickets began moving forward. As Karl and Adrian passed into the theater lobby, Adrian felt a wave of excitement. When they entered the theater, an usher showed them to their seats. As Adrian saw how close they were to the stage, he looked at Karl in appreciation. Karl smiled back at him.

When the house lights finally dimmed and the roar of conversations quieted, the curtains parted to reveal a scene illuminated by warm, low lighting. Young men dressed in black gowns and tall conical hats were seated in a circle in front of a backdrop that simulated the inside of a mosque. Three men seated at the back center of the circle held musical instruments, one with a flute, one with a stringed instrument and bow, and one with a drum. From the quiet, a voice emerged in a haunting song that was clearly a call to prayer. When the song finished, one of the musicians raised his flute and began to play a mournful but exquisitely beautiful melody. Next, a drummer beat a simple rhythm that brought all but the musicians to a standing position. Then, except for one man who stood out from the rest by his age and demeanor, each of those standing removed and put aside their black cloaks to reveal pristine white tunics and white skirts with white leggings underneath. To the rhythm of the drum, the men began to walk slowly in a circle around the older man, who was still in black, bowing to him and to one another. After they had circled three times, the flute and stringed instrument began to play as well. As the music emerged, the men began to turn, continuing to move around the circle at the same time. They held their heads tilted a little back and to one side, while their arms were outstretched, with the palm of one hand directed upwards and the other hand facing down. The teacher stayed at the center of the circle, very slowly turning in place to observe his students, one after another, as they rotated around him.

As Adrian watches, an intensity of feeling that he has never experienced before arises in him, a resonance set into motion by the music, the way the dancers move, and the stages of struggle, submission, freedom, and joy that is revealed in their faces. Gradually, the dervishes whirl faster and faster, until their white skirts lift high in response. As the tempo of their turning reaches its apogee, Adrian feels a warm current of energy circulating up and down his spine, straightening him in his seat.

When the music came to a conclusion and the dancers stopped, everyone on and off the stage were still. Adrian savored that moment, not wanting it to end. Then, without the usual theatrical bows from performers, the curtains closed. When the audience began to applaud, Adrian didn't want to move. But a nudge from Karl made him realize that he couldn't hold on to what he had experienced. He began to clap his hands, joining all those around him. Though the curtains did not reopen, a few people in the audience began rising to their feet, which brought everyone else up. When, after another minute, the curtains still didn't open, the applause subsided. The house lights went up and people began filing out of the theater.

As they moved toward the exit, Adrian looked at Karl to see how he had responded to the dervishes. Karl gave him a knowing look that signaled his shared appreciation, but Adrian wondered whether Karl had felt the same inner intensity that he had. Adrian wanted to talk with Mr. Wells about what the young men in white had been trying and ask why he had responded so strongly just by watching.

The last two weeks of the summer break passed quickly. Adrian's job at the Emporium came to an end about the same time as Margie's summer courses. This gave them the opportunity to spend more time together. As they hiked the trails of Tilden Park one clear warm day, they discussed Plato's allegory of the cave, in which people mistake shadows cast on the wall for reality.

"The thing that stands out for me is that normally we believe whatever our thoughts tell us," asserted Margie. "Our head, which is the part of us everyone seems to value the most, is the main focus of our education. But since we have such subjective ideas and images about everything, how can we trust our thoughts alone to know the truth? Maybe we should value our feelings and instinct more. I think this must be related to what Plato was pointing out. He was showing that we are like the people imprisoned in the cave, who can only look at the shadows on the wall in front of them and have lost the ability to know the real world behind them. Like them, we've grown to believe in what we imagine and are less and less able to discern what is actually taking place in ourselves and the world around us. But Plato does allow the possibility that someone could turn around and face the light, which though blinding at first, one could get used to. If we were more in touch with our feelings and instinct, wouldn't that help us to turn around and face reality, even if it was difficult?"

"I think you're on to something," Adrian echoed. "What you're saying reminds me of the experience I had when I saw the whirling dervishes. While I was watching them, it wasn't through my thoughts that I was connected to them so strongly, but through my feeling and some part I don't really understand but which I sensed through my spine. I don't think it was just imagination because it seemed so palpable. The combination of feeling and sensation brought me to a state in which everything was clearer and more vivid. Even my thoughts seemed to become more intelligent, if that makes any sense. After that experience and others I've had, it's becoming harder to look at things the same way as before, like the person in Plato's allegory who has seen the light and can no longer believe in the shadows on the wall."

Adrian and Margie took a turn off the trail which led to a view lookout. They stood quietly together, stopped by the scale and majesty of the vista spread out below them.

Margie turned to Adrian. "I want to meet a teacher in the group you're joining. I felt something when you first told me about your conversations with Mr. Wells. And I can feel you are really trying to find the truth in yourself. I love our talks, but now I want to bring those ideas into my life."

Her words rang true. Adrian felt how they were linked now by more than the feeling and physical attraction they had for one another. Another dimension to their relation had appeared. They both heard a call from within to another level of life and shared a common need to understand how to respond to it.

The Group

On the day of the first meeting of the new group, Adrian planned his departure from Berkeley carefully to allow plenty of time to get there by 7:15 to meet with Mr. Eckart. Arriving at San Francisco's Transbay terminal at rush hour, he walked to a bus stop on Mission where a crowd of people were waiting. In a few minutes, a big Muni bus lumbered to the curb. It was jammed, with standing room only. The destination displayed at the top of the front windshield didn't seem like the right one for him, but then he realized that he didn't actually know which destination he should look for. He had imagined that it would be obvious, but now he wasn't so sure.

After a few more minutes, a woman in the crowd stepped to the curb as she signaled to a small ordinary van that was approaching. It pulled over long enough to pick her up and then took off again. Noticing that it had a cardboard sign attached to the side window that read, "Daly City," Adrian thought that was probably the right destination for him and wondered if he could catch a ride in one of those vans. He asked a man waiting at the bus stop next to him what the vans were.

"Those are jitney buses," the man answered. "They're private vans that go up and down Mission all day. Where do you want to go?"

Adrian quickly glanced at a small piece of paper he pulled from his shirt pocket. "Um, I'm going to Sagamore and Plymouth."

"Then you should take a jitney bus. You can get one that branches off Mission down San Jose. It will take you right to Sagamore."

"Thanks!"

When another jitney bus came, two men waved for it. It pulled over and they got in, taking the last two empty seats. The jitneys seemed to have room for only five or six passengers. But the next one that approached, which had a sign in the window that read, "San Jose Avenue," looked to have space. Feeling hopeful, Adrian signaled to the driver, who pulled the aging gray van over and opened the door. After the driver nodded affirmatively when Adrian asked if he was going to Sagamore and Plymouth, Adrian climbed in, paid the driver, and sat down.

Though five people were jammed closely together in seats facing each other, there was no conversation. A small older man in a blue business suit dropped in and out of sleep, his eyes intermittently opening and closing and his gray head bobbing. A well built young man in a tweed sport coat was reading a newspaper, which he held open so wide that one of his elbows intruded into the space of the young woman next to him. A third man with a red face and receding hairline looked ruefully out the window, avoiding any eye contact with the rest of them. The woman seemed modest and sympathetic. She was wearing a conservative navy blue dress, very little makeup, and her dark brown hair was pulled into a bun on the top of her head. Occasionally, when her eyes met with Adrian's for a moment, each of them made awkward attempts to smile. He thought they must be about the same age.

The ride across San Francisco took much longer than Adrian had expected. Raising his voice to be heard above the din of traffic, he asked the driver how far they were from his destination. He felt a surge in the pit of his stomach when the driver answered that they were barely halfway there. Adrian looked at his watch. It was already 7. There wouldn't be time to see Mr. Eckart before the meeting. He might not even make the meeting itself.

Two of the men got off, leaving the woman across from Adrian and the man with the newspaper next to her. The woman moved about nervously, frequently adjusting her position and looking out the window as though she was anticipating a problem. Looking out, Adrian saw that the sun was setting, which made him feel his lateness even more. As Adrian had noticed the woman's interest when he asked the driver about the distance to his destination, he wondered if they were going to the same place. The man next to her folded his newspaper, put it in his brief case, and prepared to get off the bus. After he did, Adrian broke the silence.

"You don't happen to be going to Sagamore and Plymouth?" he asked her rather tentatively.

142

"Yes, how did you know?" She raised her eyebrows in surprise.

"Are you going to a meeting?" Adrian ventured a little further.

"Uh, well...yes."

"I had the feeling that you were. I'm going there too. It's already 7:20 and my meeting is supposed to start at 7:30. I didn't realize it would take so long to get there."

"I didn't either. My meeting is at 7:30 too."

Intrigued by the coincidence of being on the same bus with her, Adrian took the liberty of asking, "Are you meeting with Mr. Eckart?"

"Yes. I've met him a couple of times but this will be my first meeting with his new group. Are you meeting with that group too?"

"Yeah. I haven't met Mr. Eckart in person yet, so he asked me to come fifteen minutes early, but I've definitely missed out on that. I just hope we make it in time for the meeting."

A few minutes later the bus driver looked over his shoulder at them. "Here you go."

As the driver pulled to the curb, there was still enough light for Adrian to see a two-story Spanish style building with white stucco walls and red roof tiles across the street. Music from a juke box streamed out the door of a diner on the lower floor. The upper floor had a row of arched windows fitted with black wrought iron railings on small balconies. Leaving the bus quickly, Adrian and the woman crossed the street. As they approached the building, just beyond the coffee shop they saw an arched entrance at the street level that opened on a lighted stairway to the second floor. Adrian glanced at his watch as he followed the woman into the entrance. It was 7:26.

Just inside the entrance, at the foot of the stairs, stood a short, stocky man in his mid-thirties with unkempt red hair and wiry eyebrows. He was standing very still, like a soldier, not looking out at them at all but gazing steadily at the stairwell wall beside him. Adrian concluded that he was a doorman, but one with an inner duty.

Mounting the stairs to the floor above, Adrian was surprised but comforted to encounter Mr. Wells. With eyes drilling into his, Mr. Wells briefly acknowledged him but continued walking past. Adrian waited for a moment, looking around. He was standing in a hallway that led both left and right to a series of rooms. At the moment, the doors were all open. Adrian could see that the room at the end of the hall to his left was a very large one like you might find in a dance studio, reminding him that Mr. Eckart had said this building was the former home of the San Francisco Ballet School. People were sitting in rows of chairs in the rooms directly in front of him and to his right.

Mr. Wells returned, accompanied by a compact man with jet-black hair, horn-rimmed glasses, and a well-trimmed mustache. Mr. Wells introduced him to Adrian without ceremony and left, going into one of the rooms and closing the door behind him.

"I'm sorry I didn't get here early to talk with you before the meeting," Adrian told the man. Mr. Eckart

144

waved his arm to dismiss Adrian's apology, saying that the meeting was about to start. He motioned toward one of the rooms down the hall to his right. "Find a seat. I'll join you in a minute."

On Adrian's way down the hall to the room Mr. Eckart had indicated, he passed another room with a group of people waiting to start their meeting. To his surprise, Adrian recognized several people he had seen on campus in Berkeley. One of them acknowledged him with a smile.

Continuing on to the meeting room for his group, Adrian found about fourteen people sitting in two curved rows of seats facing two chairs that were still empty. The woman from the bus was already seated. Seeing that there was one place left in the middle of the back row, Adrian realized that he was the last person to arrive and that the room must have been carefully set up for exactly the number of people expected. He stepped over the legs of several people to get to the empty chair and sat down.

There was no conversation. On the contrary, everyone was still and quiet. Some had their eyes down on the oriental carpet that defined their meeting area. Some looked straight ahead. Others had their eyes closed. Adrian knew they were trying to collect themselves as he had begun to learn to do in the morning meditation. There was an electric sense of anticipation in the room.

Then, Mr. Eckart entered with another man, who closed the door behind him. Taking their places in the two empty chairs facing the group, they said nothing, but just waited quietly. Mr. Eckart carefully scanned the room, taking in each person. Adrian tensed as he felt Mr. Eckart's gaze sweep over him. The man with Mr. Eckart looked at them for a short time, then turned his eyes down to the carpet.

Finally, the woman from the bus spoke. "I've been trying the meditation exercise every morning for six months, but each time I become lost in thoughts. I've come to the point where I just don't think I'm capable of collecting myself and remaining present. How can I go on?"

To Adrian's surprise, Mr. Eckart smiled warmly at her. He paused, tilted his head a little to the left, and stroked his mustache. "You've taken a step," he said with kind affirmation. "You're beginning to see that you have no center of gravity that can stand up to the habitual attraction of your thoughts and emotions. Perhaps this has shaken you to the point where you feel the need for help. If you had not tried again and again, you would not have come to this certainty. So far, you have endeavored to remember principally from your head. But it is not enough. Most of all, you need the participation of your body and your feeling. How can you invite them to join your effort? You must begin by finding the authentic sensation of your body. If you can come down into your body, you will be able to stay with yourself longer. You will still be taken away by thoughts, but you will begin to see what you need to go deeper."

Mr. Eckart's response conveyed both the clarity of precise knowledge and the fire of passionate care. As

Adrian listened, he sensed something different in himself that seemed to come from the energized atmosphere shared by the group around him. After Mr. Eckart had finished speaking, he and the woman from the bus continued to look at each other for a few more moments. Then Mr. Eckart turned his attention back to the general group.

During the silence that ensued, a struggle mounted in Adrian. On the one hand, he felt he should ask a question, but on the other, all of the things that came into his head seemed false or unworthy of speaking about. When he did begin to entertain a question, he found himself rehearsing it. But he couldn't become satisfied with his formulations and worried about what people might think of him if he spoke. Realizing that he was becoming lost in these thoughts, Adrian brought his eyes up from the carpet. Mr. Eckart was glaring at him as if he knew what was going on in Adrian's mind and was challenging him to look at it. Adrian felt that he had to speak, even though he wasn't ready.

"I don't know how to relax," Adrian began nervously. "The muscles in my neck and shoulders become tense when I try to sit straight and keep still during meditation. I've tried to sense the tensions and let them go, but nothing changes, or it gets worse. So I just try to put up with the tensions and go on with the exercise. But I feel that I'm not going to be able to go deeper into myself until I'm able to relax."

"What about now?" Mr. Eckart replied without hesitation.

"What do you mean?" Adrian asked, not understanding his point.

"Are you tense now?"

His question brought Adrian back to himself. "Yes, my neck and shoulders are tense right now."

Mr. Eckart began to elaborate. "You need to see where this tension comes from. You can't make your body relax. Your mind says, 'relax', but your body says, 'the hell with you'. These tensions are armor we wear to protect ourselves. But you have to see this for yourself. And *now*, right *now*, is the only time I can see myself. *Now* is all that I have. When you are able to see where the tensions come from, relaxation will take place by itself. Do you understand?"

"I think so," Adrian answered with some hesitancy.

Mr. Eckart went on. "When you sit in the morning, or when you come to this meeting, don't try to *do* anything, don't try to change anything. Let everything be as it is. Just find the best posture you can, in which your back is well supported and you impose as little stress as possible upon your body. Then try to observe your state as it is. Your whole state, meaning the state of your body, of your emotions, and your mind. Thoughts will come, but let them go on past. They will continue to come, but keep letting them go. Sense your weight on the chair or cushion. Try to find an even sensation of your whole body. Don't try to force anything. Then watch. If the tensions are there,

148

include them but don't try to get rid of them. If you can become quiet, the tensions may begin to melt away by themselves. Try like this during the week, then tell us what you've found at our next meeting."

As he had with the woman, Mr. Eckart kept his eyes on Adrian's for a few moments after he had finished speaking. When he turned his eyes away from him and back to the others, Adrian felt relieved that the intensive demand was over but glad that he had been able to speak and received something to try.

A bearded man slightly older than the others spoke next. "I'm a jazz pianist. I spend a lot of time practicing and performing certain tunes. My problem is that, when I'm trying to sit quietly, these tunes start going around and around in my mind."

Mr. Eckart's eyes sparkled. "These tunes don't have to disturb you. They could become music to work by." He smiled. "If you turn your attention to the sensation of your body, you can let the melodies go, just as you can let the thoughts go. These tunes are not *you*. You don't have to identify with them. Let them be. Include them as you try to be aware of more of yourself."

The musician's face broke into a broad smile of understanding. "Yes, I see," he nodded emphatically. "I'll try that this week."

"Very good," returned Mr. Eckart in his refined English accent.

There were several more questions. The man who had come in with Mr. Eckart answered one of them. Adrian guessed that he was an experienced student being given the opportunity to assist Mr. Eckart with the group.

When the hour was over, Mr. Eckart asked for a volunteer to be their group secretary. The woman from the bus raised her hand. He nodded, accepting her. Then he announced that there would be practical work on Sunday. Everyone was invited to give their names to the new secretary if they wished to participate. Adrian signed up.

Sunday

Eagerly anticipating his first Sunday with the group, Adrian had no trouble getting out of bed at the first sound of the alarm. There was just enough time to make the long trek to the south end of San Francisco. The night before, as they were going to bed, he'd told Margie that he'd be getting up at 5 am and would be gone all day, explaining what it was all about. Although she'd accepted this gracefully, Margie reminded him that he'd promised to speak to one of the teachers on her behalf.

Trying not to disturb Margie's sleep, Adrian showered, dressed, kissed her softly on the cheek, and left the apartment, walking to the nearest bus stop on Shattuck. He arrived there just in time to catch the F bus, which took him to the Transbay terminal on Mission. But instead of catching a jitney bus down Mission right away, he walked across the street to a 24-hour cafeteria for breakfast. Sitting at a yellow formica-topped table by the window in the brightly lit open space of that convivial eatery, he enjoyed coffee, eggs, bacon, an English muffin and orange juice while observing the locals, who had just gotten off a night shift or were preparing for their day's work.

When he was finished eating, Adrian walked to the corner and caught a jitney bus. This time, after getting off near the meeting hall, he had to walk to a house nearby where people in the group gathered on Sundays.

Following the directions Mr. Eckart had given him, Adrian arrived at the house fifteen minutes early. The door to the garage was open. Inside, a few people were already standing around the cold but well lit space. As there were no chairs or cushions, they stood waiting, keeping their hands warm in the pockets of their jackets. Exactly at 9 o'clock, Mr. Eckart appeared with several typed sheets of paper. He paused, looked around the garage at the people there, and began to read the day's schedule and the names of those assigned to each of the teams. Everyone was designated as Miss, Mrs., or Mr., with people carefully sequenced within the team lists according to seniority in the group. Adrian's name was last. He was assigned to the metal craft team.

As everyone headed for their assigned teams, Jim, the leader of the metal craft team, found Adrian and took him into a large corrugated metal shed situated in one corner of the yard behind the house. On the way to the metal craft area, they passed through a carpentry shop with a table saw, lathe, and several work benches. Walking close to Jim, Adrian was surprised to notice that his team leader was apparently hung over from the night before. His hands trembled and his breath reeked. But when they got to their work area, Jim proceeded thoughtfully, showing Adrian how to use a special tool to curve brass rods for the base of a lamp the team was constructing. The others on the team went right to their tasks without conversation. Even while working on his own part of the lamp, Jim kept an eye on Adrian and assisted him whenever he was stuck.

At 11 o'clock, Jim quietly signaled that it was break time. Adrian followed the others as they put their work down and filed out of the metal shed to a garden patio area outside. On the way, he passed a long table with books, cardboard, colorful endpapers, stitching materials, and glue that he guessed belonged to a bookbinding project.

It felt wonderful to be outside in the sunshine and fresh air. With the dispersal of the fog, the day was warming up. Cloth covered tables in the garden offered coffee, tea, water, and snacks—rolls, deviled eggs, small slices of cheese, apple sections and nuts. People were talking quietly as they mingled in the garden, drinking their coffee. Not knowing anyone, Adrian felt awkward. He wasn't sure how much food he should take, or whether to start a conversation with someone, or if he should stand or sit. His usual comfortable roles now seemed strangely unavailable.

Without speaking to anyone, Adrian poured a cup of coffee, took a deviled egg, and stood by himself off to the side. Mr. Eckart and Mr. Wells seemed to be engaged in conversations with younger pupils. Adrian was envious, wishing that he too could have the attention of those men. A few minutes later, Mr. Eckart finished his conversation and stood unoccupied. Adrian had the impulse to try to speak to him, but he didn't have a question and was afraid to approach him. He remembered his promise to Margie to ask for an appointment for her, but decided that it would be inappropriate to address Mr. Eckart only for that. To justify his reticence, he told himself that he would only approach his teacher when he had a burning question of his own.

Linda, the woman Adrian had met on the jitney bus, walked up to Mr. Eckart and started a conversation with him. Seeing Mr. Eckart smiling at her, Adrian became jealous again and inwardly kicked himself for not taking advantage of the opportunity to approach Mr. Eckart when he'd been free. Deciding that he would speak to him about Margie at the next opportunity, Adrian moved closer and waited. Then, just as Mr. Eckart was finishing with Linda, a chime called everyone back to their tasks. Without looking at Adrian, Mr. Eckart walked past him and disappeared into the house. Adrian went back into the shed, full of self-criticism for having been so passive.

Returning to work with the brass rods, Adrian was reminded to try to watch himself. But problems with the task, along with circling thoughts about his failure to approach Mr. Eckart, continually took his concentration away. He had come there to be more collected, but it seemed as if he was more scattered than usual. Then, he was suddenly cognizant that Mr. Eckart was standing near, watching him. Feeling guilty for having been caught in what he judged to be another failure, Adrian found himself trying to appear as if he had been working attentively all the time. But when he looked up at Mr. Eckart furtively, with self-reproach written all over his face, Mr. Eckart just shook his head in apparent disappointment and walked away. Adrian felt devastated.

At 12:45, everyone put their work down and cleaned up for the lunch gathering, which was held in the meeting hall a few blocks away. Separately or by twos, most walked there, but two elderly women were transported by car. When he had arrived at the meeting hall and climbed the steps to the second floor, Adrian found the large room at the end of the hall being set up for lunch. Five tables had been arranged in a semicircle to face a sixth table set a little apart. The setup team was still busy bringing in salt and pepper shakers, cream pitchers, carafes of water, pots of coffee, baskets of bread, and ashtrays. A woman carefully placed a vase of flowers at the center of each table.

Adrian waited with the others at the side of the room until the setup team had finished their work. When they had, one of the men rang a bell. Silently, everyone found places at the five tables. Seats at the head table were still empty, as the leaders had not yet come into the room.

Soon, the kitchen team entered, carrying large pots of soup, bowls of salad and serving utensils. Taking their places behind a long table on which they set the food, they began to dish out the lunch. Servers lined up on the other side of the table to accept the completed plates and serve them in silence.

Now the leaders entered the dining hall. Apparently, they had just been meeting together in another room. They chose their places at the head table with deliberation, giving Mr. Wells, the eldest among them, the centermost position.

When the serving is completed, everyone sits still and silent. Adrian experiences a quality of listening that seems to expand to fill the room. From the alert countenances of others, he concludes that they are having the same experience. Everyone contributes to and shares in a cloud of quiet. After a minute, Mr. Wells picks up his spoon and the rest follow and begin to eat.

Gradually, sounds of quiet conversation arose at each table. In this setting, their talking did not seem completely ordinary, at least at first. The sensitivity they had felt during the silence still called them to be attentive. A middle-aged woman sitting next to Adrian asked if this was his first Sunday. Answering that it was, Adrian explained that he had just started with Mr. Eckart's group that week. As their conversation continued, questions emerged for Adrian. What was appropriate to speak about? Did he really have to make small talk about his courses at school? How much should he talk?

After a few minutes, the level of conversation in the room grew louder and Adrian noticed that the initial care and restraint with which people had approached one another had been replaced by more habitual behavior. Taking the risk of turning his gaze to the head table, Adrian found Mr. Eckart looking directly at him, as if to confirm his observation and remind him that he too had disappeared into talking.

As everyone finished their lemon custard, conversation dwindled until silence reigned again. Those who hadn't finished their dessert found themselves putting down their spoons, as the stillness in the room no longer tolerated the clink of metal on glass. Observing the watchful gaze of the leaders at the head table, Adrian wondered if they were waiting for someone to ask a question.

What could he ask about? Adrian tried to find a question from his experience during the morning, but nothing seemed important enough. He told himself that if he had really observed himself, he would have a question. Then a man at another table spoke, interrupting his train of thought.

"I see that I am constantly worried about what others think of me. At the break table, I spilled the cream as I was pouring it into my coffee and immediately looked around to see if anyone was watching me. I'm reluctant to talk to my group leader, even though I want to, because I'm worried that he will think my questions are stupid."

Adrian was immediately interested in that questioner's experiences, as they were so similar to his own. He was reminded of his own resistance to approaching Mr. Eckart. Remembering how Mr. Wells had told him that people could serve as mirrors for one another, Adrian realized that he was able to see himself in the man who had just spoken. It helped to know that the man had the same difficulties and questions as he did.

A woman, one of the leaders Adrian didn't know yet, answered the question.

"I wish to be free, but I see that I am a slave to all of my thoughts because I am identified with them. I believe in them. I say 'I' to them, as though they really represented myself. But they are not me. They are only associations, habitual and automatic associations. They represent a very small part of me. But when I say 'I' to them, I believe they represent all of me. So it is with my reactions to other people. I identify with my thoughts about what the others will think of me. A man looks at me a certain way and I begin to imagine that he dislikes me. In reality, he may not be thinking about me, or may even like me. But I believe what I imagine and act toward him in a way that reflects this belief. Later I may even become wrapped up in worries about what he thinks of me. How to be free of this constant consideration of others? First, I need to see this form of identification for what it is. I need to observe it again and again in myself. If I begin to see this tendency as an automatic habit in me, if I can include more of myself at the moment it is taking place, I can free myself. I will see that it is not me. I am here in my body, sensing my feet on the ground and giving my attention to the task in front of me. This little association is there, but I do not need to believe in it or feed it in any way. It is only an automatic reaction that has been going on all of my life. It is not me. What am I? Who am I? These are the questions that may come alive in me and lead toward moments of real freedom."

She stopped speaking and gazed intently at the questioner. The room was quiet again. Her words went directly into Adrian because they corresponded so exactly to his own experience. It was not just her words, but the way in which she spoke, from practical knowledge seemingly based on her own understanding. She was trying to show them the way toward a different way of facing life. That was what Adrian wanted, why he had come to this group of people. He felt energized and excited.

After a minute of silence, Linda asked a question. Adrian was surprised and envious, because she had already talked with Mr. Eckart at break. Now, even though this was only her first Sunday, she was asking a question at lunch.

"I've been working in the kitchen today. My task was to chop all of the vegetables for the soup. I tried to watch myself as I was working, but as usual, I kept getting lost in thoughts. How can I make use of my task to help me to be present to myself?"

Adrian looked to the head table, wondering who would answer her. When he saw Mr. Eckart smiling, Adrian knew it would be him.

"That is a very good question. I need my task, but I didn't come here just for that. How can I make use of it for my work on myself? Before I turn my attention to the task, I need to come to myself. I need to have an overall sense of my body. I need to know my posture and observe where the tensions are. Then, keeping some attention on my body, I can begin to turn the rest of it to my task. I try to have both: the sensation of my body and my work with the task. But I don't hold back. I do the best job I can, all the time trying to find better ways of doing it. Do you follow?"

"Yes, I think so," she answered.

"Good. Try like that this afternoon."

Adrian had mixed feelings. On the one hand, he was glad she had spoken about this because he had the same question. He wanted to try what Mr. Eckart has suggested. But on the other hand, Adrian was jealous of her freedom to speak not only to Mr. Eckart but in front of the whole group. But something in Adrian discerned the vanity of his reaction and he tried not to get lost in the egoistic feelings that had been revealed. He was glad when another person asked a question because the effort to listen to the speaker helped him stay separate from his emotions.

"I'm beginning to realize that all of my efforts are really only mental. For example, when I try to sense my feet on the floor, I don't really have the sensation of being in my feet; I just project a thought towards my feet and call that sensing. Or when I try to stay present, all I'm really doing is holding a thought about staying present; I don't really have a feeling or sensation of being present. The thing is, these mental efforts don't last very long, only a few seconds. And then I get swept away by my daydreams again. I don't see how this approach will ever lead anywhere. I guess it means that I'm not really working and don't know how to work. How can I go on from here?"

Mr. Wells stared intensely at the man for a moment before he answered.

"This is a very important moment for you. What you say is absolutely true. Most of the time, I live in my head. I don't really work on myself. I dream about it and imagine that I am doing it, but it is all in my head. My body and my feeling know nothing of my so-called efforts and are not

160

interested. To work, I need all of my parts to be related. But before this is possible, I need to observe my situation as it is. What is interesting is that something in you has been able to see the truth in spite of your mental manipulations. You see now that you are not working and do not know how to work. You feel the need for help. This is the beginning of work! Can you go on, staying with your question, staying in front of your situation?"

"I don't know, but right now I wish to," answered the man.

"Very good. Stay with not knowing. Most of all, stay close to your wish."

With that, Mr. Wells passed his eyes over them all for a moment and then brought them down to rest on the flower in the vase before him. Everyone in the room seemed to share the silence that followed.

A young man at Adrian's table stood up to make an announcement. From a clipboard, he read the names of people assigned to wash the dishes and clean the dining hall. Then he said they would all gather in that room again for a reading at 5 o'clock. The leaders at the head table left the room, while the rest carried dishes to bins on a table provided in the wash-up area. Full of new resolve to try again, Adrian headed back to the metal shed and his task of bending brass rods for the lamp.

Margie was studying when Adrian returned to her apartment that evening. She looked up expectantly as he let himself in.

"How'd it go?"

"It was quite a day. It's hard to put it into words. I guess I'd say that it was both excruciating and exhilarating. On the one hand, I'm totally exhausted; on the other, I'm full of energy."

His body was tired, but he sensed a fine quality of energy that had accumulated during the day. Margie noticed it too.

"There's something about you that seems different. I'm glad you had a good day. Did you speak to someone about an appointment for me?"

"Uh, I didn't get the chance," he answered guiltily. "Mr. Eckart and Mr. Wells were so busy with other people that I couldn't get a moment with either of them."

He suspected that Margie knew he was making excuses. She looked disappointed. In Adrian's mind's eye, he relived his fear of approaching Mr. Eckart during the coffee break.

"Well, I've got to get back to studying," she said, turning her attention away from him.

"I'll ask Mr. Eckart at the group meeting this week, I promise," he said, trying to make up for his negligence and retrieve the good feeling which had existed between them when he first arrived.

"It's okay. Maybe I should go to the bookstore myself and ask that woman there to put me in touch with someone."

For a moment, Adrian was relieved to think that he wouldn't have to speak to Mr. Eckart about Margie if she did that. But feeling ashamed of his passivity, he rejoined,

"No, really, I want to help make the contact with Mr. Eckart for you so we can be together in this."

"Okay, but please do it this week. I have a lot of questions I really need to ask about."

Satisfied that he had at least partly salvaged their evening together, Adrian offered to take Margie out to dinner. She declined.

"No, I have some meat loaf we can heat up. I need to stay here and study for another hour or two. Would you like to get the meat loaf out of the fridge and make us a salad?"

"Sure." Adrian remembered that he had to study too, but would now have to wait until after they had eaten. He went into the kitchen, washed his hands, and began to prepare dinner.

Fear

Adrian arrived at the group Tuesday night determined to speak to Mr. Eckart about Margie. Although he saw Mr. Eckart standing alone in the hallway as he came up the stairs, Adrian told himself it would be best to approach him after the meeting. He went directly into the meeting room and took a chair in the first row.

Mr. Eckart entered with Dr. Stein, his assistant. Soon all were still again, listening to the quiet growing around and within them. A fairly long silence ensued before anyone asked a question. Predictably, Adrian thought, it was Linda. She spoke about her attempts to follow the direction given in response to her question at lunch on Sunday.

"When I went back into the kitchen, we had to wash all of the pots and pans. At first, I found myself automatically moving to the sink and putting on rubber gloves. Then, I remembered what you said about first making a good contact with my body before turning to the task. So I stopped in front of the sink and tried to feel my feet on the floor, with my weight evenly distributed between them. That seemed quite possible, so I tried to include the sensation of my legs as well. From there, I moved up through my torso to my head. Then, I stepped to the sink again and picked up one of the pots stacked beside it. I tried to stay in touch with my body while I washed the pot, as you suggested. I picked up the sponge, dipped it in the soapy water, and began to scrub. That was the last contact I had with my body until I came back to myself later when I was telling one of the other cooks about the new vegetarian restaurant at Fort Mason. It was like I was completely gone for the whole time in-between."

Mr. Eckart looked pleased. "That was very good work, Linda. We imagine that we can be conscious whenever we want and for as long as we want, but when we try as you did we see that it isn't true. We think we are capable of great strides, but we see that we must start by taking small steps. Your effort was not wasted. Every effort constitutes a small payment. It is like putting pennies in a jar, one by one. The more you try, the more you will see yourself. Go on with this investigation, not for results, but like a student engaged in a scientific inquiry. Do you understand?"

Linda's face was alive with understanding. She simply replied, "Thank you."

Once again, Adrian's intense interest was mixed with envy of Linda's success, her courage to speak, and the attention given her by Mr. Eckart. A battle ensued between these two diametrically opposed responses in him. At one moment, he was on one side of the struggle, in the next moment, on the other side. Wanting to free himself but not knowing what to do, he looked up at Mr. Eckart. As Mr. Eckart turned to him, he knew he had to try to speak. As he began, his question materialized.

"During the exchange after lunch on Sunday, I felt a strong connection with the man who spoke about how he is always considering others. What he said about being afraid to speak with his group leader really resonated in me because I've been observing my slavery to all kinds of fears, and particularly to fear of other people. My empathy with him was more than the ordinary experience in which we say that misery loves company. It was a very freeing realization that we have the same difficulties because we have the same habits. But we also have the same wish to be free. What was most hopeful was that I was able to take everything said by the woman who answered him for my own work. What she said about asking the question, 'Who am I?' seems very important. It means something to me, but I don't really understand it. It's a mystery."

Mr. Eckart looked at Adrian for while, seemingly assessing his understanding.

"You need to see this fear of others. It's there, but it's only fear. When you see yourself entirely under the influence of it, ask yourself, 'Is this all that I am? What more is there?' Here's where the question you mentioned comes in. Who am I? You will begin to see that you are identified not only with your fears, but with everything. As long as you make excuses and imagine that you can do what you like, you will remain a slave. But if you begin to see—really see—your constant state of identification, you have a chance for freedom. Try to get very close to this fear. Look at it. Find out where it comes from. Now, you have a direction for work. Do you understand?"

Adrian felt that Mr. Eckart was now looking at the one in him who really wished to work, the one who could grow. This brought with it a new kind of happiness. At the same time, it occurred to Adrian that he also faced a new level of responsibility for himself.

He could only answer, "I'll try."

Mr. Eckart turned back to the others, but Adrian still felt the vital warmth of their exchange. His thoughts began to revolve again as he replayed his question and Mr. Eckart's response in his mind. But when a woman spoke, he dropped the thoughts to listen.

After the meeting, Adrian took the first opportunity to speak to Mr. Eckart. In a way, he felt that having asked a question gave him the right to approach him. He told him about Margie and her keen interest in the ideas and work of the group. Adrian asked if she could call him to arrange an appointment.

"I think it would be very good if your Margie could meet with Mrs. Hoyle. She's the woman who answered the man you felt so connected to at Sunday lunch. Here, I'll give your her number."

He reached into the inside breast pocket of his coat and pulled out a small address book.

"Do you have something to write on?" he asked.

"Oh sure," Adrian said, awkwardly fishing in his wallet for some small piece of paper and retrieving a dog-eared receipt from a restaurant. Fortunately, he had a pen in his shirt pocket. Mr. Eckart dictated the phone number as Adrian wrote it down on the back of the receipt.

"That's the number for her little art gallery on Union Street. Tell Margie to call Mrs. Hoyle during the week between 10 and 5."

"Okay, I will. Thanks a lot, Mr. Eckart."

"Very good, Mr. Masters." He walked away.

Adrian caught a ride back to Margie's apartment with one of the men in the group who also lived in Berkeley.

Margie opened her door. She was wearing a white peasant's blouse that dipped low. The energy Adrian had gathered during the day fueled an instantaneous wave of desire for her.

"Well, did you ask Mr. Eckart if I could see him?"

Her voice was demanding.

"Yes. But he thought it best that you meet with a woman, a Mrs. Hoyle. He gave me her phone number."

Margie looked a little disappointed.

"Listen, I heard this woman speak at lunch on Sunday. She's incredible. You'll be really glad to meet her."

Margie's frown changed into a smile. "Well, I guess it would be good to talk to a woman. And this way, I'll have my own individual contact. Thanks, Adrian!"

She slipped into his arms and they embraced for a moment in the doorway. The tide of attraction rose quickly in him. Feeling it, she stepped back and smiled.

"I think you'd better come inside."

Harmonium

The next evening, walking down Telegraph on his way to the record store, Adrian noticed an interesting musical instrument in the front window of India Imports. It had a keyboard and bellows like an accordion, but looked like a miniature piano. He went into the store to check it out.

Inside, he was greeted with aromas of incense and tropical wood. Passing by a row of carved bodhisattvas, he went to the front of the shop and asked the man there if he would take the instrument out of the window so that he could look at it more closely. The man seemed glad for Adrian's interest and went to get it. Setting the instrument on the counter, the man told Adrian that it was a harmonium, then demonstrated how to pump the bellows while striking the keys. Adrian tried it out, improvising a simple melody. As soon as he had played a little, he knew he wanted that instrument.

"How much is it?"

"Two hundred and nineteen dollars."

Adrian wasn't sure he could come up with that much money right away, but he didn't want to give it up.

"Could you hold it for me until tomorrow?"

The man thought for a moment and then agreed. "Write down your name, address, and phone number. I'll hold it for just 24 hours."

Adrian wrote down his information on the paper, thanked the man, and left the shop. There was still a little time before he had to be at work, so he decided to check out Desmond's new place.

Desmond had recently moved to a small room in a cheap boarding hotel on Telegraph. Taking Timothy Leary's slogan, "turn on, tune in, drop out" literally, Desmond had dropped out of his classes at Cal, even though he had been a brilliant sociology student with a promising future. Repeated acid trips had persuaded Desmond of the futility of his academic studies. He was now working at a warehouse in Oakland.

Adrian went down the stairs to Desmond's floor, which was situated below the street level. Desmond answered his knock, invited him in and they sat down on his bed. Through the only window in the room, which was situated at the level of the sidewalk on Telegraph outside, they watched the feet of people walking by. Soon, Desmond pulled out his long-stemmed pipe and a matchbox of grass.

"Want to turn on?"

"No, I've got to go to work." Adrian thought it was unnecessary to repeat that he wasn't using drugs anymore. He and Desmond had been good friends for a while, but now they were going in different directions. But as Adrian still hoped their relationship would improve, he didn't want to emphasize their differences.

Desmond shrugged. He filled the pipe bowl with grass from the matchbox and lit it with a lighter. The pungent odor of the marijuana filled the room. Desmond took a deep drag and held his breath.

Adrian was beginning to wonder why he'd stopped to see Desmond. Trying to make conversation, he told Desmond about the harmonium he'd seen at India Imports.

"Sounds cool!" Desmond said in an exhalation of smoke.

"Yeah, it is, but I can't really afford it. But I asked them to hold it for me for a day in case I can figure out a way to buy it."

Desmond smiled broadly. He was beginning to get high.

"We need some music!"

Desmond got up and put the new Beatles album on his turntable. He sang along as "She loves you, yeah, yeah, yeah" began to blare from the speakers.

Adrian didn't see a reason to stay any longer.

"I've got to get to work." He got up and went to the door.

"Peace!" called Desmond, holding up two fingers in a V sign and then falling into a laughing jag.

Margie was waiting for Adrian at his place when he came home from the record store later that night. They sat down with some potato leek soup she had made for them. He told her about the harmonium.

"I really want to get that instrument, but I think it's more than I can afford right now."

Margie was supportive, but practical as always. "Better wait until you aren't so strapped. It will still be around."

"But I've never seen one of these harmoniums before. The store may not have them in stock very often."

"Well, I guess you'll have to figure it out," she concluded, removing herself from further conversation about his instrument. They turned to their separate studies for the rest of the evening and went to bed late.

In the morning, they were awakened by a knock on the door. Still groggy, Adrian climbed out of bed, put on a shirt and pair of pants, and went to the door. Margie stayed under the covers.

There was a cop at the door. He wanted to come in. Taken by surprise and a little confused, Adrian let him enter.

"What is this about?" Adrian asked.

"The owner of India Imports reported a stolen article. He said that you came to his shop and showed a lot of interest in an instrument. He gave us your name and address."

"What?" Adrian was incredulous. "I didn't take it. If I was planning to steal it, I certainly wouldn't have given him my name and address!"

The cop ignored his reasoning. "Can I take a look around?"

"Sure." As soon as he had said it, it occurred to Adrian that he should have asked for a search warrant. But then he dismissed the thought because he wanted to show the cop that he had nothing to hide.

After looking through all the closets and cabinets in the living room and kitchen, the cop entered the bedroom. Seeing Margie there, he acknowledged her and then quickly turned his gaze away, apparently feeling awkward about the situation. He didn't spend much more time there, just quickly looking under the bed and in the closet.

Adrian followed him as he returned to the living room.

"Okay, looks like you don't have it here," the cop observed as he prepared to leave.

"Of course I don't," Adrian affirmed emphatically. "I didn't take it!"

The cop put his hand on the door knob, then turned back to Adrian. "Would you be willing to take a lie detector test?"

This was so completely unexpected, that without thinking, Adrian answered in the affirmative. "Yes, of course."

"Okay, I'll let you know." The cop let himself out.

Adrian returned to the bedroom and rejoined Margie under the covers.

She looked at him wide-eyed. "Wow, that was weird!"

"Yeah, I'm amazed. How strange that the harmonium was stolen so soon after I looked at it."

"Are you really going to take a lie detector test?"

"I guess so."

"Did you tell anyone else about the harmonium?"

"I don't think so... Oh, wait a minute... I stopped by Desmond's place on the way to work last night and mentioned it to him. But I don't see what that would have to do with it."

Margie sat up and raised an eyebrow. "I think you should visit your friend Desmond again and see if he has a new harmonium."

"Maybe you're right."

After his afternoon classes, Adrian returned to Desmond's place. Standing in the hallway outside the door about to knock, Adrian heard not only voices, but music, and not just music from Desmond's hi-fi system. Recognizing the sound of the harmonium, a wave of anger flashed in Adrian's gut. At the same time, this shock reminded him of the possibility of following himself in the midst of this situation. For that, he knew he needed to contain his emotion, not disappear into it's expression. He waited a few seconds to ground himself, then knocked on the door. He heard footsteps and Desmond opened the door. Barefooted, Desmond was wearing a tie-dyed tee shirt and off-white jockey shorts.

"Hi, man! Come in and listen."

Following Desmond inside, the first thing Adrian saw was a naked girl lying on Desmond's bed. Desmond sat down next to her, putting the harmonium on his lap. He pumped the bellows with one hand as he played a melody on the keys with the other. With her arms stretched straight up, the girl moved her hands to his music as though she was conducting an orchestra on the ceiling. They were both obviously high on something.

Adrian's anger began to increase, mixed with astonishment at Desmond's brazen disregard of their friendship. Desmond must realize that Adrian knew now that he had stolen the very instrument Adrian had told him about so enthusiastically the day before, but Desmond didn't seem to care in the least. In spite of Adrian's good intentions, the poison of negativity began to spread all over his body. He couldn't control it and was about to explode. Desmond, with his head thrown back and eyes closed, continued to play. The girl's movements became increasingly dramatic. As both of them appeared to be completely self-absorbed and oblivious of Adrian and his feelings, he realized that he could just leave. Without saying anything, Adrian went to the door and let himself out, barely suppressing the impulse to slam the door behind him as hard as he could. He moved with agitated speed down the hallway and up the stairs to an exit on the street.

Adrian walked at full tilt to Margie's, thoughts racing and seething with anger. When he entered her apartment, one look at his face told her the whole story.

"What are you going to do?"

"I don't know. Mainly, I'm really worried about taking the lie detector test. Now that I know that Desmond is the one who took the harmonium, my lie will undoubtedly be detected if I say that I don't know anything about the theft. On the other hand, if I tell the truth, Desmond will be arrested. Even though I'm furious, I don't want him to go to jail."

"Maybe you should ask Mr. Eckart what to do."

"No, that isn't the kind of question we bring to him. I should only ask questions about inner work."

"But isn't this a situation for inner work? Aren't you always saying that one of the main aims of your philosophy is to carry out efforts in the midst of everyday life?"

"Yes, but in this case I would be asking Mr. Eckart how to get out of the situation rather than asking how to observe myself in it."

"Well then, ask him about that."

Margie was always so simple, practical, and down-to-earth. "Maybe you're right. I definitely need some helpful advice."

This dilemma filled Adrian's thoughts for the next several days, constantly distracting him during classes and study periods. Things were a little better at the record store, as business was brisk, keeping him busy. While he was attending to customers and the cash register, his revolving thoughts became secondary.

Adrian realized that he would have to speak to Mr. Eckart about his problem and decided to do it when he saw him during the workday on Sunday. Meanwhile, Margie had managed to contact Mrs. Hoyle and made an appointment for a meeting at her gallery the following week. Both Adrian and Margie began to live in anticipation of conversations with special people that they hoped would bring the help they needed.

At last, Sunday came. Adrian rehearsed what he would say to Mr. Eckart as he rode the jitney bus to the house that morning. He planned to place the emphasis of his question not on getting out of the lie detector test, but on how to watch himself in front of such a difficult problem. But the truth was that he hoped that Mr. Eckart might offer some advice to help him with the outer situation as well.

His opportunity came during the morning coffee break. Seeing Mr. Eckart standing alone in the garden, Adrian collected his courage and approached him.

"There's something I really need to speak to you about." Adrian was surprised to hear the emotion in his voice. Mr. Eckart heard it too.

"Of course." Sensing his need, Mr. Eckart led Adrian to an area of the patio where there were two chairs. He motioned him to sit down.

Seeing now how open Mr. Eckart was, Adrian dropped his plan to camouflage his question as one about self-observation and simply told Mr. Eckart exactly what had happened. Mr. Eckart listened intently. When Adrian had finished, Mr. Eckart sat thinking for a minute before speaking.

"The only way to beat a lie detector test is concentration."

Adrian was stunned. What Mr. Eckart had said was the last thing he had expected from him. And yet, it seemed to be exactly what he needed.

"At the same time as the lie detector test is going on, while you're answering their questions, you must give the greater part of your attention to this exercise."

Then Mr. Eckart gave Adrian a difficult counting exercise.

"Let me know how it goes."

That was it. For the first time, Mr. Eckart smiled warmly at Adrian. Then without saying more, he excused himself.

This conversation with Mr. Eckart turned upside-down Adrian's fixed idea of what a teacher-pupil relationship could be. He hadn't anticipated Mr. Eckart's practical approach, free from any kind of subjective morality. Adrian felt liberated from the oppressive thoughts and feelings that had weighed on him during the previous days. Now he had something practical to help him face the lie detector test, with the full support of his teacher.

Adrian told Margie about the conversation when he returned to her apartment that night. Then he expressed his appreciation for her help.

"I really have to thank you for urging me to talk to Mr. Eckart. As usual, your practical wisdom has helped me move past my resistance. Just as it did when you persuaded me to call Mr. Wells from the Japanese restaurant."

"Okay then, why don't you take me out to dinner there again right now?" she replied with characteristic quickness.

Arm in arm, breathing in the mild evening air, they walked with lightened spirits to Kirala.

Mrs. Hoyle

Margie's appointment with Mrs. Hoyle was at 2 o'clock in the afternoon at her art gallery on Union Street. Margie had to skip a class to make it, but felt she could afford to miss it this once. Adrian offered to go with her, suggesting that he could walk and browse the shops on Union Street during her meeting. It meant that he would have to forego his Shakespeare class, but he figured he could catch up with the help of the lecture notes they sold at the student bookstore.

From the Transbay terminal in San Francisco, they walked to Powell and Market, where they hopped on a cable car that would take them to Union Street. They felt like tourists on vacation, hanging off the side of the cable car as it ascended steep Powell hill, hearing the rhythmic clang of the operator's bell, sensing the warm sun on their faces, and taking in the myriad aromas and colors of life on the street as they passed.

They got off the cable car at Hyde and Union and began the seven-block walk to Mrs. Hoyle's gallery. Holding hands and smiling, they basked in the joy momentarily granted to them. Then, as they approached the gallery, Margie began to slow down. Adrian guessed that she was feeling the same kind of nervous anticipation that he had experienced before his first meeting with Mr. Wells.

It occurred to him that she might like to make the final approach by herself. "You go on to the gallery. I want to check out a bookstore we passed on the last block."

"Okay. But where will I meet you when I'm done?"

Looking around, he spotted the perfect meeting place. "I'll be in there," he said, pointing to a coffee house across the street. "Have a good meeting."

Margie walked ahead while Adrian backtracked to the bookstore. He turned around to look back in time to see her disappear into a doorway down the street. He was excited for her.

Margie rejoined him in the coffee house a little over an hour later. She was glowing. As she sat down, Adrian saw that he was ready to inundate her with questions about her meeting with Mrs. Hoyle. He realized that the tables were turned and that now he was the one who wanted to know all about her meeting, while she must be feeling cautious about how much she said. Respecting her need to keep something for herself, he held his questions back, waiting instead for her to begin the conversation. But when she did, instead of talking about her meeting, she asked what he had been doing.

"Did you find anything you wanted at the bookstore?"

"No, I just looked around." He couldn't leave it at that. He had to ask her. "But what about your meeting?"

"Well, I can't say too much yet—Mrs. Hoyle suggested that I keep our conversation to myself—but it was an incredible hour. I've never met anyone like that before. While we were talking, I felt that Mrs. Hoyle gave me all of her attention. In fact, I don't think anyone has ever listened to me so well as she did. And so in response, it was like I was activated to give all of my attention to her. As the meeting went on, I felt I had more and more energy. I would say she helped me to respect the part of myself that wants this."

"Did she give you any exercises to try?"

"Yes, but I can't speak about them yet."

"That's okay, I understand." Adrian did appreciate her need to keep silent, but was still a little disappointed that she wouldn't share more with him.

"Well, then, shall we get back to Berkeley?" she suggested, moving her chair away from the table.

"Sure."

Retracing their steps down Union toward Hyde, they didn't speak for a couple of blocks. Finally breaking the silence, Adrian asked Margie if she had been invited to a group.

"No, Mrs. Hoyle suggested that I meet with her for awhile."

"Will you be seeing her regularly?"

"I guess so. I have another appointment with her next week."

"Did you ask for a different time so you don't have to miss classes?"

"Yes, I'm meeting with her at 4:00 in the afternoon, which should give me enough time to get here after my linguistic philosophy class."

After several more blocks of walking in silence, Adrian brought up a new subject. "I've been thinking about what to do after I graduate. You know, I'll be done in January. I've got to go to grad school or I'll lose my student deferment and be drafted. I don't think my grades are good enough to get into the English masters program at Cal. My best bet is probably San Francisco State College. They have a special humanities masters program that combines courses in literature, music, philosophy, and art. That appeals to me."

"Wow, that's a big deal," she said sympathetically, taking up the conversation. "This is really coming up soon, isn't it?"

"Yes, I've got to get my application in by the end of next week."

"San Francisco State would be a big change. Do you think you'll like it?"

"I'm not sure. But I don't really have a choice. I want to stay in the Bay Area and since I don't think I can get into a graduate program at Cal or Stanford, San Francisco State seems like the best option. I certainly have to keep my student deferment. I read in the newspaper that 60,000 men will be drafted next month to fight in Vietnam."

They reached the stop at Hyde and Powell just in time to catch a cable car down the hill. Each of them retreated into their own thoughts against the background of street sounds, the clanging bell, and the hum of the cable moving under the street. Adrian reflected on how different they were on this return trip than they had been on the ascent.

The next morning, Margie had already left for an early class and Adrian was frying an egg when he heard a knock on the door. He opened it to find the same Berkeley cop who had come before to search for the harmonium. Although Adrian had relaxed considerably about the lie detector test since his talk with Mr. Eckart, his concern now reappeared. The cop asked if he could take another look around. Adrian let him in, nervously anticipating that he might have to go to the police station to take the test.

Adrian went back into the kitchen to finish making his breakfast while the cop searched every room. He seemed to be satisfied that the harmonium wasn't there by the time Adrian was sitting down with his egg and toast. Adrian got up as the cop moved toward the door.

"What about the lie detector test? Do you want me to take it?"

"No, I talked to my chief about that, but it looks like it's not going to be necessary. I don't think I'll be bothering you again."

With that, the cop walked out and Adrian closed the door behind him. He was greatly relieved. That little saga was over now. Adrian couldn't help wondering if his relationship to Mr. Eckart and the group had influenced the way things came out. But he knew that imagination and analysis wouldn't help him understand that. He realized it was best to leave it as a question, probably an unanswerable question.

As nature abhors a vacuum, the space left by the resolution of Adrian's fears about the lie detector test was soon filled with anxiety about what he would do after graduation. He didn't really know what career he wanted in life. At one point in his undergraduate years, he had pictured himself as a college English professor smoking a pipe and wearing a Harris Tweed sport jacket with suede patches on the elbows. Now, he saw that image as a comical fantasy.

The truth was, academia wasn't for him. Adrian had become weary of classrooms, papers and exams. He wanted to be actively involved in the real world. Only the threat of losing his draft deferment made it imperative that he go on to graduate studies. He regretted not having worked hard enough to get the grades needed to be admitted to a masters program at Berkeley. San Francisco State College was the only school that made sense now, particularly as he wanted to continue with the group activities in San Francisco. And there was no question that he wanted to stay close to Margie.

Adrian filled out the forms for enrollment to San Francisco State later that week, selecting the composite humanities graduate program he had told Margie about. That still seemed like the best choice for him.

Confrontation

In mid-October, the Vietnam Day Committee—the same group of antiwar activists who had organized the three-day Vietnam War "Teach-In" on campus six months earlier—organized a march from the Berkeley campus to the Oakland Army Terminal to protest the escalating war. Though both Margie and Adrian opposed the war, they resisted participating in mass demonstrations. Still, like others, they often found themselves attracted by the magnetism of these events. On the day of the protest march, Margie suggested that she and Adrian visit her friend Sonya, who lived on the second floor of a small house at the corner of Woolsey and Telegraph, right at the border of Berkeley and Oakland. Margie thought Sonya wouldn't mind if they climbed to the roof, which would serve as a perfect vantage point for watching the march as it passed by.

Sonya gladly took Margie and Adrian up to her roof, where they watched a river of protestors flowing down Telegraph Avenue from as far north as they could see. But at the intersection directly below them, a phalanx of Oakland police stood at the border, waiting to block the marchers. It chilled Adrian to think of the similarity to the way Alabama state troopers had waited on the bridge in

Selma to intercept the marchers there. But he told himself that this was completely different. This was Berkeley. Nothing bad would happen here. As the leaders of the march drew near the police, they stopped, which gradually halted the flow all along Telegraph. The leaders stood facing the officers, seeming to weigh the risk of continuing forward. Adrian felt there was something unusually tense and threatening about these police. Uniformly outfitted in blue, wearing helmets with protective visors and grasping billy clubs, the densely packed rows of cops formed an impenetrable wall across Telegraph.

As Adrian looked down on the confrontation, he became aware of himself watching passively. It struck him that his position on the rooftop was a metaphor for his way of facing life. Rather than taking the risk of participating in this confrontation between youthful idealism and blind authority, he had chosen to look down on it from above. Just as he had during the FSM sit-in at Sproul Hall. He always played it safe. Even the interloper who gave the wrong phone number to Mr. Wells had been hedging his bets. So far in his life, no difficulty had come along that he hadn't been able to avoid.

"Look, the leaders of the demonstration are trying to decide what to do." Margie's words jarred Adrian out of his thoughts.

They could see three protest leaders at the head of the crowd, two men and a woman, talking and gesticulating. From their body language, it appeared that there were differences of opinion among them. Margie worried about the violence that might erupt if they decided to lead the marchers forward into the police line. But after a few minutes, the leaders seemed to have agreed to avoid conflict, because they signaled the marchers to turn around. The multicolored mass of demonstrators slowly changed direction, now flowing back toward Berkeley. After the marchers had retreated for several blocks, the police formation began to break up.

They climbed down from the roof and returned to Sonya's living room, where she brought out coffee and cookies. Margie and Adrian stayed for another hour, while they all talked about the war and how it had affected each of them individually. Of course, Adrian's own concern was quite different from that of Margie and Sonya, as he could be drafted and forced to fight in the war.

"But you'll stay in school and keep your deferment," Sonya insisted, waving aside any reason to be concerned about the Army.

"Yeah, I'm planning to stay in school. I've applied for a graduate program at San Francisco State. But, you never know what might happen."

"Even if you didn't stay in school, you can do what lots of other guys are doing."

"You mean, say I'm a homosexual?" Adrian was pretty sure that's what she meant.

"Sure, or a drug addict, or both. I've know several guys who've done that and now their draft classification is 4F."

Desmond had done that. He had been called for a physical right after he dropped out of school. All he had to do was check a couple of boxes on the questionnaire and he was out.

"Well, let's hope it doesn't come to that." Adrian wanted the conversation to be over. He thanked Sonya, saying that he had a lot of studying to do, and he and Margie took their leave.

As they walked home, Margie voluntarily told Adrian a little about her exchange with Mrs. Hoyle.

"She asked me about our relationship. She said that two people together can help each other in this work. I said that it was really from talking to you that I became interested. I even told her that I hoped we could eventually be in the same group. She didn't promise anything, but she didn't seem to oppose it either."

"Did you ask her when you will be invited to a meeting?"

"I don't feel it's my place to push. I'm sure she'll invite me when she thinks I'm ready. Besides, I really like being able to meet with her personally every week."

"Well, I guess I know what you mean. I kind of feel the same way. I've heard about these dance exercise classes people can attend after they've been in the group long enough. I'd like to ask if I can be in one of those, but I think that I should wait until I'm invited. It has something to do with respect."

Margie changed the subject, anticipating that they would soon have to go off in different directions if he intended to go to his place.

"Are you going on Sunday again? Don't you have some school work you have to get done?"

"Yeah, I'm going there Sunday. I have to turn in a rough draft of my Wallace Stevens thesis on Monday, so I'll go home and work on it tonight and all day tomorrow."

"Then I guess I'll be going to my apartment now. If you're done with your paper by Sunday night, come to my place for a shower, dinner and some good lovin'."

"That's a great incentive for me to finish by tomorrow! See you Sunday night!"

They kissed and parted.

Breakthrough

That night, Adrian worked on his paper until midnight, got a few hours sleep, then started again on Saturday morning. For this first draft of his thesis, he had been planning to concentrate his analysis on twelve of Wallace Steven's poems. The more he tried to understand and write about them, the more challenging they became. But forging on, he began to apprehend the depth of their meaning and to more fully appreciate the astonishing artistry of their structure and language. The poems began to show him what he wanted to say about them. The flow of ideas became so rich that he had no choice but to reduce the planned scope of his thesis to include fewer poems.

He decided to limit his study to three poems that meant the most to him: "Thirteen Ways of Looking at a Blackbird," "Final Soliloquy of the Interior Paramour," and "The Poem That Took the Place of a Mountain." Working intensely, Adrian was able to finish his analysis of the first two poems and an outline for the third by 2 am Sunday morning. He could finish writing about "The Poem That Took the Place of a Mountain" in his final draft. That left him only three hours to sleep before beginning the trek to the house in San Francisco.

Arriving there tired, Adrian wanted to sit down, but as usual everyone had to stand in the cold garage until the list of teams had been read. Hearing that he was still assigned to work with the metal shop team, Adrian went to the shed. Getting started was tough, as he faced the usual resistance to the work without his normal reserve of energy. However, the presence of the others reminded him that he had come there to struggle with himself. Glancing to the other end of the table, he saw that Jim, the team leader, was confronted with his own difficulties. His shaking hands and flushed face showed he was suffering from another serious hangover. But he had managed to make it there. As usual, he worked quietly at his task and helped others when they needed him.

This impression of Jim's attitude helped bring Adrian's own aspirations alive. Though his body was tired, he could sense it. Perhaps, he thought, he could sense it even better because he was tired. He became determined to stay in touch with his hands as he worked with the cold metal rods. But wanting to go deeper than a superficial sensation of his hands, he tried to *inhabit* them.

By the time the bell called everyone to the coffee break, Adrian had become so involved in the momentum of his work that he didn't want to stop. He was no longer tired, but on the contrary, full of energy. But seeing how he had become so identified with his endeavor that he didn't want to let it go when the bell rang a second time, he put down his tools and went out of the dark shed into the yard. The sky was overcast and the air still cool, but the freshness of the day and the colors of the garden released a flood of impressions. As Adrian was standing at the break table, Mr. Eckart came up alongside him to pour himself a cup of coffee. To Adrian's surprise, he was free of his usual fear of Mr. Eckart. He thought Mr. Eckart must have sensed this difference in his state as he reached for the teapot, because his teacher smiled at him. Then Mr. Eckart asked if they could talk. Adrian grabbed a croissant and followed him into the garden.

"How did the lie detector test go?"

"The cop came back to my place to search again. When I asked him if I would have to take the lie detector test, he said that it wouldn't be necessary. I don't think I'll hear from the police about this again."

"Good. Very good." Mr. Eckart gave emphasis to his words.

"I know I don't understand this, but somehow, I have an intuition that the talk I had with you helped influence the course of events," added Adrian. He was reluctant to say this because he didn't really know if it was true or just his imagination, but he wanted Mr. Eckart to know what he was thinking.

Mr. Eckart did not reply at once. Adrian felt that he was looking deep down into him. There was something of a hidden smile on his lips, which Adrian took as confirmation of a mystery about which they couldn't speak.

Mr. Eckart changed his posture and the subject of their conversation.

"A new dance exercise class is being formed. I think you're ready for it now. Would you be interested in that?"

"Yes, I would, very much."

"Very well. Ask Mrs. Hoyle when the class will be meeting. She will be teaching it."

"Okay, I will. Thank you!"

"Don't thank me. Just work!"

Mr. Eckart walked back to the break table, where Linda had been waiting to intercept him.

As always seemed to be the case, Adrian's excitement was tempered by anxiety. So far, he hadn't spoken directly to Mrs. Hoyle and was resistant to approaching her. But now he had to. He hoped that their common relationship to Margie might help.

Later, as Adrian was taking a seat at one of the tables in the dining room, he resolved to speak to Mrs. Hoyle right after lunch. He sat quietly as the servers placed steaming bowls of stew in front of those already seated. Everyone was waiting for the leaders to come into the dining room. Adrian's thoughts about what he would say to Mrs. Hoyle came to a standstill when he saw her enter the room. Her gaze passed to him momentarily as she sat down. The shock of that moment when their eyes met brought with it the realization that the best preparation for speaking to her was to work to be present in the moment rather than indulge in imagination about what he would say later.

When everyone had been served and there was no more movement in the dining hall, silence enveloped them. Without speaking about it, some understood that an energy of consciousness filled the room. For a minute or two, they lived together in the Now. Then, when Mr. Wells lifted his fork, everyone became animated again as they began to eat.

When they had finished the meal and conversation in the room had diminished, one of the senior women spoke.

"This morning, I tried to listen to the sounds around me as a way to stay present. I was working in the kitchen, so there was a lot going on all the time: sounds of chopping, of food cooking on the stove, of water running in the sink, of people talking. At first, this seemed to help. It was something very definite I could try, without any imagination. It wouldn't last long before I got lost in my thoughts, but then something would remind me and I could return to listening again. However, by break time, I began to lose interest in trying this. It seemed as though my original effort had turned into something else, into a kind of doing. It had become ordinary, focused on the outside. Then, after break, we were really busy in the kitchen getting the lunch ready on time. As I was bringing food to the serving table, I passed Mr. Wells. Seeing him gave me a shock, because I realized that I hadn't tried to listen at all since the break. Now, I'm left not knowing what to try."

Mrs. Hoyle answered her.

"You have seen a lot this morning. Listening is a very good way to try. It is another way of watching. But there are different ways in which to listen. You see, we are accustomed to going out to what we see or hear. When I look at another person, my automatic tendency is to go out to them. When I listen, even when I listen to music, I tend to go outside to the sounds. But I wish to include myself in my listening. At the same time that I hear the sounds coming from outside, I wish to know my thoughts, my emotions, the state of my body. So I try to listen from inside, not just from my ears, but from my whole body. I stay at home in myself when I listen.

"It is very good that you were able to see how your effort changed. It began from your wish to work, from an interest in studying yourself. But it changed into something you were trying to do to get results, a kind of manipulation. Seeing this, it was quite natural to lose interest. Later, when you realized that you had been lost for a long time in the intensity of the kitchen work, you felt the shock of that. That is important, because we need shocks to wake us up. Often we do not feel the shocks because they are buffered by our excuses and rationalizations. But because you were able to receive the shock, it brought you to a real question. You feel now that you do not know how to work. You wish to work but you do not know how to try. This is a very good place from which to begin this afternoon. Come back to listening again, but now from within, from your question, from your wish. Include yourself in your listening. Listen from your whole body."

Adrian wanted to try what Mrs. Hoyle had suggested, even though it had been specifically directed to the questioner. Here again, he saw how, in this group, the effort of one person helped everyone. They shared the same inner obstacles. Sometimes, they shared the same inner wish as well. Adrian was grateful to be there with those people. In the midst of the instability and madness of the world, this school was an island of sanity and hope.

When lunch was over and people were carrying their dishes to the wash area, Adrian left his on the table and went directly to Mrs. Hoyle as she was walking away from her table.

"Hello, Mrs. Hoyle." Adrian's momentary sense of presence from the energy gathered during lunch overcame his usual reticence.

"Hello, Mr. Masters. How are you?"

Adrian was surprised by her pleasant manner, which was quite different than what he had come to expect from Mr. Eckart, at least most of the time. Of about medium height and somewhat stocky build, Mrs. Hoyle had blond hair cut in a conventional short style. She wore a plain green skirt and simple flowered cotton blouse. A certain elegance shone from her kind smile and intelligent eyes.

"I was really touched by what you just said. I want to try to work in that way myself this afternoon."

"Yes, it's right. But you have to find your own work, which is different from the work of the woman I was speaking to."

Adrian was not sure that he understood what she meant, but he nodded his head as though he did.

"Mr. Eckart said that I should speak to you about coming to your new dance exercise class."

"Oh yes, he mentioned that he thought you were ready for the dances. We will begin on Thursday night after the theme meeting. Can you make that?"

"Definitely. I'm really interested in coming, though I really don't know what to expect."

"It is good to be unhampered by preconceptions, although I am sure those will come along soon enough. In any case, you will need to get some simple exercise shoes. You can find them at Capezio's. Get a pair with a plain suede sole, not the ones with a thick leather piece sewn on the bottom."

"Okay, thanks, I will."

He wanted to ask her about Margie, but it didn't seem appropriate to mix that in with this conversation.

"Then, I guess I'll see you this coming Thursday night."

"Yes, Mr. Masters, I will see you then. Oh, and try to come into the room ten minutes early so that you can prepare by sitting quietly."

"Thank you, I will."

Mrs. Hoyle continued on her way to the door. Looking back at the table where he had been sitting, Adrian smiled to see that someone had already carried his dishes to the wash area for him.

At the end of the day, Adrian got a ride back to Berkeley with a couple who he had often seen at the Cafe Mediterranean. Both had recently been students at Cal. Margaret, who had graduated the past June, was working as an editor for the University Press. Peter had dropped out in his senior year to start his own photography studio.

They took him right to Margie's building. Adrian hurried up the stairs to Margie's floor, anxious to tell her that he'd been invited to the dance class and had talked to Mrs. Hoyle. When he got to her apartment and opened her door, it was clear that she wasn't ready for him. Still in her slippers and without makeup, she was wearing an oversized gray sweatshirt and faded jeans. He surmised that she had been studying most of the day. However, the aroma of something fantastic told him that she had been in the kitchen as well.

"Adrian, you're here early! I wasn't expecting you for another hour."

"Yeah, I didn't have to take the bus. I got a ride with a couple who were at the workday."

They moved toward one another and embraced. Adrian's immediate sensitivity to Margie's soft body against his echoed the special quality of energy he'd come to recognize at the end of a day of work.

"Not so fast." Margie smiled, sensing his desire. She backed away from him. "I still have some school work to finish. Why don't you take a shower?"

Though it seemed to Adrian that every cell in his body wanted to make love to her right there on the spot, he admired her practicality and respected the consistent discipline she exercised in relation to her studies. Reluctantly, he accepted that his yearning would have to wait.

"What's that incredible aroma?"

"Just wait and see." She smiled.

"Okay, I'll be patient. A shower sounds good right now."

"There's a clean blue towel on the shelf in the bathroom."

After the shower, Adrian put on some clean clothes he kept at her apartment. Margie was still at her desk, writing.

"What are you working on?"

"I'm writing a paper about The Vienna Circle, a discussion group of professional people who were influenced by Wittgenstein. He came to a number of their meetings, but often disagreed with them. I'm trying to show how a study of their differences of opinion can help clarify some of the ideas in Wittgenstein's *Tractatus*."

"Sounds really interesting."

"I'll be done in a minute. I've still got a few more days before I have to turn it in. Go check out the new book I got yesterday. It's on the hall table."

Adrian found the book and picked it up. It was titled, *Her-Bak, Chick-Pea*, by Isha Schwaller de Lubicz. It appeared to be a story about a boy coming of age within an ancient Egyptian esoteric temple. Sitting down to look through it, he was particularly attracted by a center section of images taken from Egyptian hieroglyphics. What interested him most were some of the postures taken by priests and anthropomorphic creatures.

"Okay, I'm done with my paper for tonight," Margie called. "I just have to do one more thing for our dinner. Come and talk to me in the kitchen."

Putting down the book and joining Margie in the kitchen, he asked, "How did you find that book?"

"Mrs. Hoyle recommended it. She thinks it's a wonderful story that relates to a lot of the ideas we're trying to understand."

"Oh, by the way, I had a little talk with Mrs. Hoyle today."

"What did you talk about?"

"Well, earlier in the day Mr. Eckart told me that he thought I was ready to start a dance exercise class. He said to talk to Mrs. Hoyle because she's the teacher. I approached her after lunch. She had just given a really incredible answer to a woman's question. So I told her that I was helped by her answer. Then I asked her about the dance class."

"That's great, Adrian! I'm really excited for you."

"I don't really know what's it's going to be like, but Mrs. Hoyle said that it's best to give up expectations."

"What else did she say?"

"Nothing much, except that I need to buy some soft dance shoes for the class. I wanted to ask her something about you, but it didn't seem appropriate at that moment."

"So she didn't tell you that she was going to invite me to a group?"

"No! You're kidding!"

"I'm serious. She called a little while ago, just before you got here. She mentioned that she met you today. Apparently, she talked things over with Mr. Eckart and they agreed that it would be good if I was in the same group with you!"

"That's fantastic news!"

"She also said that they often separate couples because many women are so dominated by men that they need the support of their own group. But she's not worried about that with me. In fact, she felt it would be a mistake to separate us because she thinks we can help each other."

"This calls for a celebration!"

"Well then, why don't you put on some music and open the wine."

He went to the shelf where Margie kept her records. Her collection included a mix of classical, folk, jazz, and pop. Adrian looked to see if she had any Bach. He had long been a jazz fan, but the uplifting sense of harmony and order he had recently experienced when listening to *The Well Tempered Clavier* had changed his listening priorities.

Finding that Margie had one of Glenn Gould's recordings, he put on the first side and adjusted the volume. Then he went back into the kitchen to open the wine.

"Pinot Noir again?"

"Yep. Goes perfectly with Boeuf Bourgogne."

"So that's what I've been smelling!"

During dinner, Adrian told Margie about the question the woman had asked at lunch, trying to recall it as exactly as possible. Then he did his best to restate Mrs. Hoyle's answer.

"That's very helpful to hear. You know, Mrs. Hoyle has an extraordinary mind, but she's also very warm."

"Yeah, she is. I was just wondering how you're going to feel now that you will be in Mr. Eckart's group. Won't you miss your private meetings with her?"

"I will, but one has to move on to the next thing! Besides, it sounds like I'll still get to hear her point of view when I start coming on Sundays. And maybe I'll get invited to the dance class too."

"Yeah, I'm sure you will."

They looked fondly at one another. Feeling the force of Margie's attention, he became aware that, in spite of all the good news, he had lost touch with the special energy that he had sensed so strongly earlier. He felt something like remorse for having turned away from it so quickly.

"I'd like to make a toast," he announced, filling their glasses. "Here's to helping one another to remember our inner aim in every circumstance in which we find ourselves."

"I'll drink to that."

Not taking their eyes off one another, they clinked their glasses and drank.

Ideas

Peter and Margaret gave them a ride into the city for the group meeting on Tuesday night. Thinking they might like to make this a regular arrangement, Adrian tried to set the stage by paying the bridge toll. The trip took less than half the time than by bus, which would give them back precious time to study in the afternoon.

Even though Adrian had only been coming to the house in the city for about six weeks, he felt like a veteran as he led Margie into the building and introduced her to a few of the people in the group before the meeting. But once they were seated, any kind of familiar comfort went out the window. In the light of the silence that appeared, he felt exposed once again, to himself and to others. Being in question in that way was uncomfortable, but it was a condition of waking up.

Margie just listened. As each person spoke, Adrian couldn't help but listen to the questions and answers from her point of view. He envisaged how she would understand each question and what other questions it would evoke in her mind. He also surmised what she thought of each of the people in the group. As the meeting went on, he found himself just listening along with her and did not ask a question either.

Near the end of the meeting, when the exchanges were finished, Mr. Eckart introduced Margie to the others. It struck Margie how different this was from a situation in everyday life, where a new person would be introduced at the beginning, rather than at the end, of the meeting. But Mr. Eckart's approach made perfect sense. At the beginning of the meeting, they gave precedence to the silence, leaving considerations of personality aside. At the end of the meeting, when they had reached a state of sensitivity together, they could relax and allow ordinary behavior back into their mutual relationship.

As people are getting up, Linda comes over to get Margie's phone number. With some discomfort, Adrian hears a hint of false personality in the tone of his voice as he tells Margie that Linda was the first person he met in the group. In this moment, Adrian sees two sides of himself at once, both the personality speaking and the quiet awareness inside. This observation brings to mind the theme for Thursday night, which is "How to follow a living thing, wherever it leads me." Now he understands that the theme is about the work to observe oneself without interfering with one's manifestations, to allow personality to function normally while watching oneself at the same time.

The trip home with Peter and Margaret made Margie and Adrian reconsider their idea of riding with them regularly. Surprisingly, the two of them began fighting in the car like children over the choice of a radio station. Margaret punched a button for her station, then Peter changed it to his. Pretty soon, they were pushing each other's hands away from the radio controls. From the back seat, Margie and Adrian watched helplessly as this less than playful behavior distracted Peter from the road ahead. How strange that these two, who had been coming longer than them, could manifest like that right after a group meeting. Was this the way to spend the energy they had gathered? It occurred to Adrian that they might believe they were allowing their normal personalities to manifest in order to watch themselves. If that was what they thought, he felt sure they were fooling themselves. In any case, Margie and Adrian agreed afterward not to ride with them again.

Margie had been invited to the idea meeting on Thursday, but she had to stay home to study for a test the next day. Adrian made the long bus trip to Sagamore alone, looking forward to his first dance exercise class after the theme meeting. He patted his coat pocket to reassure himself that he was carrying the new white leather dance slippers he had managed to find at the Capezio's store on College Avenue.

Watching buildings, cars and people flash by as the jitney bus moved down Mission Street, Adrian thought about the theme. He didn't know what it meant to "follow a living thing, wherever it leads me." For the most part, he had been unable to freely follow his own manifestations because his attempts to observe them always seemed to get in the way. But the experience he'd had of seeing two sides of himself at once while introducing Margie to Linda at the end of the group meeting had given him a taste of what was possible. He hoped to be able to understand more that evening.

Everyone in the San Francisco groups was invited to the theme meetings. About sixty folding chairs were set up in the main hall, the same room used for Sunday lunches. Those seats faced three chairs and a table set on a low platform at the end of the room. Adrian sat down in the first row, determined to take an active role in the meeting. After most people had taken their places, Mr. Wells, Mrs. Hoyle, and Mr. Eckart entered the room, mounted the dais, and sat down. The table in front of them had been set with three glasses of water. The leaders scanned the faces in the room as they waited for the last few people to find seats. After a couple of minutes, a man closed the doors to the room and sat down.

Mr. Wells began.

"Our theme tonight is 'How to follow a living thing, wherever it leads me'. We will each try to open the theme and then ask for your questions.

"When a zoologist in the wild encounters an animal, he sets out to study it without interfering with its habits. He will keep his distance so as not to affect it's behavior, in some cases constructing a blind from behind which he can observe it without being seen. He is interested in studying everything about the animal. He is not selective about what he observes and does not turn his back on any of its actions because he wants to have as full a picture as possible of its life. He will follow this living thing wherever it leads him.

"As it is now, I reject impressions that contradict the picture I have of myself. But if I really understood that I am as unknown to myself as a new animal is to the zoologist, I would feel the need to watch myself in every situation, in every mood, in every state of mind. Then I would really come face to face with the question of *how* to watch.

"The question of how to work comes alive when I see that I don't understand what work is. Trying with others, I begin to appreciate that it is through our efforts together that a new understanding of how to work is renewed. Then, what is now a theme becomes our burning question: How to follow a living thing wherever it leads me?"

Concluding his opening, Mr. Wells took a sip of water from his glass. Mrs. Hoyle spoke next, followed by Mr. Eckart. Each developed the theme in their own way, addressing various aspects and bringing in different ideas. By the time Mr. Eckart had finished, the theme was wide open. Now it was the audience's turn to bring questions.

An older man sitting at the end of Adrian's row spoke first.

"I think that questions of behavior and morality come into play with this question. I mean this in relation to the part of the theme that says, 'wherever it leads'. The theme seems to suggest that it's okay to do anything or behave in any way we like as long as we're observing ourselves. I wonder about that. Isn't it still important to consider how we treat other people, to obey the law, and live decent lives? We can't just go off uncontrolled in the name of self-study. What would you say about this?"

Mr. Wells turned to Mrs. Hoyle, asking her to answer the question.

"Yes, I understand your point of view, Mr. Taylor. The history of spiritual groups is replete with stories about people who used their religious or psychological beliefs to justify self-serving and illicit behavior. But I do not think that is what we are addressing here tonight. Our concern is the importance of understanding the difference between consciousness and functions. 'To follow a living thing' corresponds to consciousness and 'wherever it leads' to functions. We are trying to differentiate between these two, but all we can see are our functions. We do not see consciousness, nor can we, because it is invisible to us. But we can know when it is there. We can learn to make room for it in ourselves so that it throws light on all our functions. This is the proper role destined for a man or woman—to serve as a bridge between heaven and earth, between consciousness and our functions. Our theme for tonight asks us how we can find a place within which enables us to experience both the higher and the lower at the same time."

Mrs. Hoyle gazed expectantly at Bob Taylor to see if she had gotten through to him. He looked a little puzzled, but nodded his head in appreciation for her answer. After a pause, Adrian recognized Linda's voice coming from behind him. When she had finished putting her question, Mr. Wells responded. As he did, Adrian noted with some satisfaction that he didn't bestow her with praise as freely as Mr. Eckart.

When Mr. Wells had finished answering Linda, Adrian remembered the promise he had made to himself to ask a question. He felt that the moment had arrived. Fear of speaking in front of everyone threatened to stop him as the interloper within began to make excuses to justify remaining silent. But Adrian obeyed the palpable authority of an inner intelligence calling him to settle down into his body and listen to himself as he spoke.

"I was struck by what Mrs. Hoyle said about finding a place between consciousness and functions. I'm usually never free enough to observe my functions because my attempts at self-observation are mostly mental and I guess for that reason interfere with how I'm manifesting. So I'm always sort of getting in my own way. I was really interested when I saw the theme posted on Sunday because I think I do have that question of 'how to follow'. Then, after my group Tuesday night, I had a new experience of what might be possible. I was still in touch with a certain quality of energy in me at the same time as I was talking to a couple of the women. That made it possible to hear a certain something in my tone of voice, something very egoistic and superficial. It was coming out normally, without interference, and I wasn't drawn into self-criticism about it. I simply had this impression of what seemed to be a very characteristic side of myself. Hearing myself that way was not pleasant, but I felt very alive. It really was like being in-between two sides of myself."

It was Mr. Eckart's turn to answer.

"What you say is very true, Mr. Masters. Most of the time, our so-called self-observation is purely mental. We are educated to study everything with our heads and so that is how we try to observe ourselves. We say we are searching for consciousness, but in actuality we understand even that as a mental activity. Fortunately for us, we can receive an energy that allows us to see, revealing the difference between our mental manipulations and an authentic moment of relative consciousness. As Mr. Wells said in the beginning, the dawning realization that we do not know ourselves brings us to the need to see ourselves and to the question of how to see.

"You said you felt more alive in your moment of seeing. That touches upon the words, 'a living thing', in the theme. Most of the time we do not feel fully alive. Some people have said that they came here 'to live more', or 'to live fully'. How can I feel fully alive when I am asleep? I need to wake up. And the first step is to awaken to my sleep. I need to see my life in sleep. Then, I will truly feel the question of what can open me to the light of consciousness that will illuminate and animate my functions."

Mr. Eckart reached for his glass of water and drank slowly while Adrian nodded his head several times to confirm that he had followed him. He experienced the special taste of joy that appeared with each new progression in understanding. There was time for several more exchanges before the meeting came to an end. As soon as everyone had left, Adrian joined the setup team as they put away the chairs and rolled up the carpets to prepare the room for the dance exercise class.

Dance

They had thirty minutes after the theme meeting to prepare for the dance exercise class. While the setup team was clearing the hall, those in the class went into small rooms—one for the men and another for the women—to change clothes. Adrian only had to put on his new exercise slippers, but other men were putting on pants and shirts they had brought specially for the class. Most of the men donned white clothing, but a few dressed in black.

"Why do you need special clothes?" Adrian asked one of the men.

"Well, there are several reasons. It's partly because they allow more freedom of movement. Mrs. Hoyle has said that it helps individuals to blend together into a class if everyone isn't wearing different colors and designs. But it's also because bringing these special clothes helps us to think about the class in advance, and putting aside the clothes we've had on all day helps us to let go of baggage we've accumulated and enter the class freshly."

Adrian made a note to bring a white shirt and dark pants for the next class.

When the setup team had finished clearing the room, they still had about ten minutes before the class would start. Some of the men and women had already returned to the hall and were sitting cross-legged along the side walls. Adrian did the same, remembering how Mrs. Hoyle had suggested arriving early and sitting quietly before the class. He tried to find a relaxed posture in which his back was straight, but it was difficult. Finding the best position he could, he stopped making adjustments and just tried to be quiet inside.

Mrs. Hoyle and another woman came into the room and went to the front, where a man was sitting at the piano. After speaking briefly to him, the women sat down to face the others. Then everyone in the room was still. They stayed that way for several minutes.

Mrs. Hoyle got up slowly and took a few steps forward, motioning for everyone to stand. People who had been in her class before moved confidently into position, with their arms at their sides and their feet together, looking forward. The rest fell in behind them. Some of the newest people were unsure of what to do. They grasped their hands together in front or behind them, as if that made them feel more comfortable. Adrian took a cue from the older ones and stood with his arms down.

Mrs. Hoyle asked them to begin walking around the room, just as if they were walking down the street. Each of them was to find their own natural tempo and rhythm and try to let go of tensions. They should walk as if they were in a crowded plaza, moving past others without touching them.

After the experiments that he had made to alter his walk as a way of discovering his habits, Adrian was particularly interested that Mrs. Hoyle was asking them to walk in their own way. During his efforts on the streets of Berkeley, whenever he had stopped trying to change his walk and returned to normal, he had quickly become absorbed in thoughts again and forgotten to observe the way he walked. But now, because he was with the others, he found he was able to follow himself around the room. There were moments in which he had the taste of something intimately familiar about his own way of moving.

When they had finished that exercise, Mrs. Hoyle asked them to form a large circle, facing into the center where she stood. When everyone was standing still in place, Mrs. Hoyle showed a series of postures. She held each one for a few moments, then asked the class to take it. They had to stay in position without moving for what seemed a long time as she walked slowly around the circle examining each person, sometimes stopping to help someone adjust an aspect of their position. One of these attitudes required standing on one leg, with the other leg raised in a right angle at the knee. Finding it difficult to keep his balance, Adrian struggled to keep his leg up. He thought he had it just as Mrs. Hoyle was approaching him. Keeping his eyes straight ahead, he tried to hold very still to demonstrate to her that he could do it well. Stopping in front of him, she pushed lightly against his right shoulder. Immediately, he lost his balance and had to bring his leg down. She smiled and moved on.

The next position she showed seemed easier, but Mrs. Hoyle insisted on the exactitude of every aspect of it from each person. As Adrian tried his best to take and hold the position, he found that it evoked a magical quality, reminding him of an Egyptian figure he had seen in Margie's book. He had a wondrous sense of participation in a tradition of ancient lineage.

Mrs. Hoyle showed four more positions. The class followed her, practicing until each person was able to take every position to Mrs. Hoyle's satisfaction. Then she spoke to the pianist, who then played a simple slow melody. As the class watched, Mrs. Hoyle began moving from one position to the next, holding each for four beats of the music. After going through all six positions several times, she stopped and asked the class to try it. The pianist began playing again, assisting the class by emphasizing the beat on which they were to change positions.

As everyone around the circle held each attitude, Mrs. Hoyle asked them to visualize the next attitude as a preparation for taking it. Although Adrian wanted to try this, he was still anxious and his thoughts were too dominant to allow the space needed for the effort of visualization. Again and again, finding himself caught in his thoughts when it was time to move to the next position and then moving awkwardly in reaction, Adrian became increasingly tense. Mrs. Hoyle must have seen his difficulty in others as well, as she stopped the class to speak of the importance of relaxation and a quiet mind.

"I see that I'm not quiet enough to follow my movements. I'm still distracted by my thoughts and my ordinary drive to succeed. But I haven't come here for that. Here, I wish to live differently. How can I prepare myself to let go of my thoughts and tensions to make room for a quiet attention that is capable of following the positions and movements we are studying?"

Then Mrs. Hoyle asked the class to try again. Directing the pianist to play more slowly, she counted four beats for them to begin. Adrian still didn't know all the positions well enough and struggled to find each one, often having to watch people around him to get the details. Each time he came to the position with one leg off the floor, he faced a merciless test of his centeredness. But when he took the position that echoed the feeling of the hieroglyphs, something quietened in him.

The woman with Mrs. Hoyle gave them two more exercises before the hour was over. One was a vigorous rhythmic dance and the other took the form of a waltz. At the end of the hour, everyone stood quietly in place, allowing their impressions to settle. Adrian didn't want to move, feeling the fragility of a more balanced relationship between his mind and body.

There was no conversation on the way to the changing rooms after class. When the men did eventually begin to talk as they dressed, Adrian asked if anyone was going back to Berkeley. One man, who introduced himself as Dan, said he'd be glad to give Adrian a ride. He would be leaving shortly with his wife Marie.

Adrian liked Dan and Marie right away. It turned out that they had been coming to the group for over five years. Their quiet demeanor on the ride home showed their respect for the energy they had all collected during the evening. When they did discuss their observations from the class, Adrian was impressed with their modesty, especially since they had been working with the dance exercises for what he perceived to be a long time. As they pulled up to Margie's apartment building, Adrian asked if they came in on Tuesday night as well. It turned out that they did and would be glad to give a ride to he and Margie whenever they needed one.

Margie was waiting expectantly for Adrian. Though tired from studying all evening, she asked him about the dance exercise class. Adrian told her about the exercises they had been given and described his experience. At first, she listened with great interest, but it didn't take long before her attention began to fade.

"How was the idea meeting?" she asked, yawning.

"It was really good. Mr. Wells, Mrs. Hoyle, and Mr. Eckart were on the panel in front. What they said really opened up the theme. And I was able to ask a question, which Mr. Eckart answered."

"Good for you." She yawned again.

"I guess it's too late to tell you more about the meeting."

"Definitely. I've got to hit the sack and get up early in the morning. The test is at 8 and I want to do a quick review before I leave for school."

But Adrian wasn't ready for bed. He was still full of energy.

"Do you mind if I stay up reading for a while? I'd like to take another look at that book... what was the title?"

"Her-bak."

"Right. I felt something in the dance exercise class that reminded me of a picture I saw in that book."

"Sure, go ahead. I'll leave a light on for you."

"I won't wake you up. I'll be very quiet."

"Okay. Goodnight, my love."

She kissed him and went into the bedroom. He retrieved the book and sat down with it in the living room. Thumbing through the pages, Adrian found the hieroglyph that he had connected with so much in class. It showed a woman, probably a priestess, in a position almost exactly like the one they had learned. He put down the book, stood up, and tried to find the posture again. Although not as strongly as in the class, even there, alone in Margie's living room, being in that position brought the subtle feeling of participation in something ancient and magical. Adrian sat back down, took up the book, and began to read, becoming so engrossed that he didn't put it down again for two hours.

New Directions

In meditation this morning, Adrian comes very naturally to a quiet state. Somehow recognizing the special quality of energy that has appeared, he feels that it is very important to try to stay available to it and not interfere. For that, he knows he has to let go of all thoughts, including any about trying an exercise, and simply remain still. This state deepens until, by the end of his sitting time, he has an unusually strong sense of presence. As he finishes, he feels a wave of gratitude for the activities of the evening before, realizing that there must be a reciprocal exchange between efforts he makes on his own and the work he participates in with others. He suspects that the appearance of the special energy in this meditation is related to the work in the theme meeting and dance class.

When Adrian picked up the newspaper during breakfast, what he read underlined the stark contrast between the inner quiet he had just experienced and the ongoing turmoil of the world outside. A man who opposed the rapidly escalating war in Vietnam had set himself on fire in front of the United Nations headquarters, just as someone else had the week before in front of the Pentagon. Troop deployment was increasing rapidly, so that thousands more young men were being drafted every month. Adrian's quiet state gave way to anxiety about his own Selective Service classification, as he had been looking in the mail every day for an acceptance letter from San Francisco State. It was crucial that he be admitted for the spring semester, as he might lose his student deferment if he had to wait until the fall.

With his thoughts now drawn to the rapid march of events, Adrian recalled that Margie planned to visit her parents in San Diego for the upcoming Thanksgiving break. He felt duty-bound to see his folks as well, but he wasn't anxious to go to Los Angeles. Although he'd grown up there, the culture of Southern California now seemed foreign to him. He always felt relieved to come back to Berkeley. But his parents were expecting him to come. With the holiday only a couple of weeks away, he realized that flights were probably nearly full and decided he'd better walk to the travel office on campus to get a ticket.

As he enters the campus eucalyptus grove from Oxford Street, the quiet beauty of the trees calls Adrian back to the taste of what he experienced in meditation this morning. Approaching a bench at the side of the path, he decides to sit down for a few minutes to collect himself. He has been lost in thoughts and fears for the last two hours and needs to settle down into his body again. Alongside the hum of traffic on the streets nearby, he hears the raucous cry of a crow and the dry rattle of eucalyptus leaves in the breeze. Once he begins to rediscover the magic of listening, his inner world stirs to life again. Why does he always forget this movement toward himself so easily when he sees again and again that it is paramount?

As people passed by, Adrian's intuition told him that his effort should be invisible. He wanted to appear to be sitting on the bench in an ordinary way, not as someone meditating. He crossed his legs, turned his head up as if looking at a tree near him, and moved his arms from time to time. For as long as he maintained this attempt, he was aware both of the usual flow of thoughts and his intention to stay aware of himself. But after trying in this way for about fifteen minutes, he let go of the effort. Almost immediately, he was drawn back into thoughts, which were now about his school work, especially the Wallace Stevens paper he had yet to write. Then an idea struck him. Why not remain alone in Berkeley to finish his paper over the Thanksgiving holiday? His parents would be disappointed, but he would be seeing them soon enough at Christmas. Elated at finding this simple solution, Adrian got up and began walking home. There was no need now to go to the travel office for a plane ticket.

When Adrian returned to his cottage, an acceptance letter for the spring graduate program at San Francisco State was in his mailbox. Greatly relieved, he called Margie to tell her about it. She didn't answer. Figuring that she must have stopped off somewhere on her way home from class and would be home soon, he called again ten minutes later. Still no answer. While waiting to try again, he looked through the paperwork from San Francisco State. There were two forms to be filled out and returned right away. He had to sign one of them to confirm his intention to register and list a selection of courses on the other. Seeing that he had to choose classes from three of the four disciplines in the Humanities program, he made several alternative programs with varying selections from the available literature, art, music, and philosophy classes. Then he called Margie again. This time she answered.

"Hi, what's happening?"

"Guess what? I got my acceptance from San Francisco State in the mail."

"Wow, that's great! You must be relieved."

"Yeah, I am. In fact, I was hoping we could celebrate over dinner tonight at Kirala. After all, it's Friday."

"Um, I'd like to but I'm really tired."

"Okay, I understand."

"Why don't you just come over here? Maybe you could pick up a pizza at Giovanni's on your way."

"Sure, that's a good idea. Want me to get a couple of small salads as well?"

"Perfect. But can you give me a couple of hours? There's some stuff I have to do."

"Of course. I'll be there with the pizza about 7."

"See you then."

"Bye."

As Margie opened the door, Adrian was surprised to see Karl, Sandy, Dan, Marie, Desmond and others gathered inside her apartment. When they called out,

"Congratulations!" Adrian realized that Margie had arranged a small party for him.

Beaming, Margie took Adrian's hand to lead him into the living room. The pizza box he had brought matched several others already lined up on a table.

Sandy and Karl were the first to greet him.

"Congratulations, Adrian!" Sandy chimed, smiling broadly and giving Adrian a hug.

"Yes, congrats, Adrian!" Karl joined in, putting his arm around Adrian's shoulder.

Adrian put an arm around each of them.

"It's great to see you guys here. I've been wanting for you to meet Margie."

"I was so glad when she called," said Sandy. "She thought this would be a perfect opportunity for us to come over."

"Adrian, I really like Margie," Karl said, rubbing Adrian's shoulder. "She's terrific. Just right for you."

"Thanks, Karl. That means a lot."

After they had talked for a few more minutes, Adrian left them to get a piece of pizza and greet the others.

Margie's friend Hank, who Adrian suspected still had eyes for her, intercepted him on his way to the food table. Hank wanted to know what Adrian planned to study at San Francisco State. Adrian described the program leading to a Master's degree in Humanities, explaining that it included courses in art, philosophy, literature and music.

"That sounds interesting, but what kind of career does it prepare you for? Won't you have to specialize in one discipline or another if you're going to be a teacher? I mean, a college would want you to have a master's in English if you were applying for a position as an English professor."

Adrian wasn't prepared for this question because he hadn't really asked it of himself yet. He didn't know what he wanted to do. The truth was that his main motive for staying in school was to avoid the draft.

"Well, I guess you have a point, Hank, but I'm hoping that this program will help me discover my true calling. If I find that philosophy is really what I want to specialize in, I can always transfer to a philosophy master's program."

Hank's attention was distracted as Margie brought them each a piece of pizza. Taking the opportunity to move away from Hank, Adrian went to get something to drink. Desmond came up alongside him as he poured a glass of red wine.

"Hey man, congratulations! I guess I'm glad that one of us is staying in college. But if you're only going to school to stay out of the Army, why don't you just do what I did and tell them you're a junkie? Jeff pulled the same act off without a problem. Both of us are 4F now. We don't have to worry about ever being called back again."

Adrian hadn't spoken to Desmond since the day he'd caught him with the stolen harmonium. Adrian had given up on their friendship then and was not interested in talking to Desmond now.

"Yeah, thanks for the advice. Actually, I do want to stay in school and I don't really want to have stuff like that on my permanent record. It could come back to haunt me some day. Excuse me, I've got to go talk with someone."

"Sure, man."

Adrian didn't really have anyone in mind, but as he moved across the room a man he didn't know came up to introduce himself.

"Congratulations, Adrian. I'm Mitch Crawford. I met Margie at a philosophy seminar a few weeks ago. Something she said during the class discussion intrigued me, so I sought her out during a break and we talked about a subject in which I'm extremely interested."

"Glad to meet you, Mitch. What subject do you mean?"

"Well, in a nutshell, I'd call it the psychology of man's possible evolution. I've found a lot of theory about that in books, but I'm looking for a practical approach that I can try myself. Margie mentioned that the two of you have actually been working at some exercises to develop your self-awareness. She also said that you're in a group working along those lines. I'd like to know more about it."

"I'll be glad to talk to you, Mitch, but not right now. We could meet for coffee sometime if you want. Just give me a call. You can get my number from Margie."

"That would be great. I'm really interested in everything Margie has said to me."

Nodding to Mitch, Adrian moved on to mingle, intending to talk with everyone there. During some conversations, he was reminded of an intention he had set that morning to keep a portion of his attention on his feet on the floor. He lost this contact repeatedly, but tried to reestablish it each time he remembered. Persistent effort seemed to help, because gradually he was able to stay with it longer. As he did, he caught occasional brief glimpses of himself.

After everyone had left, Margie and Adrian sat talking, sipping the remaining wine. "How did you manage to get all those people here on such short notice?"

"I'd already alerted most of them that I wanted to give you a little surprise party when you got your acceptance. I was hoping you'd hear by this weekend. So I called them and gave the green light right after you phoned me this afternoon. I didn't manage to get Jeff or Peter and Margaret though."

"Well, it was really sweet of you to do this for me. I'm particularly glad that you finally got to meet Karl and Sandy. We'll have to have them over again so we can have an evening with just the four of us."

"Yes, I've been waiting a long time for a serious talk with Karl after all you've said about him."

Adrian told Margie that Mitch had introduced himself. Margie spoke with strong support for Mitch.

"He really seems interested in the ideas we're studying. When we talk, I can feel something from him, and it's not just an intellectual interest. Because of that, I'm reminded to come back to myself while I'm with him. It's as if I have a certain responsibility to be active inside when I'm talking about these ideas to someone who really wants to understand them. So it helps both of us. I think you'll find it very interesting to meet with him."

The thought of meeting with Mitch sometime in the future reminded Adrian that he hadn't yet told Margie about his decision to stay in Berkeley for the Thanksgiving holidays. Although he explained his plan to her with some enthusiasm, she seemed dubious.

"I've been reading the transcripts of some of the earliest meetings of our group," she said. "A lot of emphasis is placed on honoring one's parents, of repaying them for what they've given to us. My relation to my parents has been pretty good, but there were plenty of times I didn't treat them well. I'm feeling now that it's really important to do everything I can to make up for those times. Don't you think that you might hurt your parent's feelings by staying in Berkeley? Thanksgiving is a day when everybody goes home. How will they feel sitting at their dinner table without you?"

"I know, I've thought of all that. But I have so much to do to finish my Wallace Stevens paper and study for finals. You'll be away, so I can spend all of my time working. I won't have anything to distract me. I'll call my parents and explain it to them. I'm sure they'll understand. Besides, I'll be seeing them soon enough at Christmas."

"Why don't you find a middle ground? You could just fly in on Thanksgiving day, have dinner with your parents, and then fly back the next day. You could work here in Berkeley all the rest of the time. Your parents would certainly understand that, especially if they know you are making the effort to be with them for Thanksgiving. Don't you think that would be a better approach in the long run?"

Margie's solution stopped him. It was both practical and thoughtful. Of course, she was right about his parents. If he didn't show up at all, they would be very disappointed. For better or worse, Thanksgiving had been built up in American culture as a day when families always find a way to be together. Also, it was not hard to picture himself alone on Thanksgiving, looking for a place to eat dinner. That could be depressing. With Margie's solution, he would have an intention that could energize the whole week. He would work hard knowing that he had to leave Berkeley on Thanksgiving. He would feel good about seeing his parents. And he could return on Friday to go back to work.

"You know, Margie, I think you're absolutely right. It just occurred to me that what you are suggesting would give me a chance to try working with intention, something that's been suggested in the group. Maybe a special intention could help me approach both my relationship to my parents and my school work in a new way. You're so good for me! You've helped me to see this situation as an opportunity to work in life instead of just taking the path of least resistance."

Cuddling up to him, Margie smiled seductively. "You're a lovely man, Adrian Masters. Just for that, I have one more way to congratulate you."

Struggle

Margie had accepted the invitation to come on Sunday, even though she had a lot of studying to do. This would be the last workday for several weeks, as none would be held on the weekends before and after the holiday. Adrian had his Wallace Stevens paper to work on, but he didn't want to miss being with Margie on her first Sunday. Dan and Marie offered them a lift.

Standing in the garage while the list of teams was read, Adrian listened for Margie's name. When he heard that she was assigned to the wood carving team led by Mrs. Hoyle, he felt a surge of gladness for her. She would be starting an interesting new craft and could work closely with Mrs. Hoyle. At the same time, he heard his own assignment with mixed feelings. Although he now felt part of the lamp team, he had discovered a lot of resistance in himself to metal work. It was a dirty craft and the brass rods were hard and cold—except during brazing, when they became hot. But of course, this resistance gave him material for struggling with himself, which was ostensibly his aim in coming there.

Mr. Eckart stepped forward with a paper in his hand, from which he began reading. The transcript of a talk given in London ten years earlier described precisely how to divide attention between oneself and an external task. Emphasis was placed first on bringing attention to one's overall situation, including the general state of the body, mind, and emotions. Only after establishing this contact would one turn to the task.

Here was a delicate moment, because one could either fall into the trap of holding back and not really engaging in the task, or one could become lost in it. For the task to help, it was necessary to do it to the best of one's ability, to bring the participation of all of the parts of oneself. But one must also remember one's intention, coming back repeatedly to be aware of oneself longer and more deeply. The reading concluded with the statement that making this effort in the artificial conditions of a workday was only a preparation for real work in the midst of the uncertainties of life.

When he had finished reading, Mr. Eckart brought the paper down to his side and stood quietly for what seemed a full minute. Adrian was filled with the excitement of a new possibility, as the reading had given him just the kind of intention that he needed.

Margie and Adrian exchanged looks of camaraderie as they passed on the way to their teams. The morning gathering had been new for both of them, as it was the first time Adrian had heard anything other than the team lists and schedule read on a Sunday morning. He went into the metal shed and joined the lamp team.

Jim was hung over as usual, but seemed unusually collected. He waited until everyone on the team was there before explaining their collective goal and individual tasks.

They sensed his seriousness, which Adrian guessed must be related to the direction given by the reading. Adrian's job for the day was to clean all of the brass rods that had been brazed into the lamps. He would have to use disagreeable chemicals, steel wool and rags to remove the tarnish already blackening the rods.

Attempting to look at his overall state as suggested in the reading, Adrian sensed the laziness of his body and his emotional resistance to the dirty task in front of him. But paradoxically, he also felt a wish to work. Trying to keep both sides in view, he picked up a rag and a can of brass polish and began cleaning the metal rods.

An hour and a half later, Adrian was glad to hear the bell for the morning break. As the day was cold and blustery, coffee and snacks were set up inside the house. Entering the kitchen, Adrian saw Margie in conversation with a tall man whose intellectual acuity had impressed him in the theme meetings. Adrian felt a twinge of jealously, but thanks to the morning's struggle to keep contradictory parts of himself in view, he was able to see both the impulse of jealousy and his habitual tendency to give it credence. Remembering what Karl had said to him that night two years ago as they lay conversing in the dark, "we are all machines," Adrian saw that his jealously was completely mechanical. But there was something else that illuminated the parts of his machine and brought alive the question of who he really was.

Margie and Adrian only had time for a quick word together before the end of break bell sounded. Margie said she had been having an extremely good morning in the wood carving with Mrs. Hoyle. Adrian was glad for her.

When lunchtime arrived, he walked to the meeting hall alone, as Margie was already over there helping with the dining room setup. While he walked, he tried to think of a question from his morning's attempts. As different formulations came to mind, he rejected one after another as being unworthy of speaking about. But he had begun to understand that it was always that way. It was necessary to speak from a question experienced in the moment.

Margie was working with a couple of other women in the dining hall, ladling soup into bowls at the serving table. As people found their places, Adrian didn't save a seat for Margie because he wanted her to be on her own and meet new people. But he had second thoughts about this when he saw her sit down next to the same man with whom she'd been talking during break. The man was smiling at her as he offered to fill her glass with water. Seeing himself about to disappear into jealousy, Adrian had enough free attention to search for the sensation of his weight on the chair. This time, the jealousy didn't go away, but because his attention was active, he was able to just let it be. As the room quietened, Adrian understood that jealousy, seen against the broad background of everything within him and around him, was only a small part of the whole landscape.

All during the meal, Adrian felt certain that he would ask a question. He didn't have to formulate one because he was living with it right then. When eventually the room became silent except for the scrapings of a few spoons removing the last of the chocolate mousse from the small glass bowls, he spoke.

"When I heard the reading this morning, I was very excited about what was suggested. I tried to look at my overall state and establish a connection with my body before I started working at my task. I can really remember that first moment when I reached for my materials while still in touch with myself. I forgot pretty soon, though, and had to start again. The thing that really helped was that I had a lot of resistance to the work I was doing. It helped because it kept reminding me of my intention. But then I'd lose it before long. During the coffee break, something happened that stirred up my emotions, but because of what we're trying there was something in me that could see my reactions and perceive how automatic they are. When I went back to work, the emotions kept coming up, and the resistance to the work was still there too. It's strange to say, but I think the emotion kept reminding me to try because I had to struggle not to be taken away by it. Usually, in everyday life, I forget completely when I get angry or something and only realize later how I reacted. But here, I was able to see my reactions as they were taking place, at least for a few moments at a time."

While speaking, at first Adrian kept his gaze on Mr. Eckart, but when he didn't look back at him he turned to Mr. Wells. But then, noticing that Mrs. Hoyle was looking at him intently, Adrian directed what he was saying to her. When he was finished, she responded.

"Without an encounter with my emotions, my effort can never continue beyond a certain point. It usually starts from my mind and then goes just so far. For my effort to go further, a certain confrontation with the emotions is needed. This morning, the reading evoked special interest in your mind, which gave you a sense of intention. You had a strong beginning with that impression of being in yourself and at the same time reaching out to your task. But then, soon, your effort began to wane. As you suggest, the appearance of resistance to the task helped you because it brought feeling into the equation. When the emotion you spoke of—you didn't say what it was—appeared during the break, you had collected enough energy during your morning's work to be able to see it. This moment of seeing was just the confrontation with emotion needed to allow your line of effort to continue to develop. This was a big step for you, but in a way I might say that it was 'beginner's luck'. It takes some people a long time to face their emotions as you did today. But now that you have, you must work even harder. There is a certain law that the more you work, the more will be demanded of you. What you discovered today is very precious. But you must let it go and not try to repeat it. Do not rest on your laurels. You will have to find your way again and again and each time the conditions will be different. This search is always new."

As he had with both Mr. Wells and Mr. Eckart, Adrian experienced a channel, a kind of tunnel, through which a current of palpable energy flowed from Mrs. Hoyle to him. Surely, he thought, this must be the esoteric meaning of "oral transmission," suggesting that something material, beyond words, can be transmitted directly from the presence of the teacher to the presence of a pupil. When Mrs. Hoyle finished, the channel between them remained as long as both of them maintained it. When his attention faltered for a moment, she looked away.

That afternoon, seeing how he could not help but try to reproduce his experience from the morning, Adrian remembered Mrs. Hoyle's words: "you must let it go and not try to repeat it." He was beginning to understand better that trying for particular results was a kind of manipulation. Only study and search stemming from a real question could lead to the opening of consciousness. He decided to simply work at his task as best he could for the rest of the day. His effort became an ongoing struggle to let go of the recurring impulse to recreate an experience and bring his attention back to the task. Trying in this way, Adrian gradually sensed a light energy in his body. When he heard the bell signaling that it was time to clean up, he felt unusually close to himself. Examining his day's work on the lamps, he had the feeling of a job well done. He put away his tools, washed his hands, and left the shed for the afternoon reading.

When everyone had gathered in the large room at the meeting hall, a tall middle-aged man with a bushy gray beard entered with a manuscript. He took his place on a chair in front of them, sipped water from a glass provided on a little table next to him, and paused for a few seconds.

Then he began to read the transcript of a rarely heard talk from the early 1920's.

Very soon, a growing lassitude told Adrian how tired his body was. His eyelids began to droop and he started missing some of the reader's words. Knowing that he might never again have the opportunity to hear this talk, he shifted his posture so that he was sitting up straight, no longer leaning against the back of his chair. He listened with his eyes closed for a minute or two, but as he started to fade again, he opened his eyes and let them rest on the reader's face. When the reader looked up for a moment, his eyes met Adrian's. The shock of their contact brought Adrian out of his lethargy into a more active state of listening and he had the sudden realization that his struggle with fatigue was directly related to the gist of the material being read. This brought such an influx of energy that he was able to listen well until the end of the reading.

After helping to put away the folding chairs, Adrian joined Margie in the hallway, where she was waiting for him with Dan and Marie. They left the building and walked down the street to their car for the drive back to Berkeley. At first, they were somewhat restrained. But soon, they began sharing moments from their day. When Adrian heard himself telling an anecdote about a situation with a person on his team, it dawned on him that he was quickly burning the fuel that he had struggled all day to collect. Recalling the point made in the reading about the necessity of conserving energy, thoughts of self-criticism began to turn in his mind. He stopped talking in mid-sentence. Dan turned his eyes from the road to Adrian in a questioning glance.

"Why didn't you finish what you were saying, Adrian?"

"Well, I suddenly realized that we are basically throwing away the energy we worked for today by all this talking. Like it said in the reading, it is essential that we begin to conserve our energy. We should allow the food we received to be digested."

Keeping his eyes on the road again, Dan nodded agreement. "Yes, of course that's true. But it doesn't help to judge ourselves. That kind of self-criticism is just mental. It's completely ordinary and useless. We're interested in seeing ourselves just as we are. We need to observe ourselves without judgment. You might say that we need to suffer seeing how we waste this energy. That kind of suffering is in the direction toward feeling our conscience, which is what we need if we're really going to change."

Adrian knew that Dan was right. As he felt the weight of Dan's experience, he was reminded of one of the important distinctions of their group. They were a community of people with more or less experience, more or less understanding. Those with more understanding helped those with less understanding, and in doing so, received help themselves.

Adrian looked at him. "Thanks, Dan. I see what you mean."

After that, they turned their conversation to worldly affairs while Marie and Margie continued to talk in the back seat.

Finals

The Thanksgiving holiday came quickly. On Monday, Adrian walked Margie to the Durant Hotel to catch the airport shuttle for her flight to San Diego and then returned directly home. Intending to follow her suggestion to work on his Wallace Stevens paper up until Thanksgiving Day, he was determined to get started. He had stocked his refrigerator with enough food to last until he left for Los Angeles on Thursday morning. All he had to do was buckle down and write.

Adrian started with "The Poem That Took the Place of a Mountain." The more he studied the poem, the more he felt that there was something he was missing, something just out of his grasp. Then, after several unsuccessful attempts to unravel the poem's meaning, he saw that it was right there in the title. He realized that, as he read the poem from line to line, his outlook gradually changed, in the same way that one's perspective changes when ascending a mountain. By the end of the poem, his viewpoint had become more expansive and informed by a sense of scale, as if he were standing at the top of a mountain. Excitedly, he wrote late into the night.

Continuing to work on his paper through the next two days, Adrian completed a first draft late Wednesday evening. On Thursday morning, he made the trip to Los Angeles. His parents were waiting for him at the airport gate. When he saw them, he immediately felt glad to be there and grateful to Margie for her sensitive and practical outlook.

After returning from Los Angeles on the day after Thanksgiving, Adrian walked up Telegraph from the shuttle drop-off at the Durant Hotel looking for a place to get lunch. As he got closer to campus, he heard the amplified sound of a man speaking on a bullhorn. He couldn't quite make out the words, but a poster stapled on a telephone pole told him that it was probably coming from a campus rally in support of the large demonstration in Washington D.C. that was to take place on the following day. Thousands of demonstrators were expected to march on the White House to protest the war in Vietnam. Adrian deduced that people hurrying past him must be headed to the support rally. Though he was momentarily attracted by the magnetism of the crowd, Adrian was determined to stay with his plan to use all of this time to work on his paper. As he was passing by Kip's Burgers, he decided to get something to go and eat it at home.

By Sunday afternoon, Adrian had managed to write a final draft of the Wallace Stevens paper and complete a first pass of the study materials for his finals. There was still more work to do, but it was a very good beginning. He recognized the key importance that intention had played in sustaining his effort throughout the holiday. This was largely thanks to Margie's influence. Again feeling grateful to her, he remembered that her plane had probably just landed at the Oakland airport. He had just enough time to walk to the Durant Hotel to meet her as the shuttle bus dropped her off there.

The days leading up to Christmas passed quickly for both Adrian and Margie, in spite of long hours of study with little sleep during finals. Adrian felt in particular that the speed with which he was being drawn to the end of his last undergraduate year seemed to accelerate daily. January loomed as an unknown for him. To his parent's disappointment, no ceremony would be held for mid-year graduates. Without fanfare, Adrian would simply stop attending classes and pick up his diploma at the Registrar's office. Soon after, he would begin commuting to San Francisco State.

On Christmas morning in Los Angeles, Adrian and his sister got up early just as they had when they were kids. There were no bicycles, dolls or Erector sets from Santa under the tree, but his sister and mother had seen to it that there were several colorfully wrapped presents for each of them. Dressed in their robes, his mother made scrambled eggs and his father began preparing his traditional Tom and Jerry batter, which he would later mix with whiskey, rum, hot water, and cinnamon.

After breakfast, Adrian's parents invited him to step outside the house. Opening the front door, he saw a light green Volkswagen bug parked at the curb.

"It's both a graduation and Christmas present," his father said, beaming. "We thought you might need it for your commute to San Francisco State College."

He definitely would. It was a generous and unexpected present that Adrian appreciated deeply. He embraced and thanked each of them. Though a bit jealous, his sister gave him a congratulatory hug. Then they all got into the car to take it for a spin.

Adrian and Margie had agreed to return to Berkeley on December 30 so they could be together for the full day of New Year's Eve. Now that Adrian had a car, he had cancelled his flight to Oakland and was ready to drive back to Berkeley on December 29. He would surprise Margie at the airport when she arrived the next day. Just as he was about to pull the VW away from the curb, the sight of his parents waving to him from the kitchen window brought him back to the first time he left home to go to Berkeley.

Peering over the clothes stacked high on the seat next to him, he takes a moment for a final look at his parents standing together in the doorway to see him off. His father is smiling, but his eyes reveal bittersweet emotion. Tears run down his mother's cheek. Filled with love for them but exhilarated in anticipation of the adventure ahead, he recalls the words of Steven Dedalus at the conclusion of Joyce's Portrait of the Artist as a Young Man: *"Welcome, O Life!"*

The movement of his father's arm still waving in the window dissolved Adrian's reverie. With tears welling in his eyes, he waved back to his parents, started the car, and pulled away from the curb.

Continuing to entertain those memories as he headed toward the freeway, Adrian recollected making the first trip to Berkeley in only six hours. That time, he had driven the white MG roadster his father gave him for his seventeenth birthday. He had loved the MG, even though it had been occasionally necessary to stop and crawl underneath with a screwdriver to get the Bosch electric fuel pump going again. Then the night he drove it to San Francisco's North Beach came into focus, leading him to relive the accident. Time had slowed down as the head-on impact of an oncoming car spun the MG around in a full circle, so that from the driver's seat he had watched the blurred world moving slowly around him as though he was on an amusement park ride. Bystanders had told him how lucky he was to have walked away without injury. The next day, when he had gone to the garage to which his car had been towed, they said that the MG was a total loss. After that, he had been without a car until now.

Adrian concentrated on the road again as he entered Highway 101. Trying for the best acceleration he could get from the VW as he pulled into the middle lane, he settled down into the seat, feeling that he was finally on his way. As his daydreams continued throughout the drive, Adrian noted that they were all concerned with people and events from the past or hopes and fears about the future. But what about the deep questions concerning his inner life that had developed during the past two years? Where were the associations about those? He realized that there weren't any. He might remember having had certain strong experiences, but he knew that the states themselves could not be remembered or repeated.

Finally arriving home in Berkeley just as it was beginning to get dark, he parked the VW a few houses away from his landlord's home. He opened the front hood, grabbed his suitcase from the tiny trunk, and carried it down the path alongside the house to his cottage in back. Standing at his front door, he fished in his pocket for the key. He always felt exposed doing this because his landlord's family could watch him from the rooms at the rear of their house. When he closed the door behind him, Adrian breathed a sigh of relief.

The next day, he met Margie as she was coming out of the arrival gate at the Oakland Airport. With her slim good looks and elegant walk, she looked like a high-fashion model in her new suede jacket and short skirt. She gazed at Adrian quizzically as she approached but momentarily dropped any questioning as she gave herself fully to their embrace.

Pulling away a little, she asked, "Adrian, what are you doing here?"

"I'm giving you a ride home."

"Did you borrow a car?"

"No, we're going in my car."

"Your car?"

"Yes, my parents gave it to me. It's a combined Christmas and graduation present."

"You're kidding!"

"No, really. It's a VW."

"Cool! Let's go! I didn't check any luggage."

Margie and Adrian traded anecdotes about their Christmas holidays as they walked to the short-term parking lot. Margie grinned when Adrian pointed out his car. He opened the door for her, tilted the front seat forward to put her bag in the back, then brought it straight again and helped her in. They were excited about driving back to Berkeley in their own car. On the way, he told her about some of the thoughts he'd had while driving.

"I've had questions like that too," she said. "Sometimes it really does seem like I have two lives. There's the ordinary life with all of my everyday wants and worries, and then there's this other life inside which I forget about most of the time. When that inner life is strong, I feel sure that it's the most important thing in the world. But later, I don't even remember that such a precious state of sensitivity existed. It's the same thing with the efforts we intend to try. When I'm talking with Mrs. Hoyle or at the group meeting, I feel sincere about wanting to work to be present to myself in the midst of my everyday life. But then later, either I don't remember to try it at all or I reject what I notice about myself because it's not what I want to see."

Adrian felt gratified that they shared the same understanding. "I've missed the meetings over the break, haven't you?"

"Yes. So much is possible with the group and it seems that I really can't do anything by myself. I'm glad we're starting up again next week."

"Did you hear about the dance exercise demonstration the advanced class is going to give at the end of January? A special teacher is supposed to be coming here from New York to prepare them. There's a chance he might even visit the other classes while he's here."

"No, I hadn't heard that," she replied. "Do you think both of us will be invited to see it?"

"Yes, I think all of the groups will be invited. We can even invite people from outside of the group if we feel they would be interested. The demonstration is going to be held at the Palace of the Legion of Honor."

"Wow! That will be a big deal if it's held there. We might have to buy tickets."

"Oh yeah, I hadn't thought about that. I guess they'll tell us about it at the meetings next week."

Margie changed the subject. "Have you heard about any of your grades yet?"

"No, but I expect we'll know in the next few days."

"Are you excited about starting at San Francisco State? It's great that you'll be able to get there in your own car."

"Yeah, I'm a little excited, but I'm also somewhat apprehensive. It's going to be a big change. It's not on the same level as Cal."

"When you do get your diploma?"

"I don't know. In a couple of weeks, I guess. It doesn't really matter to me that much."

"But your parents will want to see it. You should pay the extra money to get it framed so you can hang it on the wall."

"Yeah, I guess."

Margie spent the rest of the drive back to her apartment telling Adrian about her day of cooking Christmas dinner with her mother. At home, she put a frozen pizza in the oven and brought out a bottle of red wine. They discussed plans for New Year's Eve while they ate and then went to bed early, making love before falling asleep in each other's arms.

Posture

It took only a few weeks for Adrian to become disappointed with the graduate program at San Francisco State College. He liked his Philosophy of Religion class, but that was about it. He told himself that he had been spoiled by the world-class professors at Cal. His instructors at S.F. State were simply not of the same caliber. Adrian was particularly resistant to the teacher who served as his chief contact for the graduate program, whose bombastic lectures betrayed a weak understanding of the material.

Adrian did wonder whether his criticism of his new professors was unduly harsh. Unconsciously, he held them to the same high standard that the leaders of his group now represented for him. Ironically, the influence of those people, who he had come to regard as his real teachers, seemed to be an impediment to his acceptance of the ordinary conditions of life in which he found himself. His objections went beyond the professors, as he judged many of his fellow students to be passive and unengaged. He was particularly bothered by the way some of them habitually slumped down in their chairs during class. At the group meetings, right posture was considered to be an important support for active attention. Adrian had become convinced of this, not just because someone had said it was so, but as a result of seeing for himself how a straight spine supported concentration. He concluded that the slumped bodies around the classroom reflected an attitude of passivity that was diametrically opposite to the active engagement he was learning to value.

Adrian began to consider dropping out of school in spite of the obvious consequences for his draft status. He talked it over with Margie, who emphatically encouraged him to persevere.

"You've got to stay in school, Adrian! You don't want to lose your student deferment! You'll be drafted and will probably have to go to Vietnam."

"I know, but I can't stand spending my whole day the way I have been. San Francisco State isn't like Cal. It's much smaller, and there's not much going on outside the classrooms. People just commute there for classes and then go home again. The teachers are dull and my courses are incredibly boring."

"It doesn't matter. It's the only way you can remain a student right now. I'm sure it will get better. You have to find your own interest in your studies, even if you don't like the teachers or the other students."

"Obviously, you're right. It's really unthinkable to do something which could lead to being drafted and sent to Vietnam. But hanging in there gets harder everyday. I'm not really interested in my graduate program and I don't want to sit around in classrooms all the time. I want to be actively engaged out in the world. What I would really like to do is get a full-time job."

"What about your job at the record store? Doesn't that satisfy your need to be active in the world?"

"Not really. And I haven't told you... They're going to let me go because my work hours aren't flexible enough now. With school and the meetings, I'm in San Francisco from early morning to late evening three times a week and can't get back to Berkeley to put in time at the store. Besides that, I've told my boss I can't work on the weekends any more because I want to leave Sundays free for our workdays and I need a day off on Saturday to study."

"So what are you going to do for money? Will your parents send you enough to get by?"

"I'm definitely going to have to get another job. They have a student placement service at S.F. State. I'm planning to look for something near the college where I can work two or three hours in the afternoon."

"Okay, fine, but whatever you do, please stay in school. You're just going to have to tough it out."

Although Adrian agreed to stay in school, someone in him wanted his own way in spite of the inevitable consequences. The next day, that interloper led Adrian to the main S.F. State office to ask about the rules for dropping out of school. Adrian told himself that he was only going there out of curiosity. A clerk informed him that he wouldn't receive bad marks if he dropped out by a certain date, but would get failing grades on his academic record if he quit after that. The outlaw in Adrian made a mental note of the dropout date.

Objectivity

A few days before the dance demonstration, the members of Adrian's class were on their hands and knees in the midst of an exercise in which they had to execute quick movements of their heads, arms, and legs. The pianist had begun with a moderate tempo but gradually accelerated. Just as they were struggling to keep up with the faster tempo, the back door to the room opened and someone entered. In his peripheral vision, Adrian could see a tall man dressed in black moving with the grace and assurance of a cat along the side of the class. Arriving at the front, he stood to one side and watched them. Adrian thought it must be the dance master from New York he'd heard about. His unexpected entry at that moment intensified the already electric atmosphere in the room.

When they had finished the exercise and risen to their feet, Mrs. Hoyle turned the class over to the dance master. He swept his gaze across them, stopping to look at several people, including Adrian, a little longer. Under the penetration of his dark eyes, Adrian felt that the man was weighing his understanding and potential.

Approaching the pianist, the dance master tapped a rhythm on the wooden lid of the piano. The musician began to play, reproducing the rhythm. Then the dance master turned back to the class and executed a movement in place, marking the rhythm with vigorous steps and knee bends. The class attempted to imitate him. Once everyone was trying, he left his movement and walked along the front row, stopping in front of some people to instruct and correct them.

Returning to the center in front of them, the dance master resumed the rhythmic movement himself again, now adding arm movements. Again, they tried to follow, but the arm movements were too quick for them. Stopping the class, he showed the arm positions slowly, without music, asking the class to take them too, without the movement of the legs. After several repetitions at this slow tempo, they had learned the arm sequence.

The dance master asked the pianist to play and directed the class to take the steps and knee bends again, calling on them to allow the rhythm to circulate everywhere in their bodies. When he saw that the movement was coming alive, he added the arm positions again, encouraging the class not to lose the quality they had established. Soon, they were all taking the arms and legs together.

When the dance master directed the pianist to play faster, Adrian wondered how he would be able to follow. But the dance master had a way of making such a demand on them that they responded whole-heartedly. The class went through the whole sequence of positions again and again until everyone was breathing heavily. Just when he thought he couldn't continue through one more sequence,

Adrian sensed a surge of energy, a lightness in his body, and a new freedom of mind. He felt more awake, alive and free. He could go on without fear or tension.

As the class approached the end of a cycle, the dance master called them to a sudden stop. They stood with their arms held in the last position as his eyes passed over each one. Then he released them. Bringing their arms down, they remained standing, still and quiet in spite of their breathing, which had not yet returned to normal. The dance master gave an affirmative look to Mrs. Hoyle and left the room.

From that experience, Adrian felt specially prepared to witness the dance demonstration at the Palace of the Legion of Honor a few nights later. He sat with Margie and their guest Mitch, the man Adrian had met at his surprise party. Many other people had brought guests as well, so that most of the seats in the theater were filled.

The curtains opened to reveal costumed men and women standing in a semicircle. All wore long white tunics that reminded Adrian of the whirling dervishes, although only the women wore skirts. A musical introduction from a pianist, drummer, and flutist at the side of the stage also recalled the Mevlevi ceremony. The dancers walked slowly in a circle at first, but then moved to places in a new formation, where they paused as the music played an interlude. Then, taking precise positions as they moved, the dancers exchanged places with one another according to a definite pattern, making full turns at certain points in their progression. This continued until they had completed a full cycle of exchanges. Then, retaining their positions, the dancers began turning in place. Unlike the whirling dervishes, who tended to allow their heads to tilt to one side, these dancers kept their heads straight. But Adrian saw that their outstretched arms were very much like those of the dervishes. When the music began to slow, the dancers followed until all came to a stop. They remained standing quietly, without moving.

The audience was quiet too. Adrian wondered what impression his friend Mitch was having. Surely he shared in their common experience, even if he hadn't been prepared to concentrate in a particular way.

A shift in the arrangement of people in the class brought Adrian's attention back to them. The men had retired to sitting positions along the sides of the stage, while the women had arranged themselves into two parallel semicircles. Following an introduction from the musicians, the women moved in graceful positions to the rhythm of a waltz. As they did, Adrian realized that it was a dance his own class had studied, although they had been given only its basic rudiments. His attention was attracted to a woman in the center of the front semicircle whose movements were exceptionally elegant and precise. When the waltz was finished, the women stood still as before.

For the next dance, the women sat down along the sides of the stage and the men lined up in a V formation. The drummer introduced a complex rhythm at a very fast tempo. After several repetitions of the rhythm, the men became animated, sinking into the stage with deep knee bends as they bent their torsos to the left and right, at the same time turning their heads and executing swift gestures with their arms. As he sat riveted by the force of this dance, Adrian again sensed a warm current traveling down the whole length of his spine. He stayed still, not wanting to interfere with this movement within as the men continued on and on with what seemed to be extraordinary concentration and physical perseverance. Finally, with a crashing chord from the piano, the dancers halted in place, holding their positions until, at the sound of a final resolving chord, they brought their arms down together.

Filled with a new vitality, Adrian wanted to stay in the atmosphere of collected attention that seemed to embrace everyone on the stage as well as those in the audience. Wondering how it was for Margie, he slowly turned his head to look at her. When she met his gaze, he saw that they were both in the same state. He glanced at Mitch. Even though their guest had not met with one of their teachers and had not yet been to their meetings or classes, Adrian could see that he too was deeply touched. These dances seemed to affect everyone in the same way.

The accompaniment for the final dance reminded Adrian of choral music he had heard in a Greek Orthodox church. The dancers had resumed their positions in a circle, but now they were sitting with legs crossed. Slowly, they moved in unison into attitudes that expressed a sense of religiousness, their faces revealing deep inner concentration. They repeated a long sequence of these attitudes many times, until a soft resolving chord from the piano brought them to the completion of their effort. After sitting quietly for considerably longer than they had between the dances, the men and women rose and walked off the stage.

Those in the audience remained still for several minutes after the curtains had closed. When some people finally began to move a little, Adrian looked around him. Margie seemed free and relaxed as she turned to him. Sensing that Mitch had become a little uncomfortable at the prolonged stillness, Adrian smiled at him and stood. Seemingly relieved, Mitch got up as well. As the audience filed out of the theater, the soft buzz of conversation rose again. By the time they had passed through the outside doors, people were talking freely amongst themselves. Margie, Mitch and Adrian walked to his VW in the parking lot.

They ran into unusually heavy traffic on the freeway as they approached the Bay Bridge. Mitch suggested that it might be due to the Trips Festival, a massive psychedelic event organized by Ken Kesey, which was taking place that night at the Longshoreman's Hall. He said that thousands of people, many of whom would come high on LSD, were expected to attend. Still feeling the impact of the collected inner quiet they had just experienced during the dances, Adrian thought about the vast difference that must exist between the influences they were under and those affecting the many young people at the psychedelic rock concerts that had recently been taking place in San Francisco.

Mitch spoke again, interrupting Adrian's thoughts. He asked about one of the dances. Adrian declined to discuss it so soon, not wanting to pollute the fresh and fragile perceptions with his own subjective thoughts. Margie clearly felt the same way. Showing an attitude of openness, Mitch readily accepted their reticence. After that, the three of them talked very little before dropping Mitch off at his place in North Berkeley.

Irreversible

Adrian went to file the form to drop out of the graduate program on the last day it was permissible to do so without receiving bad marks. He knew that he should have conferred with Mr. Eckart and brought it up with Margie again, but the one in him who insisted on dropping out didn't want to be talked out of it. Adrian thought again of how he had intentionally given the wrong phone number to Mr. Wells. Was the same part of him taking the upper hand in this critical act? That time, the consequences were minor, as he had only missed a meeting during the summer and Mr. Wells had given him another chance. But this time, the outcome of his decision could change the course of his life.

At the registrar's office, Adrian ignored inner alarms of concern as he filled out the form. Then he watched himself make the irreversible gesture of handing the form to the clerk behind the counter. It was done. As he left the office, he felt lightheaded. Now, there was no going back. How long would it be before the Selective Service reclassified him? What would Mr. Eckart say? How would Margie react?

"I can't believe you didn't tell me you were going to do this." Margie was looking at him with incredulity.

"I wasn't really sure yesterday, so I didn't say anything. But today was the last day I could drop out with a clean record. I kept going back and forth in my mind about it all morning, but when classes were over and I was about to leave, I just found myself heading to the registrar's office."

"Adrian, you are an intelligent guy, but I don't understand this side of you. What are you going to do now?"

"I'll look for a full-time job."

"But who will hire you if your draft classification changes?"

"I don't think everyone cares about that."

"Of course they do!" Margie shook her head in exasperation, then began to cry. "I think you'd better go back to your place tonight. I'd like to be alone."

Adrian hadn't expected this. Feeling like he had a rock in his gut, he muttered a feeble goodbye, picked up his coat and left the apartment. His thoughts and feelings reeled in turmoil all the way home. He had assumed that Margie would support his decision. He wanted to go back and hold her and explain how he would make everything alright. But he couldn't go back to Margie's, not just then.

As Adrian drove home, he thought about how to reconcile the crisis that had arisen between them. There were still two days left before the weekend. He'd start looking for a job the next day. Then he'd find a way to stay out of the Army. He'd ask a girl he knew to introduce him to her psychiatrist friend, who would write a letter to the Selective Service certifying that he was psychologically unfit for military service.

On the way, he stopped to pick up a burger and fries at Clown Alley. As he left, he dropped a quarter in the coin box of the newspaper dispenser outside, remembering that he needed the help wanted section of the *Chronicle* to start his job search.

At home, Adrian put *Sketches of Spain* on the turntable, turned up the volume, and got a beer from the fridge to go with his hamburger. Eating and listening to Miles, his thoughts wandered repeatedly over the same territory. Although he considered ways in which he might have acted differently, he suspected that he would do the same thing all over again, even if given another chance. His quandary reminded him of another book by Ouspensky that he had read recently, *Strange Life of Ivan Osokin*. In that novel, Osokin, whose affairs have gone from bad to worse, asks a magician friend to send him back in time so he can relive his life in order to rectify all the mistakes that eventually led to his current dismal state. The magician warns him that nothing will change, but Osokin insists that he'll do everything differently. When the magician sends him back to his boyhood, Osokin finds himself repeating everything and sees events around him happening in exactly the same way as before. Adrian found an eerie resonance in himself to this story because somewhere inside he knew it was true for him too.

He wasn't sleepy and he no longer had homework to do, so he sat listening to the music with thoughts allied to self-pity revolving in his head. But then he saw with a shock that his indulgence was a waste of energy. What had he learned about facing himself? This question stayed with him until he felt an authentic need to be in touch with the presence inside that he sometimes valued so much. Responding to this call before he could drift into daydreams again, Adrian turned off the music, arranged some cushions on the floor of his bedroom, and sat down with his legs crossed. When he closed his eyes and tried to sense various parts of his body, he discovered tensions everywhere, in his face, his neck, his shoulders, his stomach, and his legs. Having learned that he couldn't force relaxation, he tried to accept the tensions. Little by little, they released their grip. But the circling thoughts returned and he disappeared into them again. The barking of the landlord's dog brought Adrian back to himself.

Momentarily awakened now, he feels alive again, seeing the ascent of the full moon through his window and hearing a passing breeze made audible by wind chimes in the garden. He is cold, but it doesn't matter. As he descends into silence, problems lose their importance, becoming secondary to the sense of being present. His thought is raised to another order, quite different from the usual revolving associations. It is like a light that shines down on him. His emotion is transformed too, as he encounters the mysterious feeling of himself. And his body, the temple in which this revelation takes place, is warm and relaxed.

The next morning, Adrian awakened early to the appreciation of a new stage in his life. Without delay, he climbed out of bed, peed, took a shower, got dressed, and sat down on his cushion. Surprised to see how quickly he was able to become quiet, he guessed that the residue of his sitting the previous night was still with him. But though he believed in the beginning that he could maintain this connection, he soon found himself lost in a vortex of thoughts and emotions again. He tried to return to a sense of his body, but quickly disappeared again into his worries. This continued until Adrian decided it was time to stop.

He wanted to talk to Margie, but when he called, she didn't answer. He resolved that before he saw her again, he would find a job. While eating eggs and toast, he scanned the help wanted ads in the *Chronicle*. He found one listed by Del Monte. Their San Francisco office was looking for a management trainee. A college degree was required. Although Adrian wasn't particularly excited by a food packing company, this opening sounded like his best opportunity at the moment. When he phoned the number in the ad, the secretary who answered offered to set up an appointment for him with her boss that afternoon. Adrian agreed, thanked her and said that he would see her soon.

Beginning to feel excited, Adrian changed into his best brown wool slacks, a blue button-down oxford cloth shirt, a red paisley tie, and his brown corduroy sport coat. He found an old shoeshine cloth in the bottom drawer of his dresser to buff up his brown dress shoes. Then he grabbed the page of the newspaper with the Del Monte ad and left the cottage. Soon he was in his VW headed for San Francisco.

The Open Door

The Del Monte building was huge. Adrian entered through one of three pairs of tall glass doors and walked into the cavernous lobby. Showing the newspaper ad to the security guard posted there, he asked for directions to the place of his interview. The guard directed Adrian to one of the elevator banks, saying that he should get off on the fifteenth floor and couldn't miss the tall wooden doors that led to the executive reception area. As Adrian stood in the elevator, the swift upward movement made him aware of his sense of balance. When the doors parted, this contact with his body continued as he stepped out onto a highly polished marble floor and saw the wooden doors ahead of him. Now he approached the doors deliberately, intending to open the right one with his left hand. Just as he neared the door, it swung open. Another young man was leaving. Adrian wondered whether this person, who had paused to hold the door open for him, had applied for the job as well. Adrian muttered a polite "Thank You" and entered the hushed reception area where the only sound was the click-clack of a secretary's typewriter.

The secretary, an attractive blonde in her early twenties, looked up at Adrian as he approached. When he introduced himself, she smiled with recognition, saying that she remembered his voice from their phone conversation that morning. She asked him to sit down and offered him something to drink. The man he had to see would be with him in a few minutes.

Adrian declined the beverage and chose a seat in the waiting area. As he eased into a chair, he had the feeling that he'd forgotten something. Then he remembered his intention to open the door with his left hand. He'd forgotten when the man came through the door and held it for him. Adrian tried to think of something that would help him to remember himself during the interview, but thoughts about what he was going to say took over. He would tell the executive that he was very interested in this opportunity to join a great American corporation. He wanted to get into management and this seemed like a good chance to get in on the ground floor. Yes, he had been to graduate school but realized that the academic life was not for him. He wanted to be actively involved in what was happening in the world.

The secretary interrupted Adrian's thoughts, saying that the Vice President would see him now. She gestured to a door that had just opened behind her. Feeling a little shaky, Adrian stood up and walked into an office with rich wood paneled walls and a large oriental rug on the floor. A man rose from behind an expansive walnut desk centered in front of a picture window view of the San Francisco financial district and came forward to introduce himself. His handshake was warm and soft. Clean shaven, with receding silver hair, he was dressed in a fine gray business suit with a red tie. He must have been in his late fifties and was probably at the peak of his career. The Vice President led Adrian to a couple of plush armchairs in the corner of the room and they sat down.

Adrian began his prepared speech, but before he could finish, the Vice President interrupted him.

"What is it that you want to do with your life?" the man asked. "Why do you want to come to work for a big corporation? As a lover of literature, are you sure that the business world is the right place for you?"

Adrian's guard dropped as he sensed that this executive was a kind and compassionate man. The approach Adrian had planned wouldn't stand up to this directness, so he decided to speak honestly. "Well, I need to get a job. I've been in college for a long time and am hungry to participate in the real world. I think Del Monte could be a place where I could do that."

The man nodded. "I see. But I have learned how important it is to do something that you like, something that really has meaning for you. At your age, you have a chance to find what you really want. Don't get stuck in the wrong business for the rest of your life."

Having paused to look at Adrian closely for a moment and to be sure that he appreciated the point, the man asked "What is it that you really like?"

"Music," Adrian said without thinking, even though he was hardly a musician. He surprised himself with this response, which came from some part of himself that didn't care at all about getting the job. The truth was, Adrian did love listening to music and liked working at the record store. He often turned to music for solace and healing. He reminded himself how much he had wanted the harmonium that Desmond had stolen from the import store.

"Then you should give all your energy to that. As a college student, you probably know the advice Joseph Campbell has given: 'Follow your bliss.'"

Adrian was stunned how quickly this Vice President had called forward what was true in him, although Adrian didn't see himself making a living as a musician. Of course he didn't belong at Del Monte corporation. He wondered if, after all these years, the Vice President still believed that he himself did.

The Vice President stood up, indicating that the interview was already over. Adrian was back to square one. Where would he go next? If he found another job opening, would the same thing happen again?

As the Vice President walked Adrian to the door of his office, he asked, as though it were an afterthought, "What about your draft status? What is it now that you are no longer enrolled in school?"

Adrian flushed. "Um, they haven't reclassified me yet."

"Mr. Masters, you must know that no company will hire you if they think you are likely to be drafted. Each day, we all read about the growing number of young men being inducted into military service. Everyone is cognizant of this fact of life."

Of course, he was right. What he was saying put Adrian's whole plan to get a job in question. Who would hire him?

"I see what you mean." That's all Adrian could say. Shaking the Vice President's hand, Adrian thanked him for his time and thoughtful directness. The man turned back into his office, shutting the door behind him. Adrian forced a smile at the secretary as he passed her desk on his way to the elevator.

Feeling completely lost now, Adrian went back to his car and drove aimlessly around the financial district. He had nowhere else to go. He didn't know what to do, but he couldn't leave San Francisco empty-handed. He was driving down Kearny when he came to a one-way cross street on his right. Noticing that it was paved with old cobblestones, out of curiosity Adrian turned onto it, seeing Commercial Street on the sign at the corner. Vehicles lined the curbs on both sides of the narrow street, so that there was barely enough room for cars to pass though. When a small van pulled out of its place ahead of him, Adrian obeyed an impulse to park where the van had been.

He got out of the car and looked around. There were no storefronts there, only faded buildings with windows covered on the inside and dirty on the outside. Peeking through a hole in brown paper meant to block one dusty window, Adrian could see several rows of Chinese women sitting at sewing machines arranged on long tables. It occurred to him that this must be one of those "sweat shops" he'd heard about where poor women worked long hours producing garments for low wages.

Walking on down the street, Adrian came to an intriguing old brick building. A brass plaque mounted by the door announced that the building was an historical landmark, the first U.S. branch mint, opened in 1854. As the tall black wooden double doors at the entrance were halfway open, he moved closer to look inside. Adrian was astonished by what he saw. A large room with exposed brick walls and plywood floor was illuminated by skylights that traversed the entire ceiling. The afternoon light revealed a pattern of hopscotch squares painted in pastel colors on one portion of the floor, an old upright player piano topped with a bust of Beethoven in another area, and antique wooden carousel animals situated around the room. The breathtakingly beautiful Adagio movement of Mozart's *Clarinet Concerto* filled the space.

Drawn like a fairy tale hero into a magical castle, Adrian had no choice but to enter that marvelous place. Then he noticed that someone was there. Alone at a table in the middle of the room, a middle-aged woman sat sewing a small cloth doll.

Without hesitation, Adrian approached her and asked, "What is this place?"

Looking up from the doll, she smiled as though she had been expecting him. "This is the art department of Single-Minded Productions."

"I want to work here!" Adrian said, without even thinking about it. As he spoke, he heard an uncharacteristic freedom in his voice.

"Why don't you apply? Our main business office is a few blocks away, on the corner of Washington and Montgomery."

"Can I say you sent me?"

"Sure. My name is Peggy. Ask to speak with Carol, our President. Tell her you'd like to work in the art department. You'll also need to meet John, our Art Director."

Adrian was elated. "Great to meet you, Peggy. I'm Adrian Masters. I'm going to go there right now!" This unfolding drama felt strangely unreal, as though he had been dropped into a scene in a Fellini movie. But it was actually happening.

Adrian left his car parked where it was and walked to the corner of Washington and Montgomery, where a small ivy-covered building had "Single-Minded Productions" printed in elegant script on a sign above the entrance. An atmosphere of whimsical elegance greeted him when he went inside. The green leaves of potted plants stood out against bright red pastel walls hung with Peter Max prints. Antique wooden furniture contrasted with the modernity of the extremely short chemise dresses worn by several women working there. A classic French bread rack was set up to showcase Single-Minded products, with children's books, dolls, felt pennants, and calendars on its shelves.

Addressing Adrian in a commanding voice, a large woman sitting at a broad Louis Fifteenth style desk asked, "Are you the typewriter repair man?"

"No, I'm here to apply for a job in your art department. I was just there, at Commercial Street, and met Peggy, who sent me here."

The woman stood up. Over six feet tall, she had a massive head of red hair, a large nose, drooping eyes with deep bags under them and a jutting chin, adding up to a stern countenance that was definitely intimidating. Although she was neither youthful nor slim like the other two women in the office, she wore the same Marimekko dress as they did.

Without the slightest suggestion of a smile, the woman looked Adrian over from head to toe. Then, seemingly accepting his request but not asking his name, she pulled out a form from a bright blue filing cabinet and handed it to Adrian on a clipboard with a pen.

"Fill this out and bring it back to me. I'll see if Carol and John have time to see you."

Adrian sat down in one of the Louis Fifteenth chairs to fill out the form. Just as he finished, the big woman announced that Carol and Jim would see him. He took the clipboard back to her and she pointed out the open door to Carol's private office. Not feeling as free then as he had been in the old mint building on Commercial Street, Adrian went in.

Carol and John eyed him as he entered. Carol's shiny platinum blonde hair, piled on her head in beehive style, echoed the gaudy white dress wrapped tightly around her short, stocky torso. Heavy mascara, eyebrow pencil and eyeliner exaggerated her dark brown eyes. Her crimson lipstick and matching nail polish joined with her white leather high-heeled boots to lend an aspect of brashness, so that overall she gave the impression of a woman in costume, conveying a coarse allure perhaps not corresponding to her nature. John's dark Elvis-style hair, slicked back into a ducktail, perfectly matched his tall slim physique. But the macho character of his black leather motorcycle jacket, black leather trousers and black leather boots were not in tune with the feeling Adrian had about the man wearing them. Standing together, Carol and John came across as caricatures of the personas they wanted others to see.

Adrian's interview with them was brief. Carol listened to his enthusiastic descriptions of their building on Commercial Street with evident pleasure. Appearing to be open to his request to work in the art department, she handed the decision over to John, as he was in charge of that part of the company. But John did not even pretend to show interest in Adrian and remained noncommittal. After Adrian reiterated his enthusiasm for their company and promised to work hard, Carol pressed John to consider him. She reminded John of a project they had been postponing, saying that Adrian might be just the person who could help them get it started.

"Do you have any experience with photography?" John asked.

"Yes, as a matter of fact I've been taking pictures since I was a kid. Photography is one of my hobbies." This was true, as he had started taking pictures with a Brownie box camera his father gave him when he was seven.

John looked at Carol to confirm the decision to hire him. She gave a disinterested nod, as if she wanted to be done with Adrian and go on to something else she had to do.

"Alright, we'll give you a try," John said somewhat half-heartedly. "I can't promise anything permanent for you right now. We'll see how it goes."

"Great!" Adrian responded with enough enthusiasm to make up for their lack of it. "When can I start?"

"Next Monday. Come to the art department at 9 am. I should be there by then. If I'm not, Peggy can give you something to do until I arrive."

"See Barbara, my office manager, before you leave," added Carol. "You can probably fill out all the employment forms we need right now."

"Thanks a lot! I'll see you next week!" Adrian said to finish the conversation. But they had already started to talk about something else and paid no attention to him. The big woman, who Adrian now knew was named Barbara, gave him another clipboard full of forms to fill out and he resumed his place in the Louis Fifteenth chair. When he returned the forms to her, Adrian realized that he hadn't even asked about the pay. No one had brought it up.

"Um, how much will I be making?" he asked sheepishly.

"Three dollars an hour. You'll get overtime if you work over forty hours. Paychecks will be issued every two weeks. We can deposit directly into your checking account if you want."

"Okay, thanks!" he said, accepting their terms without question. He started to say goodbye but Barbara turned away to answer her phone. He left the office without another word and headed back to his car.

Walking down Montgomery Street, Adrian marveled that no one there had asked about his college degree or his draft status. And they hadn't mentioned money! These people obviously lived in a different world than the Vice President at Del Monte. Turning up Commercial Street, the cobblestones reminded him of the unexpected and mysterious way he had been drawn to the old brick building. As he approached it again, he recalled the joy he'd felt in discovering that magical place. Adrian wanted to tell Peggy that he'd gotten the job and would be seeing her the following week, but as he came closer he saw that the doors were closed now. He tried the brass knob, but it wouldn't turn.

Adrian thought about what happens in fairy tales. An open door that leads the hero to what he seeks may be closed when he returns to it again. The unexpected shock of that closed entrance brought Adrian back to a sense of himself and he realized how far away he'd been most of the day. Except for a couple of minutes in the Del Monte building, he'd been on automatic pilot. He'd had his interview with the Vice President, driven around the financial district, discovered the old building on Commercial Street with Peggy sewing her doll, gone to the main Single-Minded Productions office and filled out forms for Barbara, interviewed with the eccentric Carol and John, and walked back to where he was now—all without once being aware of his own presence.

Presence

Back in Berkeley, Adrian drove directly to Margie's apartment, wanting to tell her about everything that had happened. He'd convinced himself that she would surely appreciate that the mysterious way in which he'd been drawn to Single-Minded Productions proved that he must be on the right path. Also, there was a theme meeting that night and he was hoping they could go in together. He found a parking place in front of her building and raced up the stairs.

Margie wasn't there. Adrian thought about her schedule. Her Thursday afternoon class would have been over for nearly two hours, so she must have had errands to take care of on her way home. Assuming that she would call him about going in for the meeting, he decided to go to his place so he'd be there if she did.

When Adrian had been home for an hour without a call from Margie, an impulse he hadn't felt for a long time flared up in him. Without the slightest rationale for it, the dragon of jealousy reared its ugly head again as he wondered if she could be out with Hank Stevens.

An inner voice from an unknown source brings Adrian back to himself. Instead of criticizing himself as he usually does, he finds himself more interested in understanding his egoistic emotions. The idea of study is beginning to have new meaning for him. He sits down and tries to bring his attention back to his body. Discovering tensions in his face, neck, shoulders and abdomen, he sees that they are all related to his emotional agitation. Although he isn't yet able to separate what is essential in himself from the currents of anxiety, worry, and jealousy, for a moment he is certain that those emotions do not represent the whole of him. They are part of one stream, but there is another stream, one of intelligence and sensitivity, that he only knows through intuition but wants to stay available to. He struggles to let go of thoughts about changing his state in order to accept himself exactly as he is, with all the contradictions. Very slowly, a process of inner relaxation begins to flow in him.

At that moment, the phone rang. Adrian felt the strong pull of the impulse to answer, especially as he was expecting a call from Margie. He decided to pick up the phone, but he didn't want to lose the contact that had appeared from what he had just been trying. He realized that this was another opportunity for study, a chance to listen to himself in an ordinary telephone conversation. As he stood to go to the phone, he promised himself that he would stay aware of the sensation of his body.

"Hello?" Adrian sensed his feet on the floor.

"Hi Adrian."

"Margie, it's you!" He sensed the phone in his hand as he listened to his own voice.

"How are you doing?"

"I've got a lot to tell you about. Are you going to the meeting tonight? We could talk on the way in." He felt his stomach grow tense as he waited for her answer.

"Sure, I was planning on it. Can you remind me of the theme?"

Adrian couldn't help smiling. "Yes, I'm pretty sure it's 'An entirely new understanding of the experience of being present.'"

"Right, I remember now. What time will you pick me up?"

"I'll come by at 6. We need to leave time for traffic on the bridge."

"Okay. See you then, Adrian."

"Bye, Margie." As Adrian hung up the phone, he realized that, in spite of his resolve, he'd forgotten again. He'd stayed with himself up until the point when Margie said she had been planning on going in with him. Then, in the midst of his gladness, he had disappeared.

Adrian told Margie about his magical day as they drove to San Francisco. Although she was amazed by his story and impressed that he had gotten a job, her concerns weren't resolved. She believed that he was still likely to be reclassified for the draft and didn't give much credence to his plan to avoid it by getting a letter from a psychiatrist. But Margie had forgiven him for dropping out of school. Whatever lay ahead, she was ready to go forward with their relationship.

Delayed by an accident on the bridge, they arrived barely in time for the meeting. As the big room was packed, with only a few isolated empty chairs remaining, Margie and Adrian had to find seats in different rows. Just after they sat down, Mr. Wells entered with a man and woman whom Adrian hadn't seen before and walked to the raised platform at the front of the room. The woman sat between the two men. Mr. Wells' resonate voice began the meeting.

"Our theme tonight is 'An entirely new understanding of the experience of being present.' Last week, when I was in New York, I had breakfast at a little diner named 'Eat Here Now'. This clever and somewhat humorous twist to 'Be Here Now' shows how those words have become a popular cliché in today's culture. But even we here often use the words 'being present' when we talk together without really understanding them. I realize the truth of this when I have an authentic experience of presence, because then it has new meaning for me. I recognize that the static idea I ordinarily have about presence has no real life in it. I may even see that my belief that I understand presence is one of the chief obstacles to actually experiencing it. This leads us to the basis for the formulation of our theme, because every real contact with my presence brings an entirely new understanding of the experience of being present."

Adrian felt that the directness of Mr. Wells' simple and unusually brief introduction of the theme helped to quiet his mind. After a pause, the woman in the middle spoke.

"As Mr. Wells just said, the notion of living in the present moment has become popular. We even hear it expressed in movies. The thought is that if we really value our lives, we can decide to live in the present instead of wallowing in past regrets or becoming lost in our ambitions. But what is left out is that presence is not under our command. We do not even see that it is missing most of the time. All of our functions can go on without it. For most people, it only appears in certain conditions. It may appear when we are moved by the grandeur of nature, or at times of deep personal feeling as when we witness the birth of a child, lose someone close to us, or find ourselves in danger. At those times, we feel fully alive. Later, we forget how we were and do not even notice the lack of presence. But for those who have felt repeatedly that something is missing in their lives—and I am assuming that holds true for most of us in this room—there is a possibility of developing our capacity to experience more and more moments of presence. What does it mean to be present? Who is present? To what am I present? These are the questions we need to explore further."

Everyone sat quietly, waiting for the other man to speak. He was much younger than Mr. Wells and Mr. Eckart, appearing to Adrian to be in his thirties. He had probably come from New York with the woman who had just spoken.

"I would like to continue with the questions that have just been brought. What does it mean to be present? Who is present? To what am I present? Although most of the time I don't know it, I am a creature composed of three main parts: body, mind, and emotions. If they functioned as designed, all three parts would work together, each performing those tasks proper to them at the corresponding tempo. Instead, they work disharmoniously, each part interfering with the others and even trying to accomplish the work that another part is designed to perform. For each of us, one of these parts tends to predominate most of the time. We identify ourselves with that part. If my mind predominates, I believe that my thoughts represent me. If my center of gravity is in my emotions, I identify with them. Or, if I live most of the time in my body, I take it to represent the whole of me. As a result, what is popularly known as 'living in the present' is concentrated in the part that predominates and only reinforces the illusion that this part should act on behalf of the whole person.

"To be fully present would mean to be aware of all my parts at once. What would make this possible? How can my functions be aware of themselves? Some other intelligence is needed, an intelligence that can embrace all of my functioning and bring a sense of self at the same time. When we begin to see this imbalance in our functioning for ourselves, we come to the need for a Way that can help us to be as we were made to be. Engaging with you in different activities and helped by special forms like meditation and the dance exercises, I may be brought to a state in which my parts begin to function together harmoniously, each performing its own work at its proper tempo. If this happens, and I can remain quiet enough to allow the entry of a new intelligence, I may have an entirely new experience of being present."

Adrian sensed the cumulative effect of the thought that had been developed by the three who had introduced the theme. Then, as people in the audience asked questions, he felt he was able to listen to them more openly than usual. He even found himself empathizing with a woman about whom he usually had an unfavorable opinion.

When the meeting was over, Margie waited for Adrian as he helped put away the folding chairs and disassemble the platform. Meeting her in the hallway, he saw that she was in a very sensitive state, which realigned him with a movement back to himself. They were each related not only horizontally, in the usual way one person is to another, but also vertically, to another level within that they recognized and respected in one another. Without words, they descended the stairs and walked to the car. They remained relatively quiet on the way home, only speaking briefly about their plans for the coming week.

In Margie's bedroom, they undress without words, sharing their nakedness in the flickering radiance of a candle Margie has lit. They each feel a new sense of respect for the sanctity of their bodies. Moving to the bed, they are drawn together like two halves of a whole, fitting together perfectly at every point of contact. They don't try to make anything happen. On the contrary, they surrender to the awareness enveloping them, lying still until waves of ecstasy spread out from the center of their union to the tips of their fingers and toes and to the tops of their heads.

The Letter

Adrian drove to San Francisco early Monday morning for his new job. Not wanting to pay the high price of parking in one of the lots downtown, he explored the neighborhood streets of Russian Hill until he discovered a steep street without parking limitations.

Walking down the hill, Adrian was exhilarated by the fog-kissed morning air and sounds of Chinatown waking up. On Grant Street, a truck filled with live chickens in old wooden cages pulled up to a poultry shop. The loud whack of a cleaver called Adrian's attention to the work of a man inside the shop, who was routinely removing the heads of chickens that had just been delivered. Descending from Chinatown into the financial district to Kearny Street, Adrian joined a stream of people wearing suits and carrying briefcases, hurrying to banks or brokerage houses, some stopping briefly at a curbside stand to get coffee and a pastry.

He arrived fifteen minutes early at the old brick building on Commercial Street, but Peggy was already there, still working on the prototype for a new doll. She greeted Adrian warmly and suggested he rearrange some furniture to set up a work area for himself. John arrived a little after 9. After a cursory greeting, he explained Adrian's job. He was to create a visual catalog of John and Carol's large collection of antique toys, novelties, furniture and objets d'art. Besides the things Adrian had seen sitting here and there around the room, John said there were many treasures stored in an old vault under the floor. John wanted Adrian to catalog all these objects, with a description and photograph for each.

Adrian's first task was to buy the requisite photographic equipment. Giving Adrian the keys to the VW cargo van used for picking up supplies and delivering packages, John directed Adrian to go to Adolph Gasser's and purchase the latest Hasselblad camera. As Adrian wound his way around buses, taxis and double-parked delivery trucks on the busy streets of the financial district, he felt alive again, a participant in the exuberant activity of the city. At the camera store, he enjoyed being an agent of extravagance as he charged the purchase of the very best equipment to the Single-Minded Productions account. Back at the art department, he spent the rest of the day unpacking and making himself familiar with the new gear.

Adrian described his day to Margie at the dinner table that evening. "You should see this huge vault under the floor where some of the stuff in their antique collection is stored. You have to open these heavy metal doors on the floor and then climb down an iron ladder to get into the vault room. The space really has the feeling of a different era. It's where they kept gold coins when the building was still a national mint in the middle of the nineteenth century. The air is pretty musty and you have to watch out not to get spider webs in your hair. But the cool thing is the writing on the walls by different guys who worked there. Next to their names, each one kept a running total of the money sacks he had personally loaded into the vault. They wrote down the dates, too. I think the earliest one was 1855."

"Wow, Adrian, you've really got a crazy job. Sounds pretty fun though. When are you going to start taking pictures?"

"I have to learn to use the Hasselblad first. It's a complicated professional camera. But there doesn't seem to be any hurry."

Looking down, Margie changed the subject. "Uh, Adrian, there's something we need to talk about. You know that I've applied for admission to several graduate schools for the fall semester. Berkeley and Stanford are among them, but I'm also interested in Rutgers, Yale and Princeton. I thought I should tell you that a letter of provisional acceptance from Rutgers came in the mail today. I'm still waiting to hear from the other schools, but it's possible that I might move to the East Coast in September. It's not really that different from your situation, since you might be drafted by then. This is something we really have to face."

Adrian had been so caught up in his own concerns that he hadn't confronted the possibility that Margie might leave. She was a top philosophy student with ambitious plans for her career. She could probably get into any school she wanted. But he couldn't bear the thought of losing her.

"I'm pretty sure I'll be staying," he asserted, trying not to show the pang in his heart. "I still plan to get out of the Army. I just have to get a letter from Hanna's psychiatrist friend."

"Do you think you're being realistic about that, Adrian? If it was that easy to get out of the draft, why are so many men taking far more extreme measures, like becoming conscientious objectors, or fleeing to Canada, or even going to prison?"

"Desmond got out just by saying that he used drugs. He was reclassified as 4F, which means he's permanently disqualified."

"Yes, but that was over a year ago when they weren't drafting so many men and not that many guys were trying to do what Desmond did. Now, they're wise to that ploy. My friend Alice told me that her brother tried that when he went to his induction physical last week. They didn't believe him. He's been ordered to report to boot camp next month. They need lots of bodies now."

"I'm thirsty." Adrian went into the kitchen to get a glass of water to break off the unpleasant conversation. He wasn't ready to accept the possibility he might actually have to go into the Army and couldn't face the prospect that Margie might move away.

Coming back into the living room, he changed the subject. "Have you been invited to come to the dance exercise class yet?"

"Oh yes, I meant to tell you. Mr. Eckart said I could start next week."

"Great! Will you be coming to the same class as me?"

"Yes, I think so. That reminds me—I've got to get some dance shoes like yours."

"What if I pick you up at the Transbay terminal at 5:30 tomorrow after work? We could stop to get them at the Capezio's in Union Square on the way to our meeting."

"Okay, I think I can get there by then."

"Do you have a lot of studying tonight?"

"Yes, a bunch. I need to start on it. What are you going to do? It must be weird not to have to study anymore."

"I can still study whatever I want. It's just voluntary now. You know, I never did finish *Her-Bak*. I think I'll read that while you're doing your homework."

After reading a couple of pages from *Her-Bak*, Adrian's thoughts drifted back to the unthinkable possibility that Margie might move to the East Coast. He wondered how much the uncertainly of his future figured into her considerations. He thought it was possible that she might decide on Berkeley or Stanford if she knew that he was definitely going to be around. If only he could get a 4F draft classification, then there would be no more question about his leaving. Thinking again about obtaining a letter which would certify that he wasn't suitable for service, Adrian decided to call Hanna to get the number of her psychiatrist friend. Putting *Her-Bak* down, he looked in his wallet for the scrap of paper on which she'd written her number. Adrian recognized the pink laundry receipt stuck between cards and pulled it out. He went into the kitchen to call her.

In the evening after work three days later, Adrian pulled up in front of a large Tudor style house on Grizzly Peak in the Berkeley Hills. He walked to the entrance and rang the bell. Hanna's friend Bill, a slight man with pale skin and a soft voice, opened the door and invited him in. The decor inside Bill's home reflected the fine taste of a wealthy and erudite man. Exquisite oriental rugs covered most of the oak floors in the entry area and living room. Original abstract expressionist paintings adorned the walls.

The subtle smile of a large carved wooden Buddha sitting in one corner of the room enjoins Adrian to a momentary stop. He becomes aware of his body, of his heart beating in anticipation of the request he is about to make of the psychiatrist, of his face flushed in the warmth of the house. As he moves forward again, he is aware of how quiet it is, hears the pronounced ticking of an antique grandfather clock and the dampened sound of their footsteps across the thick carpets. Bill leads him into his study, a wood paneled room with wall-to-wall bookcases. Having returned to a sensitive state after a long period of forgetting himself, Adrian resolves to stay in touch with his weight in the chair as he sits down across from Bill at his desk.

"Hanna said you are concerned about the possibility of being drafted. How do you feel about the chance you might have to fight in Vietnam?"

"I'm really worried about it. Yesterday, when I was looking through this little library they have in the art department where I work, I noticed *The Red Badge of Courage* on the shelf. I read that book in high school and still remember the part where the hero, Henry Fleming, runs from battle. For some reason, I really wanted to read that part again. Maybe I'm afraid that I might end up on a battlefield and want to know what it's like. Anyway, I looked around to be sure that the other people there wouldn't see what I was reading because I didn't want them to know I was worried about the Army. Feeling guilty, I sat down with the book and found the place where Henry flees. I read every detail of the battle because I wanted to understand what it was like for him. I could sort of put myself in Henry's shoes when he runs away into the forest and finds himself alone."

"Do you dream about being in the Army?"

Adrian thought a moment. He remembered one bad dream he'd had in which he was lost alone in a jungle after being left behind by a group of people he was hiking with. Although he hadn't connected that to being in the Army in Vietnam, that could be a valid interpretation. Besides, he needed to give the psychiatrist enough material to build a good case. He decided to make the most of it.

"Yes, I recently had a terrifying nightmare about being left alone by my platoon in Viet Cong territory."

Bill had been listening carefully. "You have a lot of fear around going into the Army. The fact that you felt guilty about reading that book and didn't want the others at work to know what you were thinking shows you suffer from an irrational level of angst. Dreaming about being caught by the enemy when you haven't even been over there indicates an unusual level of unconscious fear. I would suggest that you are a borderline schizophrenic. I think you could be pushed over the edge into psychosis and probably wouldn't even survive if you were forced to fight in the war. The people at the Selective Service need to know this. I will most certainly write a letter that explains your condition. If you give it to them, I don't think you should have to worry about being drafted into the Army."

Bill opened a drawer in his desk, withdrawing a sheet of stationery and matching envelope. He rolled the paper into his typewriter and began composing the letter. When he had finished, he removed the paper and signed it. Folding it carefully into thirds, he inserted it into the envelope and handed it to Adrian.

"This should be all you will need," he said, smiling.

"Thank you! Uh, what do I owe you?"

"We're both good friends of Hanna. I'm glad to do it."

"Wow! That's really nice of you! Thank you so much!"

"You're very welcome."

Bill saw Adrian to the door and wished him luck.

Adrian was elated. He had the letter now and the psychiatrist thought that it would work. He wanted to tell Margie right then. She would realize now that he wasn't going anywhere. She might very well decide to stay in the Bay Area for graduate school so they could be together. Most importantly, they could continue their work with the group together. What a relief!

As Adrian was getting into his car, the spell of these thoughts was broken when he caught a glimpse of the self-deceptive egoism and imagination behind them. That impression was very brief, but it came into view without being deflected by the usual defensive or judgmental reaction. The truth of what he saw was simply accepted and digested. The reverberation of the observation was strong enough that he just sat there for a minute. Thinking back about what had occurred in the psychiatrist's house, he realized that the last time he'd been aware of himself before getting in the car was the moment he sensed his weight in the chair in Bill's study. He had lost touch as soon as he started telling Bill about his fear of the Army.

Adrian started the car and pulled away from the curb. Turning off Grizzly Peak, he put the VW in first gear and coasted down steep Marin Avenue. At the bottom of the hill, he turned left on Shattuck. In a few minutes, he was pulling up in front of Margie's building. Anxious to tell her he had the letter, he ran up the stairs to her floor. On his way to the door of her apartment, he chanced to see her through her kitchen window. She was sitting at the kitchen table under a lamp, writing in her notebook. A wave of tenderness passed through him as he saw her a little more objectively than usual, as though for the first time. Her brown hair was down, spread over the shoulders of her blue sweater, conveying softness and comfort. Margie's simple beauty and the sense of active intent issuing from her expression and posture reminded him of what he loved about her. Full of feeling, he proceeded to the door and let himself in.

"How did it go?" she asked, looking up at him.

"You should have seen this guy's house. A big place, way up on Grizzly Peak with a fantastic view of the Bay, the bridges, and the San Francisco skyline. It's very refined inside, with incredible oriental carpets and original paintings. Must be lucrative to be a psychiatrist."

"But what did he say about the letter?"

"Well, first he asked me how I felt about going to fight in Vietnam. After I talked about it, he came right out and told me that it would be very bad for me psychologically to go into the Army. He said I was a borderline schizophrenic and thought it was important to make that clear to the Selective Service people. He wrote the letter for me without any trouble."

"Do you really think you're a borderline schizophrenic?"

"No, but I wasn't going to dispute it since that was the main point he was putting in the letter."

"Wow. I'm amazed it was that easy."

"Yeah, but I can't really do anything with the letter until I get reclassified and they call me in for a physical."

"We're in no hurry for that! Anyway, I'm hungry. Let's get something to eat. We can scrounge some leftovers from the fridge."

Margie's attitude toward his strategy for avoiding the draft seemed different now that he had the letter. He thought she would have to give up considering Rutgers or Princeton and start thinking about staying in the Bay Area for graduate school.

Although Adrian had begun taking pictures as a kid, he had never worked with indoor lighting. Learning to use the tools of lighting became his next task at Single-Minded Productions, as John wanted high-quality, detailed photos of every one of the objects to be cataloged. John had no problem approving the purchase of the best flash unit, several spotlights, and a reflective umbrella. Adrian even bought a special detachable polaroid film back for the Hasselblad that enabled him to take preview test shots he could evaluate immediately. If the polaroid image showed that the settings for a shot were good, he would exchange the polaroid film back with another back containing regular Kodachrome film and take the picture.

Adrian was working with the lighting equipment to photograph an antique wooden cabinet one afternoon when Alfred, the company controller, dropped by. When the two of them had met on Adrian's first day, they had hit it off right away.

Alfred came over to see what Adrian was doing. "How are you, Adrian?"

"Pretty good, thanks. What's going on?"

"I'm asking a few of our employees to take an aptitude test for some future functions we're thinking of putting in place. Would you be interested?"

"Sure, I'm game. When's it going to be?"

"The test will be held at the IBM Data Center on Front Street next Monday morning at 9 am. It should only take about an hour. Can you make it?"

"Yeah, that will work for me. Who else is taking the test?"

"So far, only David and Anita."

"It sounds intriguing. Can you say what these 'future functions' might be?"

"We're thinking of automating our accounting systems. We might get our own computer. But nothing is decided yet."

"Cool! Our own computer! Where would you put it?"

"Just between you and me, we're also considering a move to larger quarters. We've got our eye on a great office building at the corner of Sansome and Broadway in North Beach. But that, too, is still just a possibility."

"Wow, there's a lot going on! Thanks for letting me in on it."

"I want you to feel part of our family. If you do well on this aptitude test and are interested in where we're going, you could have an important role to play."

"Well, I don't know whether I have the aptitude you're looking for, but I'll be there for the test."

"Excellent. I'll be sending out a memo with detailed instructions about where to go and so forth. Now, I've got to get back to my office for a meeting. See you soon."

"Thanks again, Alfred. See you."

Adrian arrived at the IBM Data Center about fifteen minutes early. Parking in the financial district was always difficult, so he decided to park in a lot nearby. It was expensive, but he figured that Alfred would cover the cost. A secretary at the front desk directed him to a classroom at the rear of the building. Several people from other companies had already taken their places in chairs with small attached desks, on which lay sealed test booklets and pencils. Adrian took one of the places in the second row. He saw that the title on the closed test booklet read, "Programming Aptitude Test."

So that was it—they were testing them to see who might make a good computer programmer. Adrian was surprised that Alfred had selected him. Although math had been his major in high school, he hadn't taken any math courses in college. Just as he was thinking that the others from Single-Minded Productions would probably be better at numbers, Adrian saw David enter the classroom with Anita. They spotted him and found seats in the same row.

A man entered and took his place facing them at the front of the room. He went over the rules, asked if everyone was ready, and then gave them the green light to unseal their booklets and begin working. They had just an hour to complete the test.

Adrian was surprised to find how much he enjoyed the problems. They weren't so much questions of arithmetic as puzzles of logic. He sailed through the test in forty minutes. Closing his booklet and looking around, he noticed that everyone else was still at work. He wondered if he had overlooked something. Paging through the test again, he reassured himself that he had answered all the questions. With that, he stood up and walked his test booklet to the man at the front of the room. Smiling, the man took it, nodded in silence, and indicated that he was free to go. As Adrian walked toward the door, David and Anita both looked up at him from their tests. He smiled in acknowledgment and made his exit.

Three days later, Alfred came by the art department again to tell Adrian that he had received a high score on the aptitude test. If Adrian would agree to leave his position in the art department, Alfred would send him to a programming course at IBM in preparation for the planned automation of the accounting systems. Adrian didn't have to think long about it. Alfred was offering him the kind of training and experience that could lead to a real career. Surely, his pay would increase as well. And anyway, Adrian knew that his current job probably wouldn't last long once all the photographs had been taken and the catalog was finished.

The Absence of Presence

Standing in the garage on Sunday morning listening to Mr. Eckart read the list of assignments, Adrian was surprised to hear his name included with a different team. Someone had decided to put him in printing. He was glad about this, as he had been interested in the craft of letterpress in high school and had even set up his own small press in his parents' garage.

Entering the print shop in the basement of the house, Adrian recognized the various tools of the craft with fond familiarity. The wide shallow wooden job cases full of metal type attracted his attention first. These sat at an angle on the sloped tops of work tables so that someone composing type could stand in front of a case and easily withdraw letters and spaces from it. Additional job cases were stored as drawers in large cabinets set along the wall, with labels on the front of each case that indicated the size and typeface of the letters contained in it. A rack of assorted strips and blocks of the wooden "furniture" used to arrange a page of composed type sat on a metal-topped assembly table, along with the wedge-shaped metal quoins used to lock the page into the chase, a cast iron frame that was clamped into the bed of the press to hold the type in place.

At the heart of it all stood the Chandler and Price platen press. Although it was much larger than the one Adrian had as a teenager, the basic components were the same. He was eager to run it, but suspected that was a privilege to be earned. As the team gathered around the press, Robert, the leader, explained what they would be doing. Robert and another man would operate the press, printing some original material from the writing team for which type has been set on the previous Sundays. Two others were to begin composing type for a new booklet of metaphysical essays the French translation team had rendered into English. Adrian's job was to distribute type back into the job cases from projects that had been completed.

Robert was very different from the hung-over artist who watched over the metal shop. This man was one of the senior people in the group, having been there since its formation. He gave the appearance of a conventional citizen and family man, but the quality of his presence was not ordinary. Adrian appreciated his simple, matter-of-fact way of communicating, although some people found him too blunt and direct.

Adrian didn't mind the job of breaking down and redistributing type. That task helped to reacquaint himself with the job case layout, in which little wooden partitions for the different letters were sized and positioned in relation to the frequency of each letter's use. He remembered that, as the letter 'e' was used more than any other, the partition for it—larger than the partitions for any other letter—was placed in the most central and easily reached location in the job case. Quickly, Adrian regained the ability to toss each letter into the correct partition without looking at its label, if there was one. His fingers were also soon able to recognize the subtle difference between the small em quad and en quad spaces.

But what evoked happy memories of adolescent printing most of all was the smell of the ink that Robert scooped out of a can and laid on the round ink table at the top of the press. In his mind's eye, Adrian saw himself at age fifteen running the press in his parents' garage. Then, he had made a deal with the local stationery store to print customer's names inside the Christmas cards they purchased. The scent of the ink blossomed and filled the room as Robert spread it by putting the whole press in motion with the foot pedal. As the moving parts of the press progressed through their cycle, the rubber rollers moved up and down over the sticky ink on the rotating round metal table until it was spread evenly.

Adrian's reverie was cut short by another smell, that of a cigar. It meant that Mr. Eckart had entered the room. He had the habit of smoking a cigar as he toured the various team areas on Sunday. Adrian thought perhaps it might be his way of warning that he was coming. Feeling guilty that he had been lost in pleasant memories, Adrian smiled sheepishly as Mr. Eckart approached.

"Well, Mr. Masters, I'm glad that you like your new team. But is that all you came here for? Aren't you forgetting something?"

"Um, yes, I see what you mean."

Walking away from him without saying more, Mr. Eckart stopped for a brief conversation with Robert. Adrian could see by Robert's relaxed demeanor that, unlike him, he was at ease with Mr. Eckart.

Adrian turned back to his task of distributing the type. Remembering the principle of keeping part of his attention on his body and part on the task, he paused to recollect himself, trying to sense his weight distributed evenly over his two feet on the ground. Then he reviewed his posture, trying to find the sensation of his back, neck, shoulders and head. In his face, he found the habitual tensions at once, around his eyes, in his forehead, at the bridge of his nose, and in his jaw. He remembered having been told that tensions would melt away if one simply sensed them, but he wasn't finding that to be the case. As he moved his attention to his chest and abdomen, he was unable to find anything other than a superficial contact with those parts of his body.

Just as Adrian was about to give credence to a thought of discouragement, he suddenly appreciated how much more awake he was now, after having been lost in memories just a few minutes before. This reminded him that, usually believing that they are fully aware of and in control of themselves, people don't admit the possibility of a higher level of consciousness. Or, if they do, they think in terms of a leap to a dramatically different state of functioning. Most importantly, because they don't see and feel that their presence is absent, they don't look for it.

301

Most people lived their lives without knowing the subtle difference between an ordinary state and one in which there is a sense of presence. All the usual thoughts and feelings and physical habits may remain the same in both states. But if one begins to know the taste of being present to oneself, one can include a little more of life just as it is, both within and without, through an active search.

Merging with the effort he was still making to sense his body, these ideas brought a fresh perspective for resuming his task. As Adrian reached for a block of type to distribute, he realized that, to maintain his newfound presence to himself, he also needed a new intention. He decided to speed up his movements, distributing type into the case more quickly while still getting the letters into the correct partitions. Without pushing too much, Adrian tried to find a quicker tempo in which he could remain relaxed. He moved faster and faster until he was handling the type at almost twice the speed as before.

After working this way for a few minutes, the sensation of his body is more intense. A subtle inner excitement is building, but he doesn't give his attention to that. He is sensitive to the sounds in the print shop — the clink of type in the metal job sticks as the others set their lines, the cyclic whirl of the press and sticky swish of its rollers, and the murmur of occasional conversation. When it seems that he can include no more and still stay with the task, a new perception appears. Paradoxically, along with this intensity, he has the distinct feeling that something is missing in him.

302

This sense of lack lasted throughout the morning and into the break. It stayed with Adrian as he poured a cup of coffee, ate a scone, and talked with one of his printing colleagues. He considered speaking about it at lunch, but then dropped his habitual impulse to formulate a question in advance. For the moment, a different set of values were operative in him, giving priority to the need to remain open to the new intelligence that had appeared.

As his team was getting ready to make the trip to the meeting hall for lunch, Robert informed them that the lunch would be a silent one. Adrian would keep his experience to himself for the time being.

Ada

Adrian left early the next morning for his first day of programmer training at IBM. Fortunately, parking was provided for students in a lot adjacent to the training center. In the classroom, he recognized several men and a woman who had also been at the aptitude test. To Adrian's surprise, neither David nor Anita had made the cut.

IBM was known for its conservative business culture, but Eddie, their teacher, with his long hair and beard, appeared to be a hippy. Smart and lively, he kept the class interesting. He began by telling the story of a nineteenth century pioneer of programming, Ada Lovelace, the daughter of poet Lord Byron. Then he took them on a tour of the data center. When they returned to the classroom, Eddie got them started on some practical programming exercises. He said they would be writing their own code by the end of that week.

"How'd it go?" asked Margie when Adrian arrived home that night.

"It's incredibly interesting. We're actually going to start writing programs tomorrow. After we're done coding them, we get to punch them into cards with the keypunch machine. Then we'll load the cards for our program into the card reader on the big computer and it will use them to process data punched into other cards. The printer on the computer will even pump out customer invoices."

He was about to go on to tell her the story of Ada Lovelace, but she stopped him.

"Great, I'm really glad you like it. But I think that's enough computer talk for me tonight. We need to make dinner and then I've got a lot of homework. I also want to go over the new dance exercise Mrs. Hoyle gave us last week. Would you help me with that?"

"Sure." Margie's mention of the dance reminded Adrian that he had been so excited by the programming class that during the whole day he had completely forgotten to make an effort to watch himself. That amazed him. After his experience at the previous Sunday's workday, how could he have forgotten all about what seemed then to be the most important thing of all?

Four weeks later, Alfred came to a little graduation ceremony at the data center, where Adrian and his colleagues received official certification from IBM for proficiency in the COBOL programming language. Alfred congratulated Adrian and they clinked their champagne glasses. Then Alfred got serious and spoke about what he was doing to move toward an automated accounting system.

"I've hired a guy to manage the new computer system. His name is Mark. He has already set up a system at another company and understands all the steps. He's a programmer himself, so he can help you get started. But you'll be doing all the programming. We've ordered our computer so we'll have it when we're ready to move to the new office in North Beach, but that's still a couple of months away. In the meantime, we want you to get started writing the programs we'll need. Mark has located a computer at the Gift Mart that we can use at night when they're gone. You can use their keypunch machine to create your program decks and then test them on their computer. That way, we should be closer to converting to the automated system soon after our move."

This was exciting news, but there was a potential problem for Adrian. If he had to work at night, he might not be able to attend the group meetings and dance classes. That was definitely not acceptable, but as he couldn't lose this opportunity, he didn't say anything.

"That sounds great!" Adrian replied, trying not to show his mixed emotions.

"Good. You'll meet Mark tomorrow. You and Mark will have to share a cube at the Washington Street office until we get to our new digs, but you'll probably be there only a few days before you start working at the Gift Mart."

As it turned out, the computer at the Gift Mart wasn't available until 10 at night, so Adrian could still attend group meetings and then go on to work afterward. But the new schedule was difficult to get used to. He had to work all night at the Gift Mart and leave at dawn. If he could get back to Margie's by 7 am, they had breakfast together. Then she went on to school and he got into bed. He tried to sleep until 3 or 4 pm, but often woke up earlier and couldn't fall back to sleep. Just about the time he was ready to sit down for his meditation, Margie came back home. She tried to be quiet for him, but he didn't feel free to work in the way he had before. Still, they were able to talk at dinner and then drive to the city together. Afterward, Margie was usually able to get a ride home with someone while he drove to the Gift Mart.

Adrian's first task was to write a program to process new orders against the customer file and print invoices and shipping labels. He enjoyed this work and was soon ready to punch his program into cards to test it on the computer. As he had to create cards for not only his program, but also for each customer's name and address, much of his time was spent sitting at the keypunch machine. Wrong punches couldn't be undone, so any keypunch mistake meant starting over with a new blank card. This part of the job was tedious, but once all the cards for the initial customer file were done, they could be easily updated by his program. During the first week, Mark was with him most of the time to help. Later, when Mark became confident about Adrian's work, he would just join him for a couple of hours each night and then go home. Mark was planning to be married in a few weeks and had wedding preparations on his mind.

Being alone in the Gift Mart at night was eerie. The Mart was a huge place with many connected showrooms, each representing a different category of wholesale gift merchandise. There was a security guard, but he only came around a couple of times a night at set hours. As Adrian wasn't always able to meditate at Margie's in the afternoon because of their schedule, he made up for it by taking time to sit in one of the showrooms.

Having previously tried other Gift Mart rooms, one night Adrian found a small one with oriental rugs that felt right for meditation.

Sitting on a cushion he has found in the room, he listens with his whole body to the stillness in and around him. From the silence of this unaccustomed place, the appearance of a new sense of scale invites him to a widening exploration of his relation to the world around him. Beginning from a sense of the room he is in, he tries to include the whole of the Gift Mart. From there he tries to visualize the nearby buildings on Market Street, proceeding on to all of San Francisco, then the Bay Area, California, the United States, North America, Earth, the Solar System, and the Universe. The question "Who am I?" comes alive.

A New Level

Adrian's relationship with Mr. Eckart was deteriorating. Because he was afraid of what Mr. Eckart would think of him if he knew that Adrian planned to use the psychiatrist's letter to avoid the draft, Adrian hadn't told Mr. Eckart that he'd quit grad school and would soon lose his student deferment. Although personal matters did not necessarily have to be shared with group leaders, Adrian felt guilty about concealing his situation because he knew he was really guarding his self-image. Feeling this contradiction, Adrian's conscience prodded him whenever he encountered Mr. Eckart. Even though Adrian knew that he wouldn't be able to go very far without an open relationship to the man he considered his teacher, he hadn't been able to bring himself to confess the truth to him. His concealment was becoming a festering sore.

After the reading of team assignments in the garage the following Sunday morning, Adrian told Mr. Eckart he needed to speak with him sometime during the day. Mr. Eckart said he would talk to him during the coffee break. As Adrian set to work in the print shop, his thoughts went immediately into a rehearsal of what he was going to say to Mr. Eckart. When he caught himself lost in these thoughts, Adrian made an effort to bring his attention back to the type in his hands. But the force of his anxiety about their upcoming meeting kept pulling him away from the present moment and back into his thoughts.

When break time came, Adrian put down the job stick immediately and walked quickly outside. Impressions of the fresh air and beautiful garden relaxed him. Remaining where he was, he saw Mr. Eckart pouring a cup of coffee at the break table. As he prepared to approach his teacher, Adrian became aware of both the anxiety arising from his habitual fears and a wish to know the truth. He had been told to try to stay in-between these two sides, but he was usually caught in one or the other. But at that moment it was possible to be aware of both at the same time. As he did, Adrian experienced a new state of calm and confidence.

Mr. Eckart smiled as he watched Adrian coming toward him. The twinkle in his eye that had so seldom been directed toward Adrian was there now in all its glory because Mr. Eckart sensed that Adrian was in a different state.

"I'm very glad to see you like this, Mr. Masters. Get yourself some coffee and we'll find a place to talk."

As he poured a cup of coffee, Adrian saw that he was neither impatient nor nervous. In that moment, he was interested in everything, even the nuances of picking up the pot, opening the spout, and pouring coffee into a cup. Without hurry, he followed Mr. Eckart to a garden bench bathed in warm sunlight.

Adrian began his confession. Mr. Eckart's face revealed no reaction as Adrian explained about quitting graduate school and finding a job. In fact, Mr. Eckart nodded with approval when Adrian told him about his new programming position. But he frowned when Adrian described his visit to the psychiatrist and the letter characterizing him as a borderline schizophrenic.

"Don't ruin your record by doing something that will label you as a schizophrenic or drug addict. That will follow you all your life. The Army is only for two years. You have to face this intelligently. Why don't you just go in? It's true that you have to survive physically in order to survive esoterically, but at this point your fears are only imaginary. You don't know where you'll end up or what will happen. It might even be interesting."

One part of Adrian was disappointed. Because Mr. Eckart's novel suggestion about beating a lie detector test had solved another life problem for Adrian, he had been hoping that he would come up with another clever idea to avoid the draft. Instead, Mr. Eckart was asking him to accept the Army. But the new intelligence that had appeared in Adrian a few minutes ago was still there. From that more active place, he could understand and accept Mr. Eckart's advice.

"Yes, I see what you mean," Adrian heard himself saying.

"When do you think they'll call you?" Mr. Eckart asked, seemingly assured that Adrian had agreed to go in.

"I'm not sure. They have to change my draft status first, and then I'll have to take a physical exam. That might take some time. But they're calling up a lot of guys now because the war is escalating pretty fast."

"Will you keep your new computer job until you have to go?"

"Yes, at least until I get reclassified."

"Please keep me informed about your status. And let's talk again."

Mr. Eckart gave him a man-to-man look that made Adrian feel as though he had grown up a bit. Then Mr. Eckart got up to speak to a woman in the group who had been waiting nearby.

Their conversation took the force out of the anxiety that had assailed Adrian earlier in the day. More able now to engage in his printing task, he wanted to find his way back to the state he had been in during the break. But the more he tried to recreate it, the more it eluded him. Finally, he gave that up and simply tried to stay in touch with his body while attending to the typesetting. After many impressions of being taken and many attempts to return again, a more stable attention gradually appeared. He was no longer so easily distracted. His search had come alive again.

On the following Thursday night, Mrs. Hoyle brought an exercise to the class that opened a new field of material for both Adrian and Margie. The tempo was slow and the positions were simple, but the movements required an intensive inner work that had not been demanded of them before. Up to this time, all of the dances and exercises had enabled them to see the weakness of their attention and the imbalance of their parts. But now they were asked to search for and move from an inner presence. Even though they felt such presence was missing, they had to try.

In attempting to work in the way that Mrs. Hoyle indicated, Adrian saw that he didn't have the required quality of sensation or feeling. When she asked them to move an arm from the sensation of the whole arm, he had only a thought that his head directed to his arm. The same held true when asked to move from the sensation of his other limbs. In each case, a thought about sensation substituted itself for the real thing.

As Adrian continued to try what seemed an impossible exercise, he remembered what had been said about the need to know one's inadequacy. Previously, he had not understood how to approach this. But now, helped by the class, he was able to maintain his effort for short periods, even as he watched himself failing. He saw that when he fell into self-judgment, he lost his engagement with the exercise and his relation with the others. To stay with them, he had to give up his tendency to indulge in reactions. There wasn't time or energy for them. After working that way for some time, he began to recognize a new kind of suffering—not the useless tribulations he habitually abandoned himself to, but a bittersweet awareness of the truth of his being.

On the way home in the car, while they were talking about the class, Adrian suddenly felt so grateful for the group that he wanted to express this to Margie.

"You know, I'm really feeling an appreciation of all the efforts that other people have made to enable us to have the kind of experience we had tonight. I'm realizing particularly strongly that I don't know anything about the difficulties and sacrifices people have faced to find, understand and transmit what we're being given."

Margie had been nodding in agreement. "I was feeling the same kind of gratitude, Adrian. I don't think there's anything I'd rather do than work in our dance exercise class. I've never felt more alive than I do there. But then we have to go back to our everyday life. It doesn't take long before all the energy I've gathered in the class goes into the usual reactions. I want to learn how to reinvest the results of my efforts. I need to develop the ability to maintain an inner attention in the midst of life."

Adrian was touched by Margie's aim. And he was so glad they were together.

Examination

Adrian received the notice from the Selective Service the following week, much sooner than he had expected. When he recognized what it was as he pulled the letter from the mailbox, he felt a twinge in the pit of his stomach. He carried it into the cottage, shut the door, and sat down at his little kitchen table. For a moment, he just sat there, staring at the letter, reading the return address for the Selective Service and his own address over and over. Then he ripped open the envelope. Along with his new draft card, with its 1A classification, was an order to report in two weeks for a physical examination in Los Angeles. As he read it, he felt fear rise in his plexus and flow like a warm liquid through the canals of his nervous system.

In defense, Adrian's thoughts quickly went to the letter from the psychiatrist. That was his only possibility of escape from the fate represented by this other letter in front of him now. Then another opposing line of thought arose. During his recent man to man talk with Mr. Eckart, Adrian had given his teacher every indication that he would take his advice and discard the psychiatrist's letter. But now that Adrian had received a 1A draft card with his name on it and an actual date for taking his induction physical, another part of him viewed the situation differently. For nearly an hour, Adrian could only sit there, his allegiance taken at one moment by the army of associations that was intent on using the psychiatrist's letter and in another moment by thoughts in alignment with his allegiance to Mr. Eckart.

For a brief moment, a new idea appeared, that this was an opportunity for a struggle on a different level, a chance to be situated between these two sides of himself without being drawn into one or the other, at a vantage point from which he could see both at once. But Adrian was not prepared to make that effort. He would need more training, knowledge, and experience to be able to free himself from the pull of such strong influences by surrendering himself to the only force from which reconciliation could come.

As Adrian was pulled back and forth, one side began to gain the upper hand. He was startled to recognize the interloper in himself plotting how he would use the letter from the psychiatrist to fail the induction physical and escape the Army. But though he had identified this uninvited guest, Adrian was helpless to deter him, just as he had only been able to watch as the intruder gave the wrong phone number to Mr. Wells, and just as he had remained passive as the encroacher handed in the form to drop out of school. The plan came swiftly into focus. He wouldn't tell Mr. Eckart or anyone in the San Francisco group that he had been reclassified. Although the physical exam would take place in Los Angeles, the city of his home record, he would not tell his parents he would be in town.

He would handle the whole matter very quietly. He would fly to Los Angeles, rent a car at the airport, stay overnight at a cheap hotel near the Army examination center, go to the physical, present his letter at the right moment to ensure his reclassification as 4F, and then fly back to Oakland.

Now caught up completely in this new direction, Adrian found the letter from the psychiatrist and read it several times. He needed to assure himself that it would be enough to keep him out. Convincing himself that he was satisfied, he folded it carefully and put it back in its envelope. But a knot in the pit of his stomach reflected another part of him that wasn't convinced his strategy would work.

Margie wasn't either. She had just read in the newspaper that the number of American troops in Vietnam was being increased to 250,000. With that escalation in progress, she was skeptical that the Army would easily let go of prospective recruits.

"Maybe you should think about other options. If your letter doesn't work, it will probably be too late to do anything else. Have you looked into going to Canada? I've heard of several guys who have done that and seem to be fine. If you made plans to go there now, you'd probably make it."

"No, I'm not considering that at all. I want to stay here with you. And I certainly don't want to leave the group."

"Are you going to speak to Mr. Eckart about it again?"

"I implied to him that I would accept the draft, but after thinking further about it, I just don't think that makes sense. You know, he has a completely different point of view. I've heard that he was in the Air Force during World War II. After his plane was shot down, he had to make his way back from behind enemy lines. He was honored for valor. Most people in this country believed in our involvement in that war. But Vietnam is completely different. I really don't think I can get him to see my perspective."

"You have no idea what he would say. He's a developed man who understands a lot more than we do."

"Well, I don't want to tell him I've changed my mind. Besides, the physical exam is next week. That's the main thing on my mind now. I've got to book my flight today."

At the travel agent on Telegraph, Adrian bought a round-trip ticket to Los Angeles and reserved a car at LAX. Then he located a copy of the Yellow Pages for downtown Los Angeles in the library and looked up hotels in that area. Finding a cheap one just a block away from the induction center, he called and made a reservation for one night.

Adrian checked into the hotel in an old section of Los Angeles on a cool evening in early May. His small third floor room was extremely basic, with outdated furnishings, a sink and toilet but no shower, and a noisy radiator for heat. Sitting on the edge of a squeaky double bed, he ate the tacos he'd picked up at little Mexican takeout place down the street. Through the dusty window, he watched the headlights of cars moving both ways on Broadway down below. This part of Los Angeles seemed particularly cold and alien. Looking down the line of buildings across the street, he located the dimly lit sign for the Los Angeles Induction Center. He felt displaced and unprepared for the test he had to face at 9 am the next morning.

From his suitcase, Adrian took out the books he'd planned to read that night: *Early Fathers of the Philokalia* and *Inner Warfare,* translations of contemplative texts written by spiritual masters in the fourteen or fifteen century for Eastern Orthodox monks. He'd first became acquainted with that tradition from Salinger's *Franny and Zooey,* where Franny becomes intensely interested in *The Way of a Pilgrim,* an English translation of a nineteenth century Russian story about a pilgrim who journeys across Russia while practicing interior prayer. The book the pilgrim carries with him is a version of the *Philokalia.*

Having recently discovered those Eastern Orthodox instructional guides, Adrian thought they might be just the thing to help him prepare for the physical exam. Reading from the *Early Fathers,* he was struck by a strange correspondence between his situation alone in that tiny hotel room and the condition of a solitary monk in his cell. Both he and the monk felt the need for help and both were looking to the orthodox text for guidance. Adrian read until midnight and then fell right to sleep.

He woke up at 6:20, beating the alarm clock by ten minutes and shutting it off before it could ring. With no shower in his room, Adrian washed as well as he could in the sink. He wasn't interested in trying out the shared bathroom down the hall. The room was cold, as he had turned the knob on the radiator all the way off to silence it before going to bed. It made crackling and gurgling sounds of coming alive again when he opened the valve. Dressing and putting on both a sweater and jacket, he arranged a place to sit on the floor at the foot of the bed, folding the bedspread and laying it down as a base for the two pillows he stacked on top of it.

Sitting without movement, it's not difficult to approach the unknown in this foreign environment. Without doing anything, he gradually awakens to the sounds of air moving in the room, occasional footsteps in the hallway, and the early morning traffic outside. Slowly, as he is able to differentiate between thought and sensation, his center of gravity moves lower down in his body. Thoughts about the Army and related fears arise, but for the moment they are secondary to remaining available to a barely perceptible call from another part of his mind.

Adrian got up carefully, grateful for the opening that had just been granted to him. Trying to keep his thought close to his body as he moved though the room, he put the pillows and bedspread back on the bed. Then he brushed his teeth, put his wallet and room key in his jacket pockets, and left the hotel to have breakfast at a diner down the street.

Adrian took a stool at the counter and ordered coffee, scrambled eggs and bacon. While waiting for the food, he sipped his coffee and reviewed his strategy for taking the physical exam. He planned to answer affirmatively if asked if he had psychological problems. But because of Mr. Eckart's insistence that he maintain a good record, he at least wouldn't claim to be a drug user. As soon as the opportunity arose, he would tell the appropriate person that he had a letter from a psychiatrist which he needed to show to a doctor. Otherwise, he would go through the exam normally.

There was still time to go back to the hotel after breakfast. His room no longer felt alien because just a little over an hour before, during his sitting, he had been able to live more fully there for a short time. He took the letter from his suitcase and sat down to read it once more, wondering how the Army doctor would react to it. He thought it was certainly a strongly worded communication. Folding it carefully, he put it in his inside jacket pocket along with the papers for the physical. Then he packed his books, toilet kit and clothes from yesterday into his suitcase, which he gave to the hotel desk clerk to hold in case the exam went on past checkout time. It was time to go to the induction center.

As though on an assembly line, they snaked along single-file from station to station in their undershorts. Each station was marked by a white plastic sign with a black number. They had started at Station 1, where they had been given packets of forms to fill out. They had to write on clipboards, as the wooden tops of the tables were pitted from the accumulation of graffiti carved into them by draft candidates over the years. They had undressed at Station 2, where they folded their clothes to prevent wrinkles as they stuffed them into small wooden cubby holes on the wall. He had just completed Station 3, where a uniformed enlisted man had taken his height and weight and written it on the form on Adrian's clipboard while he stood on the scale trying not to show how vulnerable he felt.

Approaching Station 4, he saw a doctor with a stethoscope listening to the heart and lungs of the man ahead of him. Satisfied with what he heard, the doctor then pressed his fingers against the man's abdomen, which Adrian supposed must be to check for a hernia. The doctor said something to the man, who responded by dropping his undershorts. The man coughed a couple of times on demand as the doctor examined the man's testicles. The doctor nodded his approval and the man pulled up his shorts and went ahead to the next station. Now it was Adrian's turn to go through the same routine. The doctor passed Adrian with flying colors, adding his approval to the form on the clipboard.

At Station 5, another doctor looked into his ears, nose and throat. He asked Adrian to sit down on an examination table and struck each of his knees with a little hammer. Adrian smiled at this, as he always found it interesting to see how mechanical his reflexes were and how well they worked. Then the doctor examined his feet. It occurred to Adrian that he had heard of people getting out of the Army because of flat feet, so he told the doctor that he had a lot of trouble with his weak ankles and flat feet. Seemingly willing to follow up Adrian's complaint, the doctor manipulated his foot to check its motion, felt his ankle, and took a good look at the arch and sole of each foot. With a bored expression, the doctor just shook his head, signed Adrian's form, and waved him on to Station 6.

He had to wait outside of Station 6, which was a small office in which a gray-haired doctor in a white coat was sitting at a desk interviewing the short fat man who had been in front of Adrian. As he watched the two of them through the open door, he observed the doctor talking to the man. From the doctor's facial expressions and general manner, Adrian could see that he was not a sympathetic type but rather an adversarial one. Except for his failure to convince the previous doctor that he had flat feet, everything had been going so smoothly up to that point that Adrian had begun to feel optimistic, but now he was worried again.

The doctor stopped talking and wrote something in the fat man's file. Then he dropped the file on the desk in front of the man. When the doctor twirled his chair around to get some forms out of the cabinet behind him, the fat man waited, apparently thinking the doctor might still be attending to him. But when the doctor twirled back around and looked at the fat man with an expression that conveyed surprise that he was still sitting there, the fat man picked up his clipboard and walked out of the office.

"Next!"

It was Adrian's turn. He checked to be sure the letter was still tucked in his jockey shorts, where he had put it to keep it separate from the forms on the clipboard. He entered the office, handed his clipboard to the doctor, and sat down in the chair just vacated by the fat man. The seat was still warm. The doctor quickly reviewed Adrian's forms and then looked at him suspiciously.

"I see that you checked the box by question 12a. Why have you been seeing a psychiatrist?"

"I had to get help from someone because I was having nightmares every night about going to fight in Vietnam. I even worried about it all day as well. It was interfering with my job and my relationships."

"What's so unusual about that? We're all afraid of going to war. What makes you so different?"

"Um, I guess I should show you the letter my psychiatrist wrote about my condition. He's very concerned about how the circumstances of battle would affect me. He wrote the letter because he felt it's important that the doctors here know about my problem. Here it is."

Reaching back and pulling the letter out of his undershorts, Adrian handed it to the doctor.

The doctor frowned with revulsion as he took the warm wrinkled envelope that had been pressed against Adrian's butt. Glancing at Adrian with skepticism, he opened the envelope and took out the letter. His look gradually transformed into an expression of acute cynicism as he read it. When he was finished, the doctor practically shouted at Adrian.

"Who gave you this letter? Batman? We're going to draft you just like everyone else."

Having said that, the doctor quickly scrawled a note in Adrian's file, ignoring his insistence that the letter was genuine, written by a real psychiatrist. Then the doctor crumpled the letter in one hand and threw it forcefully into his wastebasket. Adrian was shocked. How could this doctor get away with that kind of behavior? But there was nothing Adrian could do and no one there to help him.

"Next!" The doctor motioned Adrian to leave and waved the next man in.

Adrian walked out of Station 6 in disbelief. He had not expected this. His induction into the Army seemed all but assured now. The examiner at Station 7 ahead was motioning to him to hurry up, but he was so shaken by the thunderbolt that had just hit him that he couldn't respond.

But in a minute he was at Station 7, handing his clipboard to an officer in brown khakis. He removed Adrian's file from the clipboard, checking that the necessary notes and signatures had been inserted at each of the stations. The officer seemed to think that everything was in order, because he stamped the cover sheet and signed it before placing the file in the 'M' section of the cabinet next to his desk.

"You can get dressed now. You should receive your new classification from the Selective Service in about ten business days."

"Um, what classification will that be?" Adrian asked nervously.

"You'll have to wait until you receive the letter."

"I see. Okay, thanks."

"Don't worry, you'll do fine." He smiled at Adrian, the first person there to do so.

Despondent, Adrian returned to Station 1 and got dressed. He wasted no time in getting out of there. In spite of the smog that tinged the air outside, Adrian took a deep breath as he stepped out onto the sidewalk along Broadway. He felt greatly relieved in spite of the disaster that had just occurred. The exam was over and he could go home now.

Turning Point

Adrian didn't need Margie to tell him that it was time to talk to Mr. Eckart about his new status. As before, Adrian met with Mr. Eckart during the morning break on Sunday.

They sat on the bench where they'd talked before, when Adrian had agreed not to use the psychiatrist's letter. Adrian was surprised that Mr. Eckart didn't react with disapproval when he confessed that he'd had gone ahead and done it anyway. Mr. Eckart laughed when Adrian described the Army doctor asking if he'd gotten his letter from Batman. When Adrian told Mr. Eckart about his 1A draft classification, he asked him if he could see any other way out.

"I've just started with the group. I want to continue coming here. I know this is what I need. I can't even imagine going to fight in Vietnam. That sounds crazy. There must be a way of avoiding the Army."

Mr. Eckart looked at him warmly.

"You've made progress already, Adrian. I know that you want to continue your participation in the activities here. But you have to face your life. I suppose you're worried that if you go into the Army, you'll fall two years behind the rest in your group. But if you really work on yourself in those difficult conditions, you could get ten years ahead of the others."

"But how can I approach being part of a war I don't believe in?"

"Just do your very best at whatever job you get."

Hearing the bell to return to tasks, Mr. Eckart stood up to go. Adrian got up with him. Looking at Adrian intently for a moment with his head at its usual tilt, Mr. Eckart seemed to be weighing his state.

"Maybe the Army will give you a job with computers," Mr. Eckart said with a wide smile. Then he gave Adrian a strong clap on the back and walked away.

After a full day, Margie and Adrian returned to her apartment physically tired but full of the energy that they had come to recognize as a result of intense inner activity with others. As they made dinner together, they shared what they had done on their teams that day, she with the wood carving and he with the printing. But when they sat down to filet of sole, brown rice and broccoli, the conversation turned to Adrian's new draft status.

"Do you have a different outlook about how you're going to proceed now?" she asked, pouring them each a glass of white wine.

"Yeah, Margie, I do. The talk with Mr. Eckart was short, but it helped me to accept my situation. Now that I know I'm really going into the Army, the things I want to do before I go are pretty clear. I want to continue with the activities of the group right up to the last day, but I also need to spend a few days with my parents. I'd like to visit my grandmother in Missouri, too. I have wonderful memories of living on the farm she and my grandfather had when I was little. Even though she's ninety, she's still living alone in her home in the country. And of course I want to spend as much time as I can with you. I'd like to quit my job to have the time to do these things. Money is the only problem."

"Why don't you give up your cottage and move in with me?"

He was surprised at her offer. Although he'd thought about them living together before, Adrian had never brought it up out of respect for her keen sense of independence.

"Are you sure you'd be okay with that?"

"Definitely. I've actually been considering it for awhile. Now that you only have a limited amount of time here, I think we should see what it's like to live together."

"But I insist on splitting the expenses with you."

"Can you afford to do that if you quit your job?"

"Yeah. I have enough in savings to last for a couple of months. If they don't take me by the end of the summer I might have to get another job."

"Okay, it's a deal!" They raised their glasses to confirm the agreement.

They ate without speaking for a few minutes. Adrian felt the need to ask her about her plans. They had avoided the subject since she last brought it up.

"What about you? What are your thoughts about graduate school now?"

She put down her fork, preparing what she had to say.

"Adrian, I've decided to accept the offer from Rutgers. I have to let them know this week. They have one of the best philosophy graduate programs in the country. I've talked on the phone with one of the Masters program leads there and I'm really excited about what they're trying. The program only takes two years to complete, so I'll have my Masters degree about the same time you get out of the Army. We can get back together then."

It seemed to Adrian that she was being a bit optimistic about getting back together. In fact, he was skeptical about it. But instead of voicing his doubt, he asked about her relation to the group.

"But what about your connection with the activities?"

"On Sunday, I talked to Mrs. Hoyle about the possibility of joining a group near Rutgers. She knows several of the senior people in New York and said she would speak to them about me. It only takes about an hour to go from Rutgers to Manhattan by train, so I could easily attend meetings there. Won't that be fantastic?"

"That will be great!" Adrian replied, trying not to reveal any sign of the sinking feeling in his stomach, which didn't stem solely from his sadness about their coming separation. He saw clearly that it also came from a mixture of other emotions: apprehension that she would become involved with someone else and envy of her new opportunities with the New York group. However, in spite of the disagreeable taste of these impulses, he was able to discern another feeling, one quite distinct from his selfish emotions, his wish for Margie to grow. He knew that was what he needed to remember when they were apart.

Adrian sought out Alfred to turn in his resignation from Single-Minded Productions the next morning at the new office in North Beach. Alfred, who had somehow never considered that Adrian might be vulnerable to the draft, was surprised, disappointed, and displeased. Adrian apologized for not having confessed his draft status at the time that Alfred offered him the programmer position, explaining that he'd been sure he could avoid the Army because of a letter he'd gotten from a psychiatrist. In spite of his annoyance, Alfred felt sorry for Adrian and wished him well. After gathering the few things he had at the office, Adrian made his departure. He thought about dropping by the old brick building on Commercial Street to say goodbye to Peggy and have one last look at the place that had seemed so magical to him, but he let that go. It was time to move on.

Adrian felt a welcome sense of freedom as he drove over the Bay Bridge back to Berkeley in the middle of the day. He wanted to share this feeling with Karl and fill him in about everything that had happened. Having given all his time to Margie, his job, and the activities with the group, he hadn't seen Karl for weeks. He pulled off the freeway at Ashby and headed toward the garret.

Adrian parked the VW on Blake and walked up the familiar driveway. He ascended the rickety wooden staircase to the little porch outside Karl's door and knocked on the door, but there was no response. Remembering Karl's tendency to avoid visitors, Adrian called out to him.

"Karl, it's Adrian."

There was a noise inside, then the sound of footsteps approaching the door. Karl opened it. He was in his pajamas.

"Adrian! What a surprise! Come on in."

"Sorry if I woke you up."

"Don't worry about it. I've been sleeping in a lot lately because I have such vivid dreams in those extra hours."

They passed through the tiny kitchen into the main room. Everything was the same as it had been when Adrian lived there.

"Sandy's at school," Karl explained as he put two cushions on the floor. "Would you like some tea?"

Adrian accepted and stood in the doorway to the kitchen while Karl turned on the fire under the tea kettle.

"It's already warm, so it will take just a minute. We haven't seen each other for quite awhile, Adrian. What's been happening in your life?"

"Karl, it's great to see you again. I'm really sorry that I haven't kept in touch more. With my job and all the activities with the group in the city I haven't managed to make it over here. But, believe it or not, I just quit my job! I was driving back from the city, feeling really free, and I wanted to share that with you, so I came right here. I need to tell you what's been happening with me."

"I'm glad you came. But I'm surprised to hear that you've quit your job. I thought you liked working with computers."

"Well, it's because life is taking me in a completely new direction. But let's wait until we sit down with our tea to talk about it."

"Sure. The water's already starting ready to boil. How's Margie?"

"She's really good. She's going to go to graduate school at Rutgers."

"What? Does that mean you guys are breaking up?"

"I'll tell you about that too."

"Okay, I'm pouring the water in the teapot now. Go ahead and make yourself comfortable. I'll be right there."

Sitting down on one of the cushions Karl had placed on the floor, Adrian looked around the room, recalling some of the precious moments that had taken place there. Karl brought in the teapot and two cups on a tray.

"Do you remember that first night you stayed here with me?" he asked as he sat down on the other cushion.

"Of course. I've thought of that many times. We'd been lying in our beds in the dark without talking and you suddenly broke the silence by saying that we're all machines. Do you realize that those words led to everything important that's happened to me since then?"

"Yes, I took the risk of saying that to you because I felt you were open to new ideas. I didn't know how deeply what I expressed would take root in you, but I've been glad to see that something real has grown from it. Ironically, your meetings seems to have moved us further apart, but I'm the one who pointed you to the group in San Francisco and I've accepted and respect the path you're on. Anyway, tell me about this new direction your life is taking."

"So much has happened that I'm not sure where to start. Remember the letter I got from the psychiatrist, the guy who's a friend of Hanna? Well, it didn't work." Adrian went on to tell Karl about his trip to L.A. for the physical exam and the doctor who had asked if he'd gotten the letter from Batman.

Karl couldn't believe what he was hearing. "You don't have to take that lying down. You ought to protest that doctor's treatment of you and appeal his decision."

"There's more to it. See, I'd already promised Mr. Eckart, this really special man who's my group leader, that I wouldn't use that letter. He said it might ruin my record and close off future opportunities. But I couldn't help it because I wanted to get out of the draft. So after I went ahead with it and then failed, I didn't know what to do. I felt I had to tell him what happened. He just laughed when I told him about the Army doctor asking me if I'd gotten the letter from Batman. Anyway, he convinced me that I have to face my life and accept going in to the Army."

"Adrian, you don't have to obey that group leader. This is your life. How can you even consider going to Vietnam? Even if you survive, how will you feel about being a part of what's going on over there?"

"Karl, I really trust Mr. Eckart. If you met him, you'd see how extraordinary he is. I feel like I can't go on as his pupil unless I do what he says."

"Then maybe you'd better consider asking for a different teacher. What about that other man, the one you first met? What does he say about this? Have you talked with him?"

Adrian realized that he hadn't thought about consulting Mr. Wells. He'd simply accepted the premise that since Mr. Eckart was his teacher, he had to stick with him and not go to someone else. For a moment, Karl's suggestion gave Adrian pause to look at his unquestioned loyalty to Mr. Eckart. Seeing Adrian's hesitation, Karl continued to challenge him.

"I would never agree to go into the Army just because one of the leaders said so. You started with this group because you wanted to wake up and live more fully. Now it seems that you've fallen so much under someone's authority that you're ready to go fight in some jungle! If your Mr. Eckart told you to jump off a cliff, would you do it? Maybe now you can understand better why I've resisted joining that group myself. Think well about this, Adrian. It's your life that's at stake."

"But how could I appeal the draft board's decision now? Who would I go to for help?"

"Both the ACLU and SNCC have lawyers that will help you for free. I know people who can put you in touch with them. I'm sure that there are loopholes they can find to legally invalidate your induction orders."

Karl's relentless stare called upon Adrian to challenge his belief in Mr. Eckart and his own justifications and excuses. Karl might have been right about the possibility of staying out of the Army if Adrian was willing to try. But all at once, Adrian understood that he was disinclined to go down that road. He had already accepted going into the Army. Having seen how, motivated by laziness and fear, the interloper in him had repeatedly made blind and destructive decisions that affected the whole of him, a wish to turn toward a more intelligent influence was emerging in him. He actually valued this resolve to accept becoming a soldier, for it marked the appearance of a real intention for living his life.

"I really appreciate your concern and everything you're saying, Karl, but I feel pretty firm in my decision. I'm tired of going back and forth about this. I've got to take some action. I've already quit my job and Margie has accepted her invitation to grad school at Rutgers. At this point, I think I have to play the hand that I've been dealt."

Karl sighed. "What will happen with you and Margie? Sounds like this will probably be the end of your relationship. I'll be sorry to see that because you two have something special together."

"I don't know. Margie says that she'll finish her Master's just about the time I get out of the Army and that we'll be back together then. But that sounds like wishful thinking to me. She's going to meet guys at Rutgers and in the groups in New York. A lot happens in two years. I guess there's some chance we'd get together again, but it's probably a slim one."

As Karl was about to emphasize the importance of staying close to Margie, something in Adrian's expression made Karl realize that he wasn't going to be able to talk him out of his decision, at least not right then.

"Do you know when you'll have to go?"

"Not really. But I don't think it will be longer than a month or two from now."

"Then let's spend some time together. I want to show you some of the things I've been working on. I'm sure that Sandy would like to see you as well."

"Sure. I'll have time now that I've quit my job. But I also want to stay a few days in LA with my parents and fly to Missouri to visit our grandmother."

"What about your meetings? Will you continue to go to them?"

"Absolutely."

"Adrian, I have deep respect for your valuation of that group, in spite of my view that you've fallen too much under your leader's authority. I just want you to know that I'm very glad you found it. You've obviously gotten a lot from them. But I could never join you. Do you understand why it's not the path for me?"

"Yeah, I know that you're fiercely independent and need to follow your own creative inclinations. I'm really grateful that you introduced me to new ideas and pointed me toward the group. We may not be able to share that, but we'll always be like brothers."

Adrian stood up, feeling that it was time to go. "I'd better take off. We have a meeting tonight."

Karl rose as well. "Don't be a stranger, Adrian. Come and see us."

They embraced, rekindling their bond.

Balance

The letterhead read, "Order to Report for Induction." The next line indicated that the letter was from "The President of the United States." Following the simple salutation of "Greeting" was this single sentence: "You are hereby ordered for induction into the Armed Forces of the United States, and to report at..." There, a rubber stamp had been used to insert "OAKLAND ARMY BASE" at a slight angle. That was followed by the stamped date of "JULY 21 1966" and the time of "7 AM." The order was signed by M. Gorner, Executive Secretary of the local draft board. Adrian had just six weeks to prepare to leave.

Although he'd been expecting this letter, Adrian was in disbelief that it had actually come. He read it over and over before showing it to Margie. She had no trouble believing it; she knew the order would come and had accepted the inevitability of their parting. She tried to lighten the moment by smiling and giving Adrian a playful hug. But he couldn't fully appreciate her gesture because he was in shock from the reality of the situation.

They were preparing to go to their last group meeting before the summer break. After that, he might not be able to participate in one again for two years.

"Are you ready, Adrian? We should leave a little extra time to get to the meeting because of the demonstration."

"What demonstration?"

"Didn't you hear? A man named James Meredith started a long march in Mississippi to encourage Blacks there to register to vote. He was in the second day of the march when a white man shot him. He's in the hospital, but now civil rights groups all across the country are rallying to support him. That's what the demonstration in San Francisco is about."

"Sometimes I wonder if we should join one of these demonstrations instead of going to our meeting. If our aim is to be conscious of ourselves in the midst of life, shouldn't we put ourselves in conditions like this?"

"Yes, I've had that thought too. But the truth is that we're not yet able to remain collected in a powerful situation like a political demonstration. We can barely practice being present to ourselves when we're just talking with another person. That's why we go to the group meetings. We need to develop the capacity to stay inside. Besides, you'll soon be in extremely difficult life conditions. Don't be so hard on yourself."

"Yeah, I know you're right. The group meeting tonight and the dance class on Thursday night will be the last ones I'll be able to participate in for a long time. I don't want to miss them. It's just that there's a part of me that feels we ought to support the outer movements we believe in."

"It's not always that simple, Adrian. Look at your situation: you don't believe in the Vietnam war, but instead of burning your draft card or escaping to Canada, you're about to go into the Army. You've been struggling with all the options around this for a long time and have finally realized what you have to do. It's not the right choice for everyone, but it is for you."

Everyone in the group had shown up for the meeting, sensed the charged atmosphere in the room, and felt the impact of knowing there wouldn't be another group meeting for several months. But most of them didn't know it might be Adrian's last.

As was often the case, Linda asked the first question.

"I still forget to observe myself most of the time. I do meditate every morning, but even then I'm always getting lost in my thoughts. When I know that the whole group is committed to the same exercise, then I try to make some efforts. And after I've been here, I can feel the difference in my energy when I sit alone at home the next morning. But all of this depends upon the group meetings, dance exercise classes, and Sundays. I don't see how I'll be able to work when I don't have the support of these activities. Why do we have to break for the summer? Won't that slow down our progress?"

Mr. Eckart tilted his head to one side and smiled at Linda. She was obviously his favorite in the group. Then he looked down at the carpet for a moment, collecting his thoughts.

"Inner work in everyday life is one of the ideas that attracted all of us here. I wasn't interested in living in a monastery. On the contrary, I wanted to live more fully because I felt cut off from the real vibrancy of life. So when I started coming to groups, I was willing to give up the things I used to do with my time and submit to the schedule here. For the last ten months, week after week, I've been given things to try and the opportunity to hear others speak about their attempts. Some of us have worked more, others less, but I think it's safe to say that as a group we have come to a new level of understanding. Now, it's time to go back out into life by myself, without this support.

"Continue your morning meditation. At the end of it, try to formulate an intention for what you're going to try that day. Set specific times for your efforts. We're not able to watch ourselves all of the time, but we can engage for short periods. Try your best when you remember. You may see more clearly that you can do very little by yourself. If so, this will help you to appreciate the group even more when you return. But it would be wrong to say that I can make no efforts by myself. If I believe that, I'll just become passive. I need to take the measure of what's possible for me now, to understand that although I cannot 'do' in the ordinary sense, I am responsible for a certain effort that facilitates an inward movement of attention."

Mr. Eckart stopped speaking and looked intently at Linda. "Do you understand?"

"Yes, I think so. Thank you."

Mr. Eckart scanned the group, stopping for a moment at each person. When he came to Adrian, his eyes conveyed compassion. Adrian was ready to speak.

"My question is related to what was just said. I've seen the huge difference between the way I live my life and the experiences possible when working with others here. In the morning, I'm sometimes able to be quiet enough to have a light sensation of my body and a more stable attention. Then, from time to time during the day, I'm reminded to observe myself. Usually, I forget almost immediately. But sometimes I can try more whole-heartedly. Even though these efforts never last long or go very deep, my impressions from them are undeniable.

"But on the other hand, I've found that it's more possible when we're working together. On Sunday a couple of weeks ago, I discovered what it can mean to be engaged in a real struggle to stay in touch with myself while working at a task. In the dance exercise class last week, the intensity of working together brought me to a completely new sense of myself. And directions on how to work given in these group meetings always help me.

"But now, life is about to take me to some challenging situations far from these special conditions. I'm concerned that by myself I won't be able to practice what I've learned. My very survival may depend upon being aware of myself in the midst of difficult circumstances, but I'm afraid I'll fail. How can I keep what I've understood alive? What in myself can I trust?"

Hearing the emotion in Adrian's voice, a few people turned to look at him. Paying no attention to them, Mr. Eckart spoke in an unusually forceful way.

"In the ordinary circumstances of life, we live in our heads most of the time. When I'm reminded to search for the sensation of myself, it usually issues only from my thought. I may resolve to stay in front of myself, but soon I go off into dreams about what it means to observe. Or, I may actually start to turn toward myself, but other thoughts soon attract me and I become lost in them. If a friend comes along, I disappear into my conversation with him. There's no real struggle for presence because I don't feel the need for it enough.

"But when life is difficult or in circumstances of danger, I begin to feel the necessity of having my eyes wide open, of being as sensitive as possible to everything going on in me and around me. With the appearance of real need, I can call upon my body as an ally. Meeting the outer exigency requires my best functioning, so that quite naturally I begin to respond from my mind, body and feeling more intensively, perhaps somewhat in the direction of what you experienced in the dance class.

"We here are very lucky to have these conditions. In them, we can discover what it means to live like normal human beings. If we are able to observe the truth about ourselves, we begin to verify the idea that we live in a dream. We see that we have nothing real in us. That perception can bring us to a sense of need that leads to real work on ourselves. But after we leave here, we soon become passive again. We fall asleep, hypnotized by everything around us.

344

"But I can remain active if I have a real wish to become myself and have understood something about the search for consciousness. Outer difficulties may even help me in this. Feeling the necessity of waking up in order to face life, or perhaps even to survive, I may begin to struggle much more actively to be present. But there is no guarantee of this. Confronted with outer challenges, I may become completely identified with my emotional reactions and end up falling as soundly asleep as I do when in the midst of comfortable situations.

"Your question of what I can trust is an important one. What brought me to this group? Was it only my personality or something more in me that I don't yet understand? Can I trust that? To what do I turn when I hear the inner call to open to the truth of what is taking place in myself? Who am I? These questions reanimate my search for consciousness, which is always moving and never static.

"Now that you've had a small taste of your possibilities, what do you want? An easy life or self-transformation? If you want to develop yourself, you must accept the challenges life brings. You must go forward to meet them like the heroes in myths and fairy tales. You may believe that Fate has dealt you an unlucky hand, but perhaps it's just what you need. And one more thing. There is a law: if you work, help will be given."

Listening to Mr. Eckart, Adrian moves deeper and deeper inside. More than ever, he experiences a channel between them, through which an energy is transmitted that conveys Mr. Eckart's meaning not just to Adrian's mind, but to his body and feeling as well. In the pause that ensues after Mr. Eckart has finished speaking, Adrian feels that there is no time, only Now, extending forever in a vertical plane. There is no need for Mr. Eckart to ask if he has understood, nor for him to confirm.

On Thursday night, the dance exercise class was working on a particularly difficult exercise when Mr. Eckart and Mr. Wells entered the room. It was the final class before the summer break and probably Adrian's last one for a very long time. Mrs. Hoyle had asked her students to move in a large circle as they took a series of positions. Standing in the center, she was able to see each of them well and could correct their positions as needed. Mr. Eckart and Mr. Wells sat down in chairs at the front of the room to watch. Visitors rarely came to the class, so this appearance of the two senior leaders caused a minor shock wave.

Seeing how the class had become distracted, Mrs. Hoyle stopped them and spoke with energy. "Do I care so little for what we're trying here that I let my attention be taken just because someone comes into the room? We'll begin again, but try to stay close to yourselves. It's possible to include what's happening around me without being pulled out by it."

The pianist played the introduction again and the students began moving around the circle. The difficulty of the exercise lay primarily in two areas. The first was in the contrasting qualities of movement they had to maintain in their arms. While the movement of the right arm was smooth and continuous, the left moved abruptly to each position and stopped there until it was time to move to the next. Then, the two arms switched roles, with the continuous quality now in the left arm and the static positions in the right.

Balance was the second area of difficulty. On the first beat of each measure, it was necessary to step forward with one leg while lifting the other leg off the ground into a raised position. As with the arms, the roles of the legs alternated. The ability to maintain balance became especially difficult when movements of the head were added.

As Mrs. Hoyle often did, she had them begin with one part of the exercise and then gradually added the other parts. Starting with the steps, they moved behind one another in the circle, alternately lifting their right and left legs. As they circulated around the room, the members of the class passed in front of Mr. Eckart and Mr. Wells, feeling the power of their gaze while struggling to keep attention on the movements. The intensity of demand increased when Mrs. Hoyle directed the class to add the arm movements. Seeing Adrian's difficulty in keeping his balance while attending to the arms, Mrs. Hoyle approached him.

"Trust the intelligence of your spine."

Although he didn't know how to do this, Adrian made a series of efforts to move into his back, which did gradually bring a more stable awareness from which he could better attend to his arms as he took the steps. In this way, Adrian found his balance. Then, when it seemed that he could go on no longer, Mrs. Hoyle asked the class to add the head movements. The first time Adrian turned his head, he lost his balance and was unable to keep one leg off the floor. But he kept trying to come back to his spine.

In the midst of this struggle for balance and attention, Adrian comes around the circle to the front of the room. As he turns his head to the right, he unexpectedly finds himself in direct eye contact with Mr. Wells. But this does not upset his sense of balance. On the contrary, the feeling evoked by the connection with his teacher increases his inner intensity to the point that a door within him opens to a wider vision, as though he has joined an attention which fills the room. Watching himself with a quiet mind, he is able to participate fully in all the parts of the movement. His feeling opens to the others moving in the circle before and after him and he knows their struggle.

Though this state is as fragile as a soap bubble, it endures as long as he remains available to the dawning understanding that it is not his, but given to him from another level. Now Adrian knows that all of the studies, exercises and activities are not only for his own benefit, but for the good of a higher world of being that he doesn't understand but, through an invisible intelligence within, apprehends at this moment.

He takes another step and turns his head to the left, leaving behind his eye contact with Mr. Wells. The feeling of gratitude surges into the inner space that has been created, for he knows that Mr. Wells and Mr. Eckart have come to the class tonight to support him, wishing for him to receive an impression of the real meaning of their common work that he can take with him on his journey.

The Folk Singer

In the weeks that followed, Adrian felt an urgency to live his life to the full. He started a journal and got up early every morning to write about the people, events and experiences of the past two years. Then, as Margie was free from school until the fall, they were able to spend their days together, going on hikes in the East Bay hills, taking trips to the San Francisco museums, and walking the beaches of Point Reyes, all the while sharing their innermost experiences and questions. He also made several visits to Karl, during which they renewed their kinship. The week before he had to report for duty, he flew to Los Angeles to see his parents and then continued on to Missouri to visit his grandmother.

On the morning of the long dreaded but now accepted day of induction, Margie and Adrian got up early to meditate together and share breakfast. Sitting at her kitchen table, they discussed Margie's plans. She would give up her apartment in a few weeks and fly to New Jersey to find a place to live near Rutgers University. Before they got up from the table, they promised that they would write to one another every week.

It didn't take long to drive to the Oakland Army Base, though they both wished it was otherwise. When they got there, an anti-war demonstration happened to be underway. As Margie pulled up across the street from the main building, demonstrators marched in a wide circle on the plaza leading to the front entrance. They were carrying banners with the words, "Don't Go!" and "Say No!" and calling out to young men who approached the building. Adrian realized that the demonstrators were urging new inductees like himself to turn back and burn their draft cards. Then Adrian and Margie heard the beautiful voice of that folk singer they had listened to so many times on the stereo in Margie's living room. Standing with her guitar near the entry to the building, the last portal each man would pass through as a free civilian, she sang, "There but for Fortune."

The song evoked deep feeling in Adrian, as it represented the values of the culture in which he had come of age during the past several years. Although he understood and sympathized with the ideals of the demonstrators and the singer, he had come to recognize the call of another authority, an inner one which had its source in the cosmos.

Turning to Margie, Adrian saw that she understood exactly what he was feeling. They embraced for several minutes without words and he felt the warm wetness of her tears trickling down his neck. When they finally moved apart, she saw that he was weeping too. Gently, she wiped the tears from his eyes. Then they kissed and said goodbye.

Adrian got out of the car. He had no luggage, as the induction notice had promised that the Army would issue him everything he needed. As he walked from the car toward the building, the song of the singer and the shuffle of the marchers grew louder. One of the demonstrators called out to him as he came up the walkway. Adrian smiled at the man, though the demonstrator couldn't possibly have known how he felt. Then the folk singer caught Adrian's eye and seemed to be singing directly to him as he came closer. Adrian felt the deep irony of having to walk right past her as she entreated him to go back. He slowed, stopped and turned around to see Margie, who was standing by the VW. She waved, smiling. He waved back, savoring that final picture of her. Then he turned and approached the entrance. As he was about to pass by the singer, he paused, leaned close to her, and kissed her lightly on the cheek.

Continuing to sing, she looked at him with surprise as he disappeared into the building.

Author's Note

This novel is loosely based on my own experience. Like Adrian, while still an undergraduate at UC Berkeley in the mid-1960s, I met people who gave a new direction to my life. Though the characters in Adrian's group and all their conversations are purely fictitious, their exchanges do reflect real moments of new understanding gained through a program of study with others.

For readers interested in further exploration of the ideas in Adrian's story, I recommend the two books that he discovered: P.D. Ouspensky's *In Search of the Miraculous (Fragments of an Unknown Teaching)* and G. I. Gurdjieff's *Beelzebub's Tales to his Grandson*.

William Jordan

Made in the USA
Middletown, DE
18 February 2016